ON THE RAILS

The Adventures of

Boxcar Bertie

Rosemary and Larry Mild

Magic Island Literary Works • Honolulu, Hawaii • 2022

Copyright © 2022 by Rosemary and Larry Mild
Printed in the USA by Ingram Spark (Lightning Source, Inc.)
Published in the USA by Magic Island Literary Works.

Interior book design by Larry Mild
Cover design by Larry Mild

Library of Congress Cataloging-Publication Data
Mild, Rosemary P.; Mild, Larry M.
On the Rails, The Adventures of Boxcar Bertie

ISBN 978-0-9905472-4-2
First Edition

10 9 8 7 6 5 4 3 2 1

Dedication

For our wonderful daughters—
Jackie and Myrna

For our beloved grandchildren—
Alena, Craig, Ben, Leah, and Emily

For our precious great-grandchildren—
Kai , Oliver, and Luna

For our marriage—
Soul mates, partners, lovers

Acknowledgments

We could fill an entire volume with the names of all the family members, dear friends, and acquaintances who are loyal fans of our books, essays, and short stories. And you, our readers, are all precious to us and give us the ultimate push to continue our writing.

Our special thanks and hugs to:

Sisters in Crime/Hawai'i Chapter and **Hawai'i Fiction Writers,** for their friendship, encouragement, and advice.

Diane Farkas, our close friend, for her outstanding proofreading skills.

Disclaimer

On the Rails, *The Adventures of Boxcar Bertie,* is a work of fiction. The plots and events therein are of the authors' imagination and invention. All characters therein are fictitious and any resemblance to persons living or dead is purely coincidental. A few locations have been altered to accommodate the story.

TABLE OF CONTENTS

1. Bertie's Homecoming   1

2. No Place to Go   7

3. Bridgeport and Bust   16

4. Back to Square One   23

5. Indenture's Done   31

6. Boxcar Surprise   38

7. Close Call   46

8. Just a Visitor or Two   53

9. Questionable Accommodations   60

10. Housecleaning   68

11. Chaser and Chased   76

12. Confrontation   84

13. Boston, Ever So Close   91

14. Conservation   101

15. Time to Move On   109

16. Heading East   117

TABLE OF CONTENTS

17. Recovery   124

18. More Tracks   131

19. Beyond the Fall   138

20. The Getaway   145

21. Bars and More Bars   152

22. Concussion   160

23. An Awakening   166

24. The Howling Storm   173

25. Consequences   181

26. Revelation   191

27. The Proposal   201

28. The Classroom   208

29. Challenge   215

     Epilogue   220

Also by Rosemary and Larry   222

Books Coauthered by the Milds

The Dan and Rivka Sherman Mysteries
- Death Goes Postal
- Death Takes A Mistress
- Death Steals A Holy Book
- Death Rules the Night

The Paco and Molly Mysteries
- Locks and Cream Cheese
- Hot Grudge Sunday
- Boston Scream Pie

Adventure/Thrillers
- Cry Ohana
- Honolulu Heat
- On the Rails, The Adventures of Boxcar Bertie

Short Story Collections
- Murder, Fantasy, and Weird Tales
- The Misadventures of Slim O. Wittz
- Copper and Goldie
- Charley and the Magic Jug and Other Stories

****

Books by Rosemary:
- Miriam's World—and Mine
- Love! Laugh! Panic! Life with My Mother
- In My Next Life I'll Get It Right

****

Book by Larry:
- No Place To Be But Here, My Life and Times

"**In** other periods of depression, it has always been possible to see some things which were solid and upon which you could base hope, but as I look about, I now see nothing to give ground to hope—nothing of man."

—Calvin Coolidge, 1932

"**If,** with all the advantages I've had, I can't make a living, I'm just no good, I guess."

—An unemployed Texas schoolteacher, 1933

Chapter 1
Bertie's Homecoming

POVERTY, UNEMPLOYMENT, RAMPANT CRIME, and economic dis-
cord held a major stranglehold on the nation in the year
1936. Historians labeled the surrounding years the Great
Depression. Only an unencumbered fortunate few escaped its ten-
tacles. A number of individuals even chose to end it all, choosing
death as an escape from the pain of life without privilege. Some
took unfair advantage of the existing conditions, grabbing what
they could illegally. Many took to the bottle, drowning and blurring away all their afflictions. Others shrank back, absorbing the
punishment, depending on only The Almighty's intervention to
save their ragged butts. The gallant mainstream fought back, doing with less, relying on their ingenuity, diligence, grit, and plain
hard work, if they could find it, to bolster their strained existence.
Bertie Patchet was just one young woman caught up in that horrific maelstrom.

Bertie Patchet grew up in a blue-collar family in the Hill
section of New Haven, Connecticut. At age twenty-four, she
was on the tall side—five-foot-ten and a solid 160 pounds, with
a squarish, handsome face that looked almost manly. But make

no mistake, this urban tomboy was all woman inside and out. A natural athlete, she excelled in any sport permitted to her gender. She had an appealing carefree look, with bobbed auburn hair that curled around her chin, eyes more hazel than the nut of the same name, and orange-brown freckles galore.

With the help of her mentoring high-school teacher, Bertie had won a three-year scholarship to Central Connecticut State Normal School to become a teacher. As a scholarship recipient, she was able to find part-time work in the school cafeteria. This job didn't pay all that much, but it did cover her expenses and gave her a bit left over. She took advantage of that free schooling and employment to become an independent soul—or so she thought—for the first time in her life.

Bertie graduated with honors in June of 1936. On Graduation Day she headed home to an alcoholic mother and an abusive, sporadically employed stepfather. These were the nightmares she had intended to flee from ever since she was old enough to consider escape. But with her meager funds, where else could she turn but homeward?

The Great Depression began in 1929 and still held its ironclad grip on the nation. A woman with a bachelor's sheepskin couldn't necessarily find employment in dire times like these. A man would find it almost as difficult, but with more choices. So many occupations were closed to females by virtue of the existing culture of the times. Bertie's cherished independence now faced new challenges.

* * * *

The ramshackle flatbed tobacco truck rumbled down the Berlin Turnpike toward the city of New Haven. Abe Merrill, the driver, was an elderly tobacco farmer. Clad in blue riveted bib overalls and a woven straw hat, he had kindly picked up a lone hitchhiker on the outskirts of New Britain. The widowed farmer craved a little company along the lonely road that wandered through broad fields wafting a pungent mix of cow manure and sun-drying tobacco leaves.

Abe's passenger, Bertie Patchet, sat next to the farmer in the doorless cab to his truck. Wearing a seersucker jumper over a white blouse, she attempted to chat with him as he made his way into the city, but his humble conversation was limited. She cringed a bit but hid her feelings while Abe complained about the drawn-out death of his wife a year earlier and the nasty pests that ate holes in his precious tobacco leaves. Mostly, though, he talked about the penny postcards from his twenty-something son who told of his adventures riding boxcars across the country. His son's exploits as a hobo mildly interested her. She had heard that a hobo was a homeless person who willingly traveled to find work; whereas a bum was a beggar adverse to working.

The flatbed truck slowed, left the pike in Westville for Whalley Avenue, and followed it all the way to Church Street in downtown New Haven. Abe coaxed the truck toward the railroad station and the loading docks nearby. They had reached the end of the line for Bertie. After her hearty thank-you and goodbye, she began the long walk up the hill from the station to the Patchet house. Or was it the Stoltz house now that her mom had married Frederick Stoltz?

The downstairs two-bedroom apartment in that gray, two-story house was the only place she had ever called home. She considered "home" to be the place of her birth and early years, the time with her real father, who died from pneumonia just before her fourteenth birthday. To steer clear of her hateful stepfather, Bertie used every excuse possible to avoid going home on weekends and school holidays. She missed her mother, or rather the woman Zelda Patchet once meant to her. Zelda was no longer the mother she knew, but an automaton subservient to the will of her husband.

After three years without showing up at their doorstep, Bertie wondered what kind of reception she would receive. Yes, she had sent postcards, and even phoned her mother birthday wishes, but scarcely anything else.

Bertie stopped out front at the great oak tree. Its invasive but tolerated roots had torn up the cement sidewalk in exchange for yielding abundent shade. She gazed at the house. *The paint's faded and peeling now, and some roof shingles need to be replaced. I wonder about Mom and Fred, if the two of them have changed for the better. Oh well, I can hope, can't I?* She climbed the six worn steps to the door and tried her key. It went in, but her key didn't turn—a subtle unwelcoming message. Pressing the doorbell, she heard the dull ringing inside, then the sound of footsteps. The door swung open to reveal her weighty, barefoot stepfather in suspenders draped over a shabby tank shirt and unpressed pants. A bewildered look hung on his roundish face, as well as several days' growth of graying beard stubble.

"Well, look who decided to come home to roost."

"Hello," Bertie said weakly, as she stepped across the threshold and left her one suitcase by the door.

Fred reached out to embrace her, but Bertie shuddered and sidestepped his arms in a well-practiced maneuver. His perplexed, hurt look turned to a stiff smile as she slipped past him.

He yelled, "Hey, Zelda. You'll never guess who's showed up at our doorstep, hon. It's your long-lost lovin' daughter."

"Bertie, Bertie, oh my Bertie," Zelda called from the kitchen. Mother and daughter rushed to meet in full embrace in the middle of the dining room. "Let me look at you, darlin'." Her hands went to Bertie's shoulders and held her at arms' length. "You look so filled-out and elegant. I missed you terribly, dear."

"Momma," said Bertie. "I graduated Normal School. I'm a full-fledged teacher now and I have my sheepskin to prove it. Now I can earn my own way."

But Zelda Stoltz seemed disinterested; her mind was not on her daughter's accomplishments. She licked her lips and swallowed repeatedly as though there was a thirst needing to be quenched. But a mere thirst couldn't describe the alcohol addiction she had fallen into.

Stepping back, Bertie gave a searching once-over to her mother's degraded appearance—mousy brown hair in tangles, surely from weeks of neglect, dark rings beneath tired gray eyes, and the faded, grimy housecoat.

"What's wrong, Momma? Why are you neglecting yourself? You're unhappy. You've been drinking again!"

"Things ain't been so good for us lately, dear," said Zelda Patchet Stoltz. "Yeah, I take a drop of medicine now and then."

"Oh, Momma," said Bertie with watering eyes. "You're still boozing it up?"

"It helps when things ain't right," moaned Zelda, "so I cover it all up with a bit of tasty gin or rye or whatever is left in the house."

Bertie's eyes darted about. "You know it will be the end of you yet. But why are you living this way? The house is filthy, and you both look like hell."

"My Fred, he lost his job and can't find work anyplace. And I ain't so young any more. I know there ain't anything out there for me neither."

"Never mind you. Does he even look?" asked Bertie.

"He did for a while, but there's no use, so he gave up months ago," said Zelda. "You have no idea what it's like out there."

"I haven't exactly been hiding in a paper bag, you know. I'm aware of what's going on in the world. Fred should clean himself up and continue looking. It isn't fair to you."

"It's none of your goddamn business what I do or don't do, missy," grunted Fred, eavesdropping from the kitchen.

"It sure is when it affects my momma," said Bertie. "But I'm not going to stand here and argue with you. All I want to do is make sure she's okay."

"Screw you," he mumbled under his breath.

Bertie spent the rest of the day doing chores: cleaning house, doing laundry, and making a trip to Pegnatarro's Grocery around the corner, so the icebox might yield something edible for supper. Putting the food away in the lower chamber, she recalled the icemen in rubber aprons, carrying monster ice cubes with huge scissoring tongs and depositing them in the upper chamber of the icebox. At Pegnatarro's she spent nearly all her personal cash out of her last pay envelope from the cafeteria job. The only things she bought for herself were three five-cent Baby Ruth candy bars.

While housecleaning, she came across her old camping backpack and a short camping hatchet with its hammerhead and cutting edge. Bertie deposited them next to her bed.

At suppertime she scrambled eggs and made toast for each of them. A hostile silence punctuated the meal. Still, Zelda helped with the dishes and cleanup afterward. Later, she and Bertie sat on the blue horsehair settee in the parlor while Fred kept adjusting the tuning dial on the tall RCA radio that stood on the floor. The music station kept drifting off tune as the newfangled tuning-eye indicator beam widened. Bertie always thought of that indicator as an evil eye, probably since her mother remarried.

Her old bedroom looked smaller than she remembered it, and some of her favorite posters had been taken down. But that night she fell into her bed exhausted. She slept soundly until near dawn, when a familiar squeak of her bedroom door's hinges jarred her awake. The door opened. A bulky silhouette appeared. As the dark figure came closer, Bertie knew who it was. The headlights of a passing car momentarily lit up the bedroom long enough for her to be sure. She already knew Fred's disgusting intentions. This morning wasn't the first time he'd attempted to assault her. His past failures didn't keep him from trying once more. His hand pulled back the covers as he stood beside her bed, with his naked beer belly overflowing his polka-dot boxer shorts.

Chapter 2
No Place to Go

BERTIE'S LEFT ARM slid from under the pillow toward the night-stand and the hatchet's handle that stood vertically against it. Her fingers curled firmly around the handle, awaiting Fred's next move. While he concentrated on pulling back the bed-covers, she began raising the hatchet with the hammerhead down. As he lifted one leg to climb into bed with her, she targeted the one foot still on the floor and slammed the hammerhead down on his toes with all the might she could muster. Fred crashed to the floor, doubling up, howling in pain for a good two minutes while she held the hatchet over him in case any spark of revenge burned within him.

"You lecherous old bastard," she shouted. "You still can't keep your pecker in your pants! You're revolting! I don't know what my mother sees in you. After three years away, I've learned how to take care of myself. I should have used the other edge of the hatchet on your damn pecker. That would have fixed you for good."

Bertie triumphantly waved the hatchet back and forth over him. She kept flipping the edges—hammerhead up, then cutting edge, and back again. His murky gray eyes opened wider and wider with sheer fright. Still howling, Fred tried to scoot away on his backside, but could only make it by inches. Eventually, he scrambled up onto his good foot, hobbled, then hopped out of the bedroom, still moaning. Bertie heard the bathroom door slam shut behind him. She laid down the hatchet, let out a deep breath, and relaxed. The corners of her mouth turned up in a hint of a grin. Finally, she had won a long-overdue skirmish with her stepfather. *It feels so good to get even,* she thought. *Who says revenge is evil?*

Daylight began seeping into the room, and Bertie made some quick decisions. *Momma will have to fend for herself. I can't save her. As long as she wants Fred, the child molester, to stick around, there's no room for me in the same household. I'm in no position to support three people even if I want to. Which I don't.*

Bertie washed, dressed, and placed her suitcase on the bed. She picked up the empty backpack lying on the floor and set it next to the suitcase. The color of Army khaki, it was roomy, made of tough canvas, and had a large outside pocket where she could stow the hatchet. Transferring all that she owned from the suitcase took only a few minutes. Slipping into the backpack's shoulder straps, she furtively left the house, room by room. As she passed the closed bathroom door, she heard Fred caterwauling inside. As she passed their bedroom, she saw her mother still under the covers, turned toward the wall, shrinking in guilt. *So she's known all along about Fred's horrible behavior.* Bertie couldn't get out of the house fast enough.

She wanted to believe her departure wasn't based on anger alone, but on good sense and logic that drove her from the only place she had ever called home. Her stifled anger at repeated harassment attempts had boiled over last night. She should have known. Bad apples never get better. Instead, they turn even more rotten.

Out on the street in front of the family house, she had to decide where to go. It didn't matter much as long as it was far away. She turned left, the direction she had always taken while walking to the elementary school of her childhood. Approaching Dewitt

Street, the first intersection, she looked to her right and saw the brick edifice of Horace Day School. The job to teach third grade there had been tentatively promised to her, but she had been told nothing concrete yet. Schools would start in three months, the first Monday after Labor Day, but she wasn't going to wait around. *Away, away, away from this awful place.* She drummed those words into her head.

It wasn't always like this, she thought as she crossed the street. *My stepfather's actions have stolen precious memories from me. Now the first thing I think of is Fred standing over me. Because of him, I can't easily recall my happy early-teen days when my real daddy was alive and Momma hadn't yet taken to the bottle.*

* * * *

As Bertie walked farther, her agitation cooled, and in the next block her brain gave her a break and began to trigger pleasant memories. She heard Meyer the fishmonger tooting his conical tin horn with a full-breath's blast, announcing his arrival to his customers. He stopped his two-wheeled wooden pushcart on the blacktop street, and eased the rear down to rest on its two leveling legs. Two flip-top compartments, one on each side of the cart, held freshly caught fish packed in chopped ice. His pull-down scale hung from a hooked bar. After he weighed the fish, the pan remained swinging for several seconds. Meyer, an elderly man with a full gray beard and peaked cap, spied Bertie standing on the curb and waved his hello.

She fondly remembered other men with their pushcarts. Luigi, the vegetable man; Theo, the seltzer bottle man; Jesse, the rag man who collected old clothes and metals; and Dave, who sharpened knives and scissors and repaired umbrellas. *Gosh, I'm surprised I can still remember all their names. Three years—it seems like such a long time. Those guys must have made a hell of a deep impression on me, carting food and amenities right to our front door.*

Crossing Howard Avenue brought recollections of her real daddy taking her to the Howard Theatre, a block to her right. A child's admission was only a dime then, and with it she received a comic book with the cover clipped so it couldn't be resold. Usually, they saw a full-length feature and a medley of short subjects, including serialized adventures and the newest cartoons. In the lobby there were penny candies, sold by the pound or individually for one copper coin. She remembered pointing through the glass case at the assortment, and her real daddy would pay.

Love and good times reigned in the Patchet family when Lance Patchet had headed their household. A lump filled Bertie's throat as she painfully recalled the day she lost him. Phone calls, especially long-distance, demanded a hush from all those present, and telegrams usually heralded bad news. One such long-distance call to her mother informed the family of terrible news. Carpenter Lance Patchet was at work in a nearby town when a faulty piece of scaffolding lumber split in two, sending him four stories to his death. Her daddy was only forty-eight years old. The sudden family-only funeral took place three days later. His death devastated both mother and daughter. Zelda Patchet had few skills outside of homemaking. She struggled, taking in other peoples' sewing, laundry, and ironing to meet expenses. Bertie returned to her school studies. Her mother turned to habitual drinking. Hardly a year later Zelda found pedophile Fred Stoltz and blindly leaned on him while continuing to abuse the bottle.

* * * *

Bertie continued walking briskly but with no clear destination. To the right, the avenue dead-ended at City Point Park and Long Island Sound. A turn to her left would have sent her closer to downtown, but for what earthly purpose? None. Nothing promising there for her. She looked straight ahead. A mile down the hill, the road passed the railway station.

Hey! Her pace quickened as a fresh thought popped into her brain. While hitchhiking with the farmer, he had told her about the penny postcards from his son, a hobo riding the rails across the U.S.A. Suddenly, the hobo idea excited her. *Traveling and seeing the country like that? What an adventure!* But thoughts of caution braked her enthusiasm. *How can a lone woman like me survive riding boxcars around the country? Is it even safe for a female? With my looks, could I ever pass for a man? Well, I'll never know 'til I try.*

At the next corner Bertie stopped in front of Wagoner's Drugstore and set her backpack down on the sidewalk. She pulled out her checkered newsboy cap, stuffed her bobbed auburn hair inside it, and yanked it down hard over her forehead. Looking at her reflection in the display window, she twisted her face in several directions—and grinned. The likeness in the glass had truly turned her into a handsome young man. Her clothes worked, too. Flannel shirt, loose dungarees, and flat shoes—no actual gender distinction. *I can just as easily be a guy.* Slipping into her backpack straps once more, that imaginary young man started down the hill full of grit and determination.

At the base of the hill, with the railroad station looming on her right, she had more decisions to make. Once she entered the station, she'd have to show a ticket in order to access the boarding platforms, and then figure out a way to get to her rail yard destination. The buildings, mostly factories to the right of the station, abutted the rail yard with their rear walls—so no access there. To the left of the station building, the grade rose sharply, protected by an eight-foot-high wooden fence with peeling black paint—quite impossible to climb. Somewhat dejected by her goal being hindered so quickly, she crouched down on a large rock to rest. Tears came to her eyes.

Then Bertie noticed movement at the lower end of one of the boards in the fence. The single piece of wood tilted outward, and the woolly muzzle of a dog emerged, followed by the rest of him squeezing through. The mutt approached her with a wagging tail and the hope of a handout, but when the petting he received was not exactly what he was looking for, he drifted away to forage elsewhere.

Bertie decided to explore the dog's egress from the fence. Avoiding the protruding rusty nails, she pulled the bottom of the board far enough toward her until she could fit her head inside for a peek. She discovered a narrow footpath running along the inside of the fence that followed the falling grade back to the station's platforms. *The hole made by one loose board is too narrow for my body to squeeze through, but a second board might do the trick. My hatchet is just the tool I need.* Bertie tapped the nails back out of the first board with the hatchet's hammerhead and then pulled them the rest of the way out with a notch on the blade side. She hammered out the bottom of the second board and dispensed with those nails as well. Pulling both boards out far enough allowed her to wiggle through to the footpath. Reaching through the hole, she brought her backpack over to her side. Not wanting to attract any attention to her handiwork, she pulled the boards back into their original position, leaving only a barely tilted opening at the bottom of the first one where the dog had squeezed through. She left the rusty nails on the ground; they weren't needed.

Bertie slipped into her backpack's shoulder straps once more and scampered down the narrow path to the platforms and track level. She knew the platforms were there for passengers and not for freight cars, so she continued to where they ended, hoping to find a rail yard where freight boxcars were actually loaded. Beyond the platforms, the space widened into a broad rail yard, and the number of tracks multiplied at least sixteen times. She trotted past track-switching apparatuses and train-signaling devices. Everything around her appeared charcoal-gray or black. Even her hands looked sooty. She breathed in the soot as she high-stepped over rail after rail, crossing the yard. She saw men working. A flashing white light indicated that someone had started welding. It drew her attention like a magnet, and she slowed to watch hypnotically. Then she remembered that watching that flash for any length of time could be harmful to the eyes and wisely turned away.

"Hey you, are you crazy? What the hell are you doin' out there?" yelled a voice behind her. "It's dangerous! There's movin' equipment all over the place. Git your arse outta there!"

Bertie turned around to see a tall, heavyset man with glasses wearing an official-type cap, hop-stepping the tracks, trying to catch up with her. Not wanting to be caught trespassing, she increased her own hop-stepping and soon outdistanced her pursuer to the point where he gave up the chase. No doubt the years doing calisthenics in high school were coming in handy now. She hurdled the last track and sprinted toward a line of work sheds, thinking to hide among them.

"In here," croaked a voice coming from nowhere in particular.

Confused, Bertie stopped. An arm reached out from between two sheds, and a large hand grasped her own arm, gently pulling her inside the narrow space left between the sheds.

"You can't go running around a rail yard in broad daylight, lad," said the same gravelly voice. "The workmen don't often mind, but there are rail yard cops out there, too. They'll beat the living tar out of your ass if they catch you."

"Thank you, I think," said Bertie. "But who are you and why are you giving me all this free advice?"

"Arnie Folsome at your service, lad." The guy in faded jeans and denim shirt did a mocking bow from the waist. "I believe they coined the word 'hobo' for the likes of me. Most of us are riding the rails looking for work wherever we can find it. The rest are lazy bums looking for free handouts. As for the advice, I believe that even a plebe hobo deserves a fair start. It's a pretty risky world out there."

"Which kind of hobo are you?" asked Bertie, then bit her tongue for being so brazen.

"Now you're getting way too personal," replied Arnie. "But I'll answer anyway. I'm one of the bums, mostly, but I'll work when I get hungry enough. To tell you the truth, I'm in it for the camaraderie. My whole life as a clerk in a brokerage firm, I never made so many friends as I have as a hobo. I'm almost glad I was laid off. I'm having fun, lad."

Arnie sat down on the ground with his back resting against the shed, and Bertie followed suit. As the sun moved from east to west, it now cast a beam of light for Bertie to get her first good look at Arnie Folsome. *In his mid-forties*, she decided. *Balding except for a salt-and-pepper fringe. A beardly growth and bushy brows to match the fringe and watery brown eyes the color of late autumn in the rain. Quite pleasing, actually.*

"What's your name, lad?"

"Bert, for Bertrum Patchet, but some of my friends call me Bertie," she said after a hesitation to adjust the gender voice. It was her first time needing to validate her male identity.

"Glad to meet you, Bertie," he returned with a smile and the offering of his right hand.

"How do you eat and where do you sleep?" asked Bertie as she shook his hand. "I'm new to all of this. What did you call me—a plebe, a beginner?"

"Yeah. About eating. I knock on back doors and humbly beg for a bite. If they hesitate, I let them know I'll do chores. Sleeping is another story. I'll lie my head down wherever I feel safe and it's not too hard. The best sleeping is underway in a boxcar with straw on the floor or in a dry, grassy meadow before the dew arrives."

"That all sounds rather iffy to me," said Bertie.

"There's a lot of iffy to becoming a hobo," said Arnie, "especially getting on and off a boxcar that's moving faster than you would like it to."

Bertie's heart fluttered. "That on-and-off thing sounds pretty risky. Just how do you do it without getting maimed—or even killed?"

Arnie settled in like a lecturing professor. "The first thing you look for is a boxcar to board. The train has to be moving a bit slower than your regular running speed. Then you look for an open door with a vertical handrail next to it and an iron-rung step below it. Next, you run like hell alongside, keeping up with the moving boxcar. You lunge forward, and with two hands, grab the car's handrail. You pull yourself up until you get a foot in the rung step. Then, using the handrail, you can pull yourself up the rest of the way. Lastly, you roll your body all the way into the car. You'll get used to it."

Oh my God, she thought. Trying not to betray her sense of panic, she asked, "What's your next direction? West or northeast?"

"West, I think," he replied. "Maybe tonight, when the cops have a tougher time keeping watch on us."

"Mind if I join you?" she asked. "That way I can see how an expert does it."

"You're welcome to, lad."

Just then, a dark shadow flitted past one end of the space that concealed them and a figure reappeared, staring in at them.

"Oh-oh!" yelled Arnie, as he sprang to his feet. "Get moving!"

"It's that same guy who chased me before," she shouted, jumping up.

Arnie grabbed her arm and pulled her to the short side of the shed. She could hear the thudding of heavy work boots only a few feet behind them. *What's this guy gonna do if he actually catches us? Is he a supervisor or guard or something? Will he beat us or arrest us and throw us in jail? This whole hobo thing is a bad idea.*

Chapter 3
Bridgeport and Bust

ONCE AGAIN, Arnie tugged hard on Bertie's arm, yanking her around the corner of the shed before the lumbering man could reach it. As they dashed down the opposite long side, Bertie began to see the game Arnie played—cat and mouse. They would round corners of the sheds and stay at least one side ahead of the chasing man until he tired. And Arnie did win the game for them, as twice around the shed proved to be the limit for the heavyset man. Bertie breathed a sigh of relief when she saw him limping slowly off, shaking his head in defeat. The about-to-be-inducted hobo and her mentor rendezvoused back at their original spot between the two wooden work sheds to wait for nightfall.

* * * *

The sun had gone down hours ago, and the rail yard had taken on an eerie façade of faint shadows. The bleakness of cloudy weather melded completely with the darkness of a moonless night. The roar of rolling stock seemed so much louder in the absence of the work-a-day din. Sounds and shapes appeared without warning and disappeared into the black void. The smell of burning coal perme-ated the air—the offensive, inescapable stench of fire-eating locomotives.

A fast-moving passenger and freight train chose that moment to thunder into view. The locomotive's oscillating head beam, almost blinding, appeared first. The lion-like roar of the engine and hyena-like screeching of steel wheels on the tracks blasted their ears. The rush of riled-up dust and bitter smoke stung their noses. A streak of blinking lights trailed to a pinpoint before the train disappeared, leaving behind an eerie silent aftermath.

Bertie now feared that boarding a boxcar at night would be even harder to do. "How do you know when the right train is coming through?" she asked.

Arnie tried to reassure her. "There are four or five each night, but we're only interested in those that actually stop or are assembled here. If you pick one that's slowing down or at a standstill, you run the extra risk of being discovered by a rail yard cop. What we're looking for is a moving train that's slowly accelerating." From his back pocket he pulled out a pint bottle of booze, tilted it to his mouth, and imbibed a long slug. He saw her watching him closely, and he felt a tinge of guilt. "Just a little bit of bottled courage, lad," he added as he wiped his lips with the back of his hand.

"I thought alcohol was prohibited," scolded Bertie, then regretted her tone.

"*Was* is the key word here, lad," Arnie reminded her. "Prohibition ended three years ago, and I approve. Why should anyone care what I put in my gut? Those temperance ladies should mind their own damn business, shouldn't they?"

"Do I have to answer that?"

"No, Bert. I was just sounding off. Sorry."

"I think I hear something coming, Arnie."

"You've got a good ear, lad. You're right, and it's coming in slow from the East, very likely stopping for passengers."

The locomotive appeared, chugging in ever-slowing beats, followed by a coal tender car, a mail car, and five passenger cars. Then came a chain of eight freight boxcars, five sealed and three with open doors. The train halted, aligning the people carriages with the station's passenger platforms. This arrangement logically left the boxcars exposed in the rail yard. One of the yard cops appeared out of nowhere and began checking each boxcar for stowaways. Finding none, he disappeared like a ghost into the night.

"I'm going for the second one," said Arnie. "Try for the same car, and we can ride together."

"Okay," said Bertie.

At the end of twenty-minutes they heard the first few chugs of the locomotive's engine and the screaming slippage of steel wheels on the tracks.

"Now!" cried Arnie. He leaped ahead of her and ran toward the second open-door boxcar at full speed with Bertie close behind. He reached for the handrail, boosted himself into the air, and slipped one foot into the iron rung step below like an old pro.

It was Bertie's turn, but the train was moving faster now. She couldn't keep up with the second boxcar, so she allowed the third car's opening to come within reach. When the third open doorway came abreast, she grabbed the upright handrail, ran as fast as she could alongside, pulled herself off the ground with two hands, and threw her legs forward until she caught her right foot into the iron rung. Bertie let go of the handrail, one hand at a time, and with fingernails scratching and grabbing, righted herself over the foot rung. Throwing herself forward, she fell onto the boxcar deck. She landed with her stomach balanced precariously on the metal edge. Thanks to her inherent athleticism, she managed to wriggle and creep forward on her stomach, inch by inch, until totally inside the boxcar.

Immersed completely in darkness, a frightened Bertie crawled to the after-end of the car and sat with her back against the rear bulkhead. Lights appearing out of nowhere cast massive shadows through the open door, whipping across the entire car with great speed. With a sudden terrifying roar, trains flew by in the opposite direction.

Bertie had experienced loneliness before, but it was always among strangers. There was a certain abruptness in her disposition that allowed her to lead a group, but rarely make a friend. Now she was truly alone, without a soul in sight. The novice hobo sat in a near-fetal position, hugging her knees against her chest—fearful, tearful, and exhausted. Her breath became shallow and quick. She regretted not boarding the train in the same car as Arnie. *Will I ever see him again? I already miss his old-hand advice and wry humor. He's interesting, but he's still a hobo who could be—and was—something more. How am I anything better than him, cowering here like a little baby? Where's the Bertie Patchet with the budding spirit of independence, the woman I thought I'd become? I want to be that woman again—even if I do have to pass myself off as a guy right now.*

She began to relax, taking deeper breaths. Wiping the stale tears from the corners of her eyes, she vowed to keep a level head from now on. Keeping a cool head had actually come naturally to her as a high school standout. She loved calisthenics and thought herself as good as most of the boys. Academically? In Normal School she'd ranked higher in her graduating class than most any of the men, proving herself more than worthy of her three-year full scholarship. At this moment, she drew herself up straight against the wall of the boxcar and decided, *I can do this, whatever it is, whatever it takes.*

The lights and shadows slowed and the wheel noise changed to a lower pitch as the train lost speed. *We're approaching a station again. This would be Bridgeport,* Bertie figured. The train came to a full stop with all eight boxcars still in a rail yard, in a series of bumps as each car came to a bouncing halt up front. What she didn't expect was a major bumping noise in the rear of her car. Without warning, she felt movement and heard chugging once more, but this time backwards, the direction from which they had come. She watched signal lights and minutes pass, then the movement forward again onto a siding. Moments later, her car stopped.

Bertie jumped up and peeked outside. Her boxcar was one of the three empty ones, parked beside a dimly lit, deserted platform. The platform didn't stay deserted for long. A tall man in a peaked hat and bibbed overalls appeared out of nowhere. He continually slapped a nightstick across the palm of his other hand as he walked. Approaching the first open boxcar doorway, he pulled a long flashlight from his hip and turn the beam toward the opening. He disappeared inside and reappeared a minute later. As soon as she saw his flashlight beam pointed out of the car, Bertie ducked back inside, out of his line of sight. *Oh God*, she thought, *he'll find Arnie.*

She heard a ruckus in the car up front and she knew Arnie had been discovered. *Thud. Thud. Thud.* It had to be the watchman's nightstick, striking him over and over again. Arnie bellowed and cried out after each of the inflicted blows. His cries and pleas got louder as the beating moved out to the platform of the loading dock. Bertie stuck her head out just far enough to see her friend under ceaseless attack from a man almost twice his size. Arnie's arms rose to block the blows, but his defensive moves were ineffective.

Am I next? she worried. The bully was facing the opposite direction. Grabbing her backpack, she stole out of the boxcar unseen and darted across the loading dock, away from the two men and down a small flight of steps leading who knew where? She didn't care, as long as the space was dark and she wouldn't be seen. She found what she needed. At the base of the steps, Bertie discovered an open space under the loading dock and crouched to hide there. She wanted to remain close by in case she could be of help to whatever remained of Arnie.

By the time she'd found a place to settle, the beating sounds had ceased. Bertie heard the cop's heavy work shoes trod across the deck away from the steps and eventually disappear. She waited as long as she could, but when the mothering instinct in her could wait no longer, she crawled out from the end of the dock and stood up, scanning the loading dock. But she found no one. The cop had taken Arnie with him. There was nothing more that she could do for Arnie Folsome.

Bertie remembered seeing several broken wooden pallets, emptied of their former loads. Glancing around to make sure she was alone, she slid the best sides of two of the pallets together to make a bed for the rest of the night, and covered it with packing dunnage to fill in the gaps. But anxiety kept her awake for hours. First, grieving for her lost new friend. Second, she hadn't figured out her next move. Third, she needed to make a decision before dawn. These thoughts kept racing through her mind like a track star racing for the finish line. Bertie wanted to travel south—but not alone. She didn't want to face the complex underground rail yard of New York without Arnie and his know-how.

So what to do instead? Reverse her direction and head northeast. But she'd have to get to the tracks on the near side of the station. She supposed that boxcars were usually at the end of a mixed-car train. Her supposition implied that passenger cars would arrive first and align with the platforms. Using this logic, Bertie had a rough idea of where to wait for a boarding opportunity. The planning finally ended in a turbulent sleep.

A jarring clamor, prolonged and growing louder, disturbed her sleep and jump-started her brain. Within moments she was fully awake and functioning. The workday had begun on the loading dock above her. Workmen were loading the boxcars brought in the night before. Dawn had barely broken, and the sun lingered close to the horizon, casting a highlight on a series of homes before it, a skyline of sorts.

Bertie slipped on her backpack, crawled out from underneath the end of the dock, and skirted around to the other side of the first boxcar without being seen. She followed the siding's tracks back to where the train tracks were denser and turned in the direction where she believed the station to be. The footing presented Bertie with a damnable choice. She could walk from wooden track tie to wooden tie. Or walk the underlying subgrade of packed but uneven gravel, traprock, and coal. Or walk a similar mix in the gully next to the tracks. The measured choices meant tiring work for both the legs and the mind. It would be too easy to trip or slip if one daydreamed and didn't stay fully alert. She chose the grassy gulley.

Bertie soon entered a wide underpass with street traffic and the accompanied din above, and there the number of tracks paired to four. Looking beyond the other end of the concrete underpass, she could now see the station and the passenger platforms at least a mile ahead of her.

About halfway through this cavernous underpass, she heard a train whistle off in the distance and the faint chugging of a loco-motive's engine. She didn't think much about it. But the locomo-tive chugging seemed to be getting louder, closer, begging for her attention. She could easily determine the direction the train was taking, but on which of the four tracks? She was in the middle of a wide, walled underpass with at least fifty steps on either side to get out. Going forward or backward was just too far. Now she was stranded with yet another quick decision thrust upon her young mind. She stopped, turned, and saw the smoky rail horse puffing, grinding, bearing down on her at many miles per hour. It had no mind to stopping—it was a passenger express train bound for the big city beyond. *Will this iron horse gallop over whichever track I choose and trample me? What have I done?*

Chapter 4
Back to Square One

HORRIFIED, Bertie saw the monstrous train thundering straight toward her. But on which track? She froze, but only for a split-second. Four tracks. Two for coming and two for going, just like the lanes on the street above her.

She jumped two tracks to her right, lunged fifteen feet to the concrete wall on her right, and plastered her body flat against it. The locomotive entered the underpass, packing it with a choking cloud of gritty black smoke while spitting scalding steam from the wheels. Bertie squeezed her eyes shut and pinched her nose closed with one hand. She could feel the heat from the steam as the bellowing engine rumbled past with a deafening roar.

As the smoke began to dissipate, the wheel-on-track din throbbed in her ears. In one minute, the entire dozen carriages, engine through caboose, had whipped by her, never knowing that a woman came close to dying there. As proud as she was of her quick thinking, she hurried to the end of the underpass as fast as her legs would carry her.

Bertie walked the last mile to the station platform, where the crowd awaited the morning commuter train to New York. She turned quite a few puzzled heads as she picked her way across the tracks onto the platform, but no one seemed to care enough to do, or even say, anything about her. Excusing herself a half-dozen times, she pushed her way to the opposite end of the platform, and stepped off it onto the tracks once more, eliciting the same kind of curious head-turning. About a hundred yards farther, she spied a lone, open-door work shed up against a slight slope and headed to it. *This shed might be the best place to hide until evening*, she thought. *I can get closer to the main track under cover of darkness.* She ducked inside and sat down on the dirt floor—amid an array of tools hanging from clips on the walls. She was surprised that the door had been left open—and grateful for the negligence. The tools made inviting targets for thieves. Exhausted, she closed the door most of the way to allow for a little ventilation, slumped down against a wall, and dozed off.

Two hours later, Bertie jumped up, alerted by a rumbling noise. She peeked out the door. A mixed freight-and-passenger train had arrived. But for how long a stop? She had an inkling it might be only a few minutes. From her hiding place, she stared at the one open boxcar. The more she looked, the more tempting it became, like a three-course meal one salivated for. She scanned the area and saw no one. With several minutes already expended, she raced toward the open car. Grabbing the vertical handrail, she leaped onto the step and flung herself inside. Seconds later, the train jerked into motion. First a bump backward, then several forward as the train took up its slack and accelerated.

Bertie got to her feet and boldly stood by the open door as the car moved past the platform. A little girl, perhaps no older than five, waved to her from the platform. Bertie smiled and eagerly waved back. Beyond the station and its rail yard, the scenery mostly became a series of modest homes with their backyard fences lining the tracks. The yards held laundry strung on long clotheslines; abandoned junk cars and trucks; and a tire swing hanging from a great oak tree.

Occasionally, Bertie would see a patch of green and brown

farmland, and that made her think of food. She hadn't eaten for a day and a half. She still had the three candy bars she'd purchased; they were her last resort. When she tired of the repetitive backyard scenery, Bertie ambled to the rear bulkhead of the car and sat with her back to it. What to do next? She decided to get off in New Haven, the next train station, and forage for more substantial food. At least the city had a walking path she knew to and from the rail yards. And she knew the town as well.

Twenty or so minutes later the train began to brake again. Bertie sprang to her feet and rushed to the open door. The moment the train stopped she surveilled the area and saw a work crew of four men about fifty yards behind her, bent over their shovels and picks. Clutching the handrail, she set one foot on the step and leapt to the ground. But where to go next? Pangs of sadness enveloped her as she thought bitterly, *My home town and I can't go home.*

Thirty feet ahead of her, at the top of a substantial grade, she saw the eight-foot fence she'd encountered before. But from the rail yard she couldn't reach the footpath; the grade was too steep. She followed it downhill until she found an easier access—a trail of packed sand and stone leading up to the fence. *Ah.* She gratefully spied the loose board where the dog had crawled through— and where she had entered days before. Juggling the two boards she had pried open, Bertie pushed her backpack through and then squirmed through after it. To catch her breath, she plunked herself down on the familiar flat rock and drew her knees up to her chin. Sobs choked her throat and she blinked back tears as she thought of Arnie, how brutally he'd been treated. But Bertie scolded herself. *Get a grip, girl. You can't sit here forever.* She knew it wouldn't be long before a city cop came by and arrested her for loitering.

She slid into her backpack straps, and headed away from the commercial area surrounding the station toward the residential neighborhoods. The thought of knocking on doors and begging for a decent meal turned her stomach. Here she was, a college graduate, hitting the lowest point in her life. But she had no choice.

A half-dozen homes rejected her pleas; two residents even yelled, "Get the hell away from here!" Ready to give up, she knocked on one more door, and to her great surprise, got a wholly different answer. A rotund middle-aged woman wearing rimless glasses had opened the door to her. The woman had a pleasant, round-cheeked face and high-pitched, almost shrill voice as if she'd taken some of that new happy gas dentists use to bury patients' pain. At first the woman hesitated, but when Bertie remembered Arnie's pitch, she offered to do chores for putting something in her stomach.

The woman thought for a moment, then declared, "Well, I'm on a bare-bones budget, so I certainly couldn't pay you in cash, but maybe I could spare a meal or two. All alone and getting older, you know, and can't clean as well as I used to. Do you do cleaning? I mean really clean house and wash clothes, too?"

"Yyyes, ma'am!" stammered Bertie. "I can do some gardening and a little indoor painting, too. But, ma'am, I sure could use something to eat and drink right now and in between all that work you've got planned for me."

"I don't like being called ma'am—it makes me feel older than I really am. My name is Tessie Burns. You can call me Tess." She took Bertie by the hand and led her through the back hall, where the icebox sat, and into the kitchen. "You can start on that sink full of dishes while I fix you a sandwich."

"Okay, Miss Tess." Bertie took one look at both deep sinks and thought, *I'll bet there's two-weeks worth of dishes in there. She lives alone. How can anyone leave dishes for that long?* Bertie unbuttoned the cuffs on her flannel shirt, rolled up her sleeves, and dove into the pile. A few minutes into the task she removed her baseball cap and shook out her hair before resuming.

"My goodness, you're a young woman," declared Tess, returning from the icebox in the hall.

"Yes, but I bet I can do your chores as well as any man." She set the last of the dishes in the rack to drip-dry and started on the silverware.

"I'm sure you can, young lady. Frankly, I feel more comfortable with a woman in my house than a man. I didn't want to get too personal with you as a man, so I didn't ask your name."

"It's Bert when I'm a man and Bertie when I'm a woman." She grabbed a dish towel to dry everything she'd washed.

"Why are you traveling as a man?" asked Tess.

"Since I can't find a job in my profession, I decided to see the country by riding the rails, and it's much safer to travel as a man." She dropped the silverware into their proper spaces in the designated drawer.

"I see," said Tess. "And just what profession is that?"

"Schoolteacher. I graduated Normal School only a few days ago. I'm young, eager, and a good teacher, but no one has hired me yet. I even tried to get several jobs in retail, but all those positions were already taken. It's even harder for a woman to get employment these days."

"Well, I've got several days' work for you, if you're interested. I can give you three meals a day, if you're willing." She pointed to the kitchen table. On a plate sat one slice of cheese on a single slice of buttered white bread next to half a glass of milk.

"I'm both interested and willing," Bertie replied. "But are you willing to let me sleep in the back hall overnight?" *Maybe the woman's got some better place in mind*, she thought.

"First we'll see how good you are."

Bertie sat down at the table, ate, and drank—wondering, as she did, whether she had the courage to ask for more. "Please, Miss Tess, would you kindly spare a second slice of buttered bread. I haven't eaten in two whole days now."

"Of course, you poor dear, but remember I don't have much else to give you. That was my last slice of cheese. I need to go to the grocer's."

Tess buttered another slice and set it on the plate in front of her. When that was gone, she led Bertie into the living room and dining room and turned her loose with a carpet sweeper and dust cloth. These rooms had been as neglected as the dirty dishes. The dust was at least a quarter-inch thick, and the carpet sweeper had to be emptied way more often than normal. She worked hard and when she finished two hours later, it was clean as a whistle, like her father used to say. But she hadn't finished; Tess handed her a tin of furniture wax. Bertie took the wax in stride, smeared it on, and applied plenty of elbow grease until she had each piece glowing with a shine.

"How's that?" Bertie asked, when Tess came to inspect.

Tess was extremely pleased with the result, but didn't want to let on, so she replied, "Swell."

Bertie's arms were sore from all the rubbing, so she sat at the kitchen table to rest and the two chatted easily for a while. Tess kept looking up at the clock and, after thirty minutes, she said, "There're still two bedrooms and a bath to be done before suppertime."

Bertie slowly left her chair and thought, *These will be the most expensive meals I've ever had. The old bat's really taking advantage of me. I bet she's just too damn lazy to do her day-to-day chores. I haven't seen her wear an apron yet. I wonder if she even has one. But, then again, maybe I shouldn't be so catty.* Bertie tackled the two bedrooms and had them freshened in an hour. Upon finishing, she stepped into the back hall to retrieve her backpack and carried it into the bathroom.

Watching her, Tess asked, "What on earth are you doing?"

"When I finish scrubbing the bathroom, I'd like to take a bath, clean myself off, and put on fresh clothes. Surely, you won't deny me that. I've had these clothes on for several days now."

Tess considered the request for a minute or two and then said, "I suppose so, but make sure you scrub the tub well afterward and don't use too much hot water. You'll still have to do the supper dishes."

"I just know you'll want me to do the laundry in the morning," said Bertie. "Well, won't you? And I'll throw my stuff in with the lot."

"Your filthy rags in with my fine clothes and white sheets? Certainly not. I won't have it. You'll do them separately and scrub the washtub and wringer afterward. Do you understand me?"

"Sure, Miss Tess, perfectly." The heavily stained toilet, floor, and sink repulsed Bertie, but an hour's scrubbing transformed the bathroom to bright, shiny, and almost like new. It smelled better, too. Afterward, it didn't take long for Bertie to shed the grimy clothes and ease her tired body into the tub's lukewarm water. From the other side of the bathroom door, she heard her taskmaster's annoying voice.

"Bertie, don't you think you've been soaking in there long enough? Your supper is on the table."

"Yes, Miss Tess, I'll be right there." She stood up in the draining tub, dried with the cleanest towel she could find, added it to the laundry basket, and stepped onto the tile floor. Bertie dressed quickly and put her grimy things on the floor next to the basket. When she sat down at the table, she found a plate with two frankfurters, two slices of white bread, and a generous helping of baked beans straight out of the can. A glass of water and a jar of mustard stood within reach. Her first bites of everything on her plate told her that it had been left standing too long; they were cold. She ate silently, thankful that she had anything to eat at all.

"There are still things to be done," said Tess, hoping to squeeze more work out of Bertie.

"Tomorrow is another day," Bertie responded. "You've worked me hard enough for one day. You've gotten a fair exchange, haven't you? I'll continue tomorrow if you'll find me a decent place to sleep."

"Fair? Maybe so," said Tess. "You'll sleep in the back hall. I've put a pillow and a couple of blankets out there on the steps. If you lock the outside door, it will be safe enough out there."

"Yes, thank you," Bertie said aloud, but at the same time thought, *You lazy witch! You have a perfectly good extra bedroom, with a nice soft bed, and you exile me to the hard floor of the back hall?* She pushed her chair back and got up to leave the kitchen.

"Where are you going?" asked Tess. "It's early."

"I'm exhausted. I thought I'd get some sleep so I can get a

good start tomorrow." *What does she want from me now?*

"You know, being a lonely widow is a damnable life," Tess spoke in a whisper. "My husband has passed, and my children hardly ever visit. I sit in this big house day after day with no one to talk to. Won't you stay a bit and chat?"

Her practiced widow's voice, no doubt. No squeezing sympathy out of me, thought Bertie. "Thank you, but I'm afraid I'd fall asleep on you. My day started at daybreak in Bridgeport, and I had very little sleep the night before. Please excuse me." Bertie took hold of the glass doorknob, pulled open the door, and let it shut behind her. In the hall she removed the blankets from the steps to the second floor and spread them on the floor. She puffed up the pillow with several good whacks before lying down and placing it behind her head. She fell fast asleep in minutes.

But sometime later, a strange noise jarred her awake. The clinking noise seemed to come from outside. Had she forgotten to lock that door? She saw the knob turn and the door open a crack. Her hand went to the backpack lying beside her and slipped the hatchet out of it loop. There was no time for her to stand up. Heart thumping against her chest wall, she gripped the weapon under the blanket and waited.

Chapter 5
Indenture's Done

THE OUTSIDE DOOR SWUNG OPEN the rest of the way, and the starry night sky beyond filled the back hall with dim light. Two adult silhouettes appeared just inside the hall at Bertie's feet: a man and a woman. One of them snapped on the overhead light, momentarily blinding her. Bertie sat up and slowly made out a well-dressed man and woman, who were just as surprised as she was.

"Who are you and what the hell are you doing in our back hall?" demanded the man, sliding his key in his pants pocket.

"I've been doing some chores for Miss Burns," answered a nervous Bertie. "She's letting me sleep here for a night or two. But who are you folks and why are you here?"

The woman stared down at Bertie as if she were less welcome than a stray dog. "We live upstairs in the apartment on the second floor. Now, if you'll move your blankets, we can get by."

Bertie stood up and pulled her blankets to one side. Waiting until they climbed the steps and she heard a door close on the second floor, she re-locked the back door, spread out her blankets once more, and turned off the light. She kept the hatchet close

31

by, just the same. Squeezing her eyes shut, this time it took nearly an hour before she fell asleep again. During that hour, she heard several train whistles. *Tess's house isn't so far from the railroad station. It's as though they're calling to me. Have I made the wrong decision stopping back in New Haven?*

Early morning brought with it a new soreness in her limbs, borne of both the hard floor's sleeping surface and muscle-memory of yesterday's physically different chores. Her wristwatch displayed 7:32. She folded and stacked the blankets and pillow on the stairs and replaced the hatchet in its backpack loop. Ready for breakfast, she tried the knob on the door to Tess's apartment. It was locked, so she resorted to knocking.

"Who is it?" said the squeaky voice on the other side.

"It's me, Bertie. Can I come in and have some breakfast?"

Bertie heard two deadbolts slide back, then the key turning in the lock, before the door opened a crack. Tess checked the knocker's identity and undid the chain to let Bertie inside.

It must be hell to live with all that insecurity, thought Bertie. She stepped into the kitchen and saw partially eaten eggs and toast on one plate and an empty plate across the table. Bertie headed for the bathroom to pee and wash. After noting what she'd seen on Tess's plate, she was having the best of thoughts about her own breakfast. When she returned to the kitchen, there was a filled bowl sitting atop that plate.

"What's this?" asked a disappointed Bertie.

"I made you some hot nourishing oatmeal," replied Tess, with an added shrill to her voice. "Something to get you all fired up and ready to do today's chores."

Ye gads and little fishes, thought Bertie. *The old woman's gone off her rocker if she thinks I'm getting all fired up about her chores.* She picked up her teaspoon and dug into the oatmeal. Well, at least it's still hot and nourishing, and she did provide a mug of coffee.

"I was thinking that once you get the laundry going, you could wash and wax the kitchen floor," Tess preached. "Then there's all my brass knickknacks that need to be polished, but be careful you don't drop any. Some are quite fragile."

"Yes, Miss Tess. Can I finish my breakfast first?"

"Sorry, dear, I was just thinking out loud. Would you like some more oatmeal? There's a bit more left in the pot and it will only harden there."

"Sure," said Bertie.

But Tess made no move to serve her, so Bertie got up, brought the pot to the table, and scraped the gooey remains into her bowl. She put the pot in the sink and sat down to finish eating. Scooping up the last spoonful, she saw Tess hunched over, busily writing a list. Making the final notation, she handed it to Bertie. It was midafternoon before Bertie completed that list of chores and headed for the bathroom to clean up. Tess had been taking a nap when she went in, but was waiting at the bathroom door when she came out,

"You went through my list pretty quickly, dear. I have a few more things for you to do before suppertime." Then she noticed that Bertie wore a blue short-sleeved shirt and dark blue pants with wide legs and high waist, her backpack, and newsboy cap. "Where are you going, dear?"

"I'm leaving town," said Bertie.

"Why?" she asked. "Haven't I treated you fairly?"

"I have never worked so hard in all my life. I did everything you asked of me and I did it well. That part I can take okay, but jeepers, woman, you've treated me like a pariah. You barely fed me, and you have plenty of food in that old icebox out in the hall. Plus bread going stale in the breadbox on the counter. You made me sleep on the floor out there when you had a perfectly good bed going to waste. A fair transaction? No way! Look, I'm grateful you gave a hungry woman a bite to eat at all. But I have a college degree, and I'm looking for greener pastures and decent employment. I have to leave."

"I'm sorry you feel that way. Is there something I can do to make it up to you?" whined Tess.

"There's that hunk of stale rye bread in the breadbox you'd

never miss. How about that?" asked Bertie."

"You'd stay for that piece of bread?"

"Nope. I was hoping you had it in your heart to give it to me as a parting gift."

"I suppose I could," Tess said. "I wouldn't want you to go away thinking poorly of me. The bread is yours." She went to the breadbox, removed the half-round rye, dropped it into a brown bag, and handed it to Bertie.

"Thank you," she said.

Bertie surprised Tess with a big hug for her gift, and tucked the rye bread into her backpack. It would make at least two suppers.

Tess watched her leave with a pang of regret. *Maybe if I hadn't piled on so many chores. Maybe if I'd fed her better and had let her sleep in the extra bed. Then maybe she'd have stayed longer.*

At the back door Bertie turned and waved, then walked down the driveway to the street. She chalked up her stay in New Haven to a bad experience. *I'll never become anyone's slave again.*

On her lonesome once more, she half-trotted back toward the railway station and spotted the wooden fence—the special entrance to the tracks that she'd made for herself. She ducked easily through it and propped up the boards again. The path back to the platforms proved uneventful. The only passengers she saw were on platforms much closer to the station than the one she traversed.

Upon entering the rail yard, she encountered laborers in clusters of work parties. One was using a long prybar to move a rail; two men assisted him by pulling crowbars in the same direction. In another group, a single welder repaired a broken brace while three men idly looked on. There were other work parties, but she wasn't close enough to see exactly what they were doing. One man, wearing a somewhat battered fedora, appeared to be a foreman and observed her walking by herself. He took a few steps in her direction. and looked as though he might confront her. Bertie picked up an abandoned battered bucket and started throwing scraps of waste metal into it. Even though she wore a backpack, she had somehow convinced this man that she belonged in his particular work sphere. He turned away.

Bertie spotted the space between the two sheds that she and Arnie had shared just two days before, so she headed straight for it. Arriving at the space, she slipped out of her backpack and set it aside. The presence of so many work crews between the main tracks and where she took refuge meant that any attempt to board a train before nightfall would be pretty foolhardy. With at least a few hours to wait, she made herself comfortable on the yellowed, thick grass. Puffing up the backpack, she created a soft spot to place her head. After her physical workout as an exploited maid, she fell asleep.

A three-quarter moon and a trillion stars had arrived during the time that she'd slept. Bertie awoke to the stale odor of consumed alcohol, combined with a noxious whiff of bad breath. An unwelcome intruder had decided to share her makeshift pillow while she slept. She shook him off, yanked her backpack away, and stepped out of the space into the open rail yard. The workmen were gone and the yard was quiet. The most used tracks reflected the moonlight and shone where they were worn. Bertie decided to get closer to those main tracks. She moved to a sizeable switching box and crouched down behind it to hide.

She had only half an hour to wait before the first train came to a passenger stop. *How can I tell whether there are any freight cars, let alone any open boxcars until it starts moving again? At least it's headed northeast, in the right direction. But that could be a problem, too. I'll be running to my right for the first time and I'll have to use the opposite hand and foot.* The train started to move. Bertie sprang up, fixing her eyes hard on the locomotive and carriages as they passed her. But there were no freight cars on this train, nor on the next one. *Oh no! I'm on the wrong side of the station! I have to get my butt over to the other side.*

In the pre-dawn haze, Bertie had only walked fifty feet when she sensed movement to one side and behind her. She turned, stopped, and steadied her eyes on a guy sitting on a wooden box in front of a dilapidated woodshed, a mere freight car's length away. He was wearing a black railroad cap with a large blue and white logo on the front. She watched as the guy wiped his brow with a colored handkerchief. Then he pulled the cork out of a bottle, tilted his head back, and drew long on it.

I have to be careful, she thought. *I don't know how drunk he is, but this one's got to be the yard security, The next train could come through any minute and daylight will be here soon. I need to get to the other side without him seeing me. I don't have Arnie here to advise me. Arnie. I wonder if he's even alive. I hope so. He was such a nice man.*

Bertie moved silently to her left, stepping carefully so as not to disturb any of the noisy rubble underfoot. Circling around a lone sidelined freight car, she changed direction, crossing the first track and the second, then trotted a hundred yards down the track to the platforms and another hundred yards beyond them. This was the spot where she needed to be.

Almost dizzy from the exertion, she made it to the other side. Now she was counting on an opportunity to board a train while it stood still to let passengers on and off. Freight cars were usually at the rear of the train to facilitate coupling and uncoupling at the cargo destinations. The next train had six boxcars in tow— two with open doors. It bumped to a stop, each car slamming into its neighbor. Bertie chose the first boxcar. *Arnie warned me not to board a halted train, but I don't see anyone around, and it sure is a lot easier this way.* She put one foot in the rung below, and with five fingers gripping the hand rail, heaved herself into the car with a twist. Landing hard on her rump, Bertie lay there for a few moments to catch her breath. *Phew, what's that awful smell?*

The boxcar smelled of animal dung and soiled straw. Bertie knew an open door meant the car was being aired out. She stood with her back against the wall opposite the door to take advantage of the fresh, predawn air. As the train began to move, she slid down to sit. Bertie could see the sky as it began to lighten, and a tinge of orange marked the direction where the sun would soon be. Gazing up, she saw a few black crows flying in awkward circular patterns, likely in search of food. *How like me,* she thought, *these scavengers of the sky.*

Bertie was dozing off when she heard a snorting noise coming from the shadows at the trailing end of the car. *Could it be a stray animal someone forgot to remove? I can't tell if I'm sharing the car with a cow or a pig or a human. And that odor! Yuck! It sure smells like an animal and there's all this loose straw, or is it hay, spread on the floor? I'm not even sure I know the difference. I s'pose animals eat hay and sleep on straw.*

There's that sound again. No, now it's more human-like. A snore maybe? Whoa. I'm not alone and, at this speed, there's nowhere I can escape to. Good grief, how do I keep getting into all these damn messes?

Chapter 6
Boxcar Surprise

AS BERTIE'S EYES ADJUSTED to the pale early-morning light, the ill-defined lump on the floor became more discernable. *Oh crap. it's a man*, she decided, as she made out the dark shape curled in the fetal position only a few feet away from her. A man snorting and stinking. *If I leave him alone, maybe he'll do the same for me.* His snorts eventually abated, so that all she heard was the *clickety-clacking* wheels against the track, now more regular as the train attained its cruising speed. Through the open door, she saw occasional lights in homes and businesses streak by in hypnotic flashes.

A June rain shower with swirling winds broke loose outside. As the winds blew fresh but chilling air into the reeking boxcar, Bertie began to tolerate the peculiar odors—but not the closeness of the creepy figure. Silently, she made her way to the opposite end of the car. Her knees buckled as she sat her shivering body down and leaned back against the car's bulkhead. Sensing the unknowns she faced, brought on a fatigue like she'd never known before. She just had to lay her head down. She scratched together a meager amount of the cleaner straw—until the pile made a crude pillow to rest her head. Lying down, she tried to get comfortable on the prickly, itchy straw, so it took a while for her to fall asleep, but when she did, she dropped into a welcome dreamland.

But not for long. Something or someone pulled and yanked at her left foot. Resisting, pulling her right foot back didn't help. She rolled away from the bulkhead and opened one eye to find a large figure of a man looming over her, trying to get the sneaker off that foot. She sat up quickly, only to have the bearded figure shove her back down again.

"Gimme yer shoes," he bellowed as he moved to straddle her.

Bertie managed to keep her tightly laced shoe on during the struggle that followed. First, she kicked him in the face and then in the chest with her free foot, while deflecting his attacking fists and arms away from her face. They rolled over a few times as she fought him off. He backed off into a kneeling position to gain leverage for a major swing. Bertie took advantage of the momentary break to draw both her sneakered feet up and back to kick out at him. The kick caught him squarely in the chest, throwing him backward against a vertical steel brace in the nearest wooden bulkhead. The back of his head slammed into the brace hard enough to be heard. He slumped to the floor like a wet rag.

Bertie scrambled to her feet and scanned her surroundings quickly for any convenient weapon. A pitchfork strapped to the opposite bulkhead caught her eye and she grabbed it from its metal clip. She stood over her assailant at the ready, but soon realized that he was unconscious and blood was pooling on the floor at the back of his head. She laid the pitchfork down.

Locating her backpack, Bertie discovered that her assailant had dumped its entire contents onto the boxcar floor, seeking booty as well as her sneakers. *He's a mean, smelly old bastard, but I can't let him bleed to death.* She searched among her scattered belongings until she found a mini package of Kleenex tissues. She wiped away the bulk of the blood, starkly red on the dirty blond hair, but she soon learned that wiping too close to the wound only brought fresh blood to the surface. Among her things, she picked out a woolen scarf and wrapped it around his head to secure two of her folded tissues directly over the wound.

There really isn't anything more that I can do, she thought. *I don't have any water to wash his wound. I hope it won't get infected.* She sat cross-legged and rested his head gently in her open lap. Examining his face more closely, looking beyond the scraggly blond beard, she realized that he was much younger than she had originally thought. *He's got a youthful face hidden behind all that fuzz— handsome, too. He could use a haircut. His hair is longer than mine. What makes a young guy turn to thievery?*

She sat there daydreaming, listening to the rhythm of the tracks going *clickety-clack, clickety-clack*. It was the unique music of leaving home and never never going back. It was also the chorus of not knowing what the veiled future had in store. Once more, blurred backyards slipped by outside, and the clouded skies attested to the uncertainty of the next day's weather. Bertie Patchet, schoolteacher, and this unknown man in her lap, had made a hobo's pledge to accept whatever crossed their paths. Whatever had brought them together, it was this pledge and common decency that compelled Bertie to attend to him.

The patient's eyes fluttered open—and landed on her ample, round breasts filling out her high-necked shirt. He blinked hard. "Hey, you're a girl!"

"Yep, a real girl just like my momma," returned Bertie with a dash of sarcasm. "And, no doubt, you're boy under all that fuzz." He tried to sit up, but couldn't. His hand automatically went to the back of his head. "Oooh!" He moaned loudly several times and rolled right and left, squirming in discomfort.

"But you!" she said. "You're a would-be thief with a nasty gash on the back of your head. You need medical attention. I think I've stopped the bleeding for the time being, but maybe you need some stitches for it to heal properly."

A long deep-pitched whistle and the continued *clickety-clacking* on the rails let them know their train didn't plan to stop anytime soon.

"How long was I out of it?" he asked.

"About thirty minutes."

"How'd it happen?"

"You don't remember?"

"No. I wouldn't have asked otherwise." He rose up on one elbow, so he could get a better look at her. "I do remember you calling me a thief."

"You tried to steal my sneakers while I was asleep, and we fought until you hit your head on that brace over there. You can't just go around taking anything you want. Besides, there's no way my size-eight woman's shoes would fit you. You have to be at least a man's size twelve."

"Twelve-and-a-half, actually. I apologize for everything I did. I didn't know you were a woman at the time. I still don't remember doing anything like that. I must have been desperate over a little hole in my right shoe. Did I hurt you at all?"

"A few minor bumps and bruises," she answered. "I'll survive, but my being a woman shouldn't have mattered."

"I'm sorry."

"You shouldn't steal from anyone," she lectured on.

"I guess I failed my first attempt at Thievery 101. I've never done anything like that before."

"What's your name?" Bertie really needed to change the subject.

"Stanford Milhouse, Stan. What's yours?"

"Bertie, Bertie Patchet." She suppressed a smile. "That's a pretty fancy first name for a rookie hobo-thief."

"Yeah, I know," he said with a sour look on his grizzled face. "My parents had big ideas that came to nothing. Where're you headed, Bertie?"

"Any place I can land a job."

"I thought I'd try Boston," said Stan. "I got a cousin there working on one of them big old estates. I'm kinda handy at a lot of things. I figured maybe he could put in a good word for me, to take me on, too."

"Boston sounds pretty good to me, too," said Bertie. "I thought I might wait tables or clean rooms or cook for somebody, anything during the summer months. Then in the fall I'd like to get a teaching job. I've got a teaching degree from a college to back it up. A school would be nice, but I'd be willing to tutor some rich brats. I'd sing for my supper, but nobody's got the patience for a sweet little voice anymore."

"You're a singer?"

"More like *was* a singer. But I don't think anyone would pay to hear me."

"You any good at it?"

"Some people thought so. I paid good money to take a few lessons. I can even teach a little basic music to elementary students. But hey, Stan, where are you from and what can you do?"

"Norwalk, Connecticut. But what do I do? Not a damned thing. I never had to do anything except chores around the house in return for a piddling weekly allowance of twenty-five cents. I've never held any kind of job in my whole life." Stan lowered his eyes and paused as if continuing would be a struggle. "Dad made just enough as a house painter to pay the rent and put food on the table. And mom cooked and cleaned. It was all she knew how to do. Then Dad got laid off. He also got drunk one night after that and crashed that freakin' old Buick of theirs. Killed the two of them. I was eighteen, of legal age, so the landlord threw me out of the house with a few of my things after one free month."

"You poor dear," she sympathized. "How long ago did you get evicted?"

"Just last week. I hung around for a bunch of days, hoping some kind of job would turn up, but it didn't, and then my cash ran out. Yesterday, I decided to try my luck at hopping freight trains. So here I am."

"So, you're new at this hobo life, too," she said, having no idea how to continue this conversation.

"Yeah. Hey, the train is slowing down," he said. "We must

be coming to a station."

"Probably Old Saybrook," Bertie said. "There must be some passenger cars up ahead. Can you stand up yet?"

"I think so," he replied, struggling to his feet. "But why?"

"The rail yard cops will be searching all the empty boxcars looking for freebee riders like us."

"Couldn't we just shut the door?"

"Nope," she replied. "Then they'd know for sure we're in here."

"Then what can we do?"

"We hug the bulkhead on the platform side and make ourselves as skinny as possible, hoping they don't look too closely."

"What happens if they do find us?" asked Stan.

"The ruthless cops come inside and drag us off to beat us to a bloody pulp like that sadistic guy that got hold of my friend Arnie in Bridgeport yesterday." Bertie felt a shiver of nerves run through her. "They're a brutish, relentless lot. I think they get hired for their size, muscles, and downright meanness."

"Who's this Arnie?" he asked. "And what happened in Bridgeport?"

"Arnie Folsome's a pretty nice guy I met in a rail yard a few days ago. We seemed to have something in common, so we decided to ride the next freight together. When the right train came through, it was still not slow enough for me to hop the same car as Arnie, so I was forced to get aboard the car behind his. We wound up in different cars on the same train. Would you believe, fifteen minutes later both our cars were part of a three-car group that got decoupled and routed to a Bridgeport commercial siding for loading. It couldn't have been worse for us. When we got there, a railway cop was lying in waiting at the loading dock. He searched Arnie's car first because it lined up closest to him when the three cars stopped. The bastard dragged Arnie out onto the dock by the collar and whipped him with his truncheon and kept kicking him in the ribs while he lay unconscious on the loading platform."

Sobs caught in Bertie's throat. She wiped away a few tears

with the back of one hand. "I knew I couldn't help Arnie. The brute would have turned on me, and I was certainly no match for him. So I took advantage of the fact that the big bully was otherwise occupied. I snuck out of my car, ran across the platform, and hid under the dock. Stayed there all night. Next morning I didn't see a sign of either one when I came out from my hiding place. What I did see—it was horrible—was a clotted pool of Arnie's blood that had soaked into the platform timbers."

"So you have no idea if he ever got away?" Stan asked.

"No. I don't know where he is today or even if he's still alive, but I sure hope he survived. I was afraid to hang around that rail yard, so I skedaddled while I still could. I feel kinda guilty about it."

"You had no choice," said Stan. "I would've high-tailed it, too."

The train slowed to a full stop and reverberated a few times as the individual cars bumped together for their final statement. The two hobos leaned against the door-side bulkhead and listened. For a while, all they heard were the normal outside noises: street traffic, other trains in the distance, a few chirping birds, and a voice here and there. Then a loud clunking sound—hardwood on metal, the dreaded signature of the rail yard cop making his rounds. The billy club truncheon, striking the iron-rung car step, struck terror intended as a warning for any hobo riders. Bertie and Stan were no exception. The clunking got louder and louder as the billy club sounds got closer and closer—the next car, then theirs. The cop swung a powerful flashlight beam through the open door of their car. The sharp beam began its sweep at their end, then swept to the opposite end, leaving only a marginal space for them to cower in. The beam hesitated at the far end, settling on some questionable articles. The small unidentified heap appeared to be something left behind.

Is the rail cop suspicious? wondered Bertie. *His flashlight is lingering longer than necessary. He might have seen something of inter- est. Is it enough for him to enter and investigate further? Will he drag us off and beat us bloody like the cop in Bridgeport did to Arnie? Oh God.* With hearts pounding, the two cringing fugitives hugged the bulkhead wall and waited.

Chapter 7
Close Call

FOR A FEW TOO MANY SECONDS the powerful flashlight beam vacillated around the ill-defined heap on the floor at the opposite end of the boxcar. Bertie and Stan dared not breathe. The wait for something decisive to happen seemed forever. Then the beam bounced wildly across the boxcar and disappeared as the rail yard cop withdrew it. Either the heap on the floor looked too insignificant to investigate or the cop was too lazy to climb into the boxcar to inspect it. He slammed his truncheon down with a *clang* on the iron rung step and strode past.

Minutes later the train whistle blew a warning blast. The string of boxcars stretched until every last one strained, squawked, and then inched into motion, allowing the whole train to roll as one. It gathered momentum, starting with the engine's *chug-a-chug* and the tracks' *click-a-clack*, accelerating, closing in on, and eventually reaching, its normal *clickity-clack* rhythm.

"Whew, that was close," said Stan.

"What's down at the other end of the car that the rail cop was so interested in?" asked Bertie.

"Just my duffel and my guitar," said Stan. "I didn't think he could see that far in the dark."

"A flashlight covers a lot of ground. If he'd taken more time to examine your stuff, he would've had a good reason to come in. Luckily, he didn't recognize anything."

"That stuff is all I've got in this world, every stitch." Stan shuffled to the other end of the car, gathered up his belongings, and brought them back.

"You said something about a guitar. Do you play?" she asked.

"Yeah, you wanna hear something?"

"Sure. We've got nothing else to kill the time."

Stan already had the instrument half out of its canvas casing, when she said, "Or maybe not. It's only twenty minutes to New London. We should get off there and get your head gash taken care of."

"You really think that's necessary?" he asked, while sliding the guitar back into its case.

"Yeah. Maybe I should have another look at it."

Stan unraveled the scarf for her to see. "How's does it look?"

"It's still an ugly gash," Bertie said, "but the bleeding has stopped. Still, I think we ought to get that wound cleaned out before any infection sets in. Maybe it needs iodine or hydrogen peroxide or something. I can't tell whether you need stitches or not, but it's sure going to leave one helluva nasty scar."

"I can live with the scars," said Stan. "They're reminders of the dangerous lessons we've learned in life. I just don't want too many of them. I don't know why you're so caring for me when I treated you like shit."

"Maybe it's the mothering instinct in me. I'd better wrap that scarf back on. You'll need it when we jump."

"Jump?" His voice quavered.

"Yeah, jump." She handed him a wad of tissues and he held it in place over the gash while she wound the scarf twice around his head and tucked in the end so it wouldn't unravel.

"We don't know what to expect in New London. We could stop in a fully exposed area, and I don't want to take any chances."

The time to New London passed quickly, and Bertie prepared them for a pre-station debarking. They positioned themselves next to the open door and waited for the train to slow to a reasonable, non-crippling speed. First, they flung their belongings out the door. Bertie gave him an encouraging little shove and Stan leaped out. She followed. They both landed hard, stumbling to the rough ground and rolling to a final stop in the sooty gravel about a hundred feet from their tossed gear. Brushing themselves off, they rubbed their bruises and trudged back to collect their belongings. They had to walk more than half a mile to get to the rail yard on the opposite side of the station. The fair-sized city came into view on their left, with the waters of Long Island Sound on their right.

They had crossed a number of tracks when Bertie spotted a rail yard work shed. She pointed. "Look, there's some shelter over there."

"Yeah," said Stan, "There's actually a black rubber hose coiled up on the shed wall. Could be some water close by." As they approached the shed, they saw a water spigot on the end of an iron pipe coming out of the ground. Bertie rummaged around in her backpack and retrieved a spare clean sock. She tried to turn on the water, but discovered the wheel handle was missing. "I don't think we can turn the valve on," she said.

"Isn't that the handle up there on a nail?" asked Stan. "Under the eave?"

"Right on," said Bertie. "Just what the doctor ordered." She reached up, grabbed the handle, fitted it to the valve stem, and turned counterclockwise until the water flowed. Soaking the sock, she dabbed at the dried bloody mess at the back of Stan's head, gently cleaning it as she went. When she finished, she told him, "It's the best I can do for you. Any more and I'm afraid I'll start the bleeding all over again." She rinsed her lone sock in the stream of clear water and wrung it out several times until the pink stain turned almost white again, then hung it on a backpack ring to dry.

"Maybe I won't need stitches after all?" he asked in a hopeful tone.

"I don't know, maybe," she said. "Or maybe it'll leave a larger and uglier scar for you to carry around for the rest of your life."

"I don't care," he said. "I told you how I feel about scars." He smiled for the first time since she'd met him. "Besides, I can't see it."

"I guess we should get our fill of water while it's so available," she said.

They each slurped a drink—she with cupped hands, while he positioned his mouth under the tap for a more direct intake. She reached over him to turn off the water when he'd enough and pulled back.

"Thanks. Say, there's a patch of thick green grass behind that shed that looks like it might be good for sleeping," said Stan.

"I guess we both could use a little sleep, especially under that shade tree," she agreed, looking more than ever like a twenty-four-year-old tomboy.

That's exactly where they headed. Stan fell asleep first, while Bertie lay there thinking, staring up at the clusters of crab apples in the full tree above them. They were almost ripe, she noted, before dozing off. The sun was warm and the breeze cooling. They slept for hours, taking advantage of the soft bed of grass. When they awoke, the sun had gone down. About fifty yards away, they saw at least three small lights flickering on the grassy knoll that lay alongside the tracks. Gathering their gear, they cautiously strolled toward the lights.

As they got closer, Bertie realized they had stumbled on one of many established camps in a hobo-friendly community. The lights were actually cooking fires. Large tin cans hung over these fires, suspended by wire threaded through nail holes punched near the tops of the cans. Perhaps some of the cans were filled with weak coffee or a makeshift soup or the rare hobo stew—if the ingredients had been either pilfered or begged from local gardens. They encountered four young men, huddled close to the nearest fire, probably to get warm and wait for whatever was in the pot to be ready.

There was some risk in approaching hobo strangers, especially groups. For the more stingy types, the treasured food in the tin can was worth getting nasty over, maybe even fighting over. For others, the tin's treasure was worth sharing in return for much-needed socializing. The latter group saw it as a hobo fraternity. Like it or not, they were all stuck in this situation together. Bertie and Stan had no idea what reception they'd get.

"May we sit in?" asked Stan.

The man wearing a black watch cap motioned silently to an open spot, so they put down their gear and joined the ring around the fire. Minutes passed. The same man looked up at them. "Do you have anything to contribute?"

Bertie fumbled through her things and came up with the chunk of rye bread she'd acquired from the reluctant Tess. Stan cut it into six equal pieces with his pocket knife and passed the pieces around to the men. After a time, a bald man stirring the tin can with a large hunting knife, declared: "The stew's done." One by one, each man dipped into the tin for a half-fill with his own tin cup. It didn't take long for every one of those pieces of rye bread to disappear into their individual cups. While the men dipped and chewed, the man in the watch cap looked over to Bertie and nodded his assent. She dipped into the can with her own cup and then she looked to Stan, who merely shrugged—he had no cup. Bertie dipped her bread and drained her cup, savoring every morsel, then passed her cup to Stan, who dipped it in and ate his meager share of stew as well.

Stan unpacked his guitar and strummed a few odd bars before moving on to "She'll be Coming Round the Mountain." Bertie started to sing the words. In a short time everyone joined in, following with whatever lyrics they could remember to "You Are My Sunshine" and "I've Been Working on the Railroad." The singing attracted other men and soon the circle widened to accommodate them. There were more songs, and after one lull, the bald man broke the short silence to sing "Love Letters in the Sand." He sang in a clear tenor voice. All the prior music had put everyone in a good mood, but when the bald man finished, a few of the men were overtaken by nostalgia. They were lonely, among other lonely men, and it didn't take much to set them thinking about themselves and the sorry fortunes they'd been dealt.

A train whistle blew several short blasts—the next freight north and east. By the time it arrived, it was still moving slowly enough for boarding. All the men in the hobo camps had their eyes on the six boxcars with open doors. The man in the watch cap ran alongside the second open car, grabbed a bar, and swung inside.

The bald man and one other hobo ran together and landed in the same car. Bertie and Stan weren't so lucky. By the time they got their opportunity, the train was moving too fast for them to board.

The bald man waved from the open door and yelled, "Don't worry, there's another freight train coming through in about an hour."

At least a half-dozen disappointed men walked back to the other campsites. All four members of Stan and Bertie's little circle had made the first train out that night; Stan and Bertie were left with the embers of their campfire. Stan found a small portion of watery hobo stew left in the tin. He wiped the bottom of the can with his fingers and licked them clean until it yielded too little to bother.

"I've got just the dessert to go with that," Bertie said, as she brought out one of the three Baby Ruth bars stowed in her backpack. Stan cut it in half and they shared it while waiting for the next freight train to come through. Together, they stood up and dutifully stamped out the remaining embers.

Sure enough, the minutes passed quickly. More savvy now, they arrived at the adjacent track before the others. They broke into a run. Bertie hopped on, rolled in, and made it onto her knees.

The train of boxcars had been moving faster than Stan expected. By the time he threw himself at the open door, he almost missed his target altogether, but managed to roll in next to her.

Catching her breath, Bertie sensed something wrong. They were not alone. Someone else was hidden in the deep shadows in the after-end of the boxcar. The cloud-covered night sky made it even more difficult to see. But she knew someone was there—she could smell the unwashed body from the distance.

"Who's there?" cried Bertie. "Come out where we can see you."

"Up yours! Seeing me is none of your damn business," answered a gruff voice with neither a face nor form in the depths of darkness. "Stay away from my end of this boxcar and you won't get hurt."

"Hey, we've got as much right to be here as you have," yelled Stan.

"I've got a gun in my hand that says you don't," replied the voice. "Now keep your distance or I'll blow a few holes in your gut."

Chapter 8
Just a Visitor or Two

BERTIE and Stan were jolted by the threat from the after-end of the boxcar. They looked at one another, each unsure how to respond. Some minutes later, Stan gathered up the courage to try.

"We mean you no harm," he said. "We just want to know who and what we're dealing with."

"Just stay in yer end of the car, and we'll get along jes fine," said the same harsh voice out of the darkness.

"What if we don't want to stay where we are?" argued Stan. "We've got just as much right to be in the rear as you do."

"Remember, I was here first. Besides, I've got a gun that will make sure you keep your distance," said the voice.

"How do we know you're not lying about the gun?" taunted Stan.

They heard a metallic click that sounded to Bertie like a pistol's safety being removed. "Don't antagonize him, Stan," she murmured, moving closer to the front of the car. "I can live with his conditions. We'll keep our space and let him have his."

"That's a swell idea, Toots," said the voice.

"I don't like being intimidated," mumbled an angry Stan as he too moved to the front. "But for your sake, Bertie, I'll go along with a truce. You hear that up there?" he shouted.

"Yeah! A very wise decision on your part," replied the gravelly voice.

Bertie and Stan settled into their corner. Because they couldn't trust the threatening guy at the far end of the car, they had to take turns dozing—who sat up and who laid their head in the sitting person's lap. Alternating, each of them snatched an hour or two of sleep on the way to Providence, Rhode Island. As they approached the city, daylight began to fill the car, affording some visibility. Bertie was taking her turn on watch. She couldn't move because Stan's head was in her lap. She noticed something weird at the opposite end of the car. Not only was the form becoming clearer, there seemed to be another form lying flat on the car's wood flooring without benefit of straw.

Seems like they're both asleep, Bertie thought, squinting to get a better look. *I don't see a gun anywhere. Maybe he was bluffing. Why didn't the other person speak?* Her eyes strained through the still-dim light trying to see more detail. *The guy on the floor hasn't moved. Is he even breathing? Jeez, everything appears wet under him. I wonder if it's blood, and the guy is actually dead.*

Bertie wanted to wake Stan up, but she had to do it quietly and carefully. If he awoke with a loud start, she'd wake the guy across the way as well. She looked down at Stan and stroked his cheek with her forefinger. His hand flew up immediately to brush away the annoyance. He tried to sleep through the brushing but she persisted. Each time she stroked, he was a little more awake until one eye after the other popped open and stared into her face. With a finger to her lips, she whispered *Shush* and murmured, "There are two people down at the other end. It looks like at least one is sleeping and the other one is dead."

Stan lifted his head for a quick look, then sat up straight. "How do you know the other guy's dead?" he said.

"Check out the liquid pool under him," whispered Bertie.

"Looks like blood. I think the one we spoke to murdered the other guy, so we have to be careful. We can't claim *not* to have seen the dead man, so if he wakes up and sees us gawking at what he's done, he'll have to deal with us. I think we have to move first and get the upper hand."

Stan nodded. They both got to their feet and slowly, silently, approached the smelly stranger. As they got closer, the smell got worse. Stan stood, ready to pounce, but the guy woke up and stared back at him. Suddenly, he produced his gun out of nowhere.

Stan jumped at him anyway and deflected his hand. The shot went wild, ricocheting through the car several times before embedding itself somewhere in the wood siding. The two men wrestled for the gun and two more wild shots rebounded throughout the car. Finally, the gun came loose. As they both scrambled for it, the gun scooted out the boxcar's open door. In a wild, stumbling attempt to recover his weapon, the smelly stranger crazily followed it out the door and disappeared into the passing scenery.

Bertie and Stan looked at each other in mixed shock and relief. As the train approached the Providence suburbs, it began to slow. Neither one had repacked their belongings. They were stuck in a boxcar with a bloody murder victim.

"We'd better get off here," said Bertie. "We don't want to get caught with a dead body. They'll think we did it and got rid of the gun. They'll never believe the bit about the murderer going out the door that way."

"You're right," said Stan. "Soon there's gonna be cops all over the place. And maybe we should stay away from the tracks for a few days as a precaution."

Watching him venture to the other end of the car, she asked, "Where the hell are you going, Stan?"

"I'm just having a look around—to see what the murderer left behind.," said Stan. "There's a canvas tote here that I need to open. Jeezuz! There's a whole lot of paper money inside—could be hundreds or even thousands of dollars here. We can't leave this behind." He zipped up the tote and carried it to their end of the car.

"But that's not our money," declared Bertie. "That's stealing, isn't it?"

"Well," he reasoned, "if we don't take it, the next person that comes along will scoop it up, anyway. This is an opportunity speaking to us. Besides, we can always turn it in later, if we have to. Maybe there will even be a reward."

"Hurry. Get your things together," she said. "The train's stopping and there's a short fence over there." When the last car jerked to a stop, they threw their stuff outside and climbed down out of the car. People were wandering around the fenced-in area, so the two vagabonds picked up their tossed baggage and rushed to the fence, away from the milling passengers. Tossing his duffel over first, Stan required a boosting shove from athletic Bertie to get over the top. With her muscular arms, she pulled herself up, swung one leg over the top, rolled over to the other side, and dropped to the ground.

They found themselves in a small but well-tended backyard.

"Hey, you people!" A gray-haired woman in a faded housedress stood at the open screen door. "Get away from here!" she yelled, shaking her finger and stamping her foot. "You're in my garden, trespassing, crushing my flowers and vegetables!" Bertie and Stan slunk away and ran down her driveway to the sidewalk and street.

"This is definitely a poorer neighborhood," said Stan, scanning the row of paint-peeling bungalows. "No use looking for work or a handout around here."

"Don't worry, Stan. There are plenty of super-rich mansions in Providence. All we need to do is find them. Let's walk toward the bay."

"Aren't you thinking of the Newport mansions, Bertie?"

"Yeah," she grinned. "You're right about that. But both cities are on Narragansett Bay. Providence is too big not to have some mansions as well."

"I like your idea of heading for the water," Stan said.

An hour and a half of walking didn't reveal any mansions, but it did put them in the center of town. As they passed coffee shops, greasy spoons, and more appealing restaurants, the wafting aromas attacked their empty stomachs. Stan reached into the canvas bag and pulled out a handful of paper bills, mostly fives and tens. "Maybe your pristine conscience would let us spend a little of this loot on a decent meal."

A growl responded in Bertie's deprived stomach. She wasn't about to argue. Asher's Soup and Sandwich Shop proved to be the only incentive they needed. A blackboard with just a few items took the place of a hands-on menu. They feasted on heaping bowls of matzoh-ball soup, thick corned-beef sandwiches on fresh rye, and slices of dill pickles. Accompanied by Dr. Brown's Cel-Ray soda, the lunch was the only substantial meal either one had eaten in a week. Although the restaurant's aluminum-piped chairs were not the most comfortable, they felt like royalty compared to the wood floors of the boxcars. They decided to linger awhile.

An elderly man in a smudged white apron took their orders, served them, and bussed the table afterward. He serviced the five other noon-hour patrons, too. Stan noted that this stooped man with a deeply lined face seemed to be running the business all by himself. Did he do the cooking as well? He looked stressed and weary, walked with a slight limp, and constantly pushed his rimless glasses up his crooked nose.

"Are you the proprietor?" asked Stan.

"Yes," he replied. "I am Mordechai Asher, the owner. How can I help you?"

"I was thinking you might need some help washing dishes and waiting tables. We—"

"You mean you can't pay for the food you've eaten?" asked Asher. "I call the police on you."

"No, no, we have the money. See?" said Stan, as he flipped a five-dollar bill on the table. "I was asking because we need jobs."

"Sadly, I had to let all my people go," said the old man.

"Not enough business to pay anyone. Times are tough. People can't afford to eat out so much. The few customers I get at noon keep us going. My wife, Ida, has to come in now and do all the cooking. We keep the menu simple, tasty, and reasonable in price."

"I just thought we'd ask," said Stan. "The best of luck to you, Mr. Asher."

"Lunch was wonderful," said Bertie. "By the way, what part of town do the wealthy people live in? I'm a certified teacher without a school. I thought I might tutor some rich kids while I wait for a school position."

"And where I might be useful as a groundskeeper," Stan added.

"All the big historical mansions are over on Benefit Street," said Mr. Asher. "There's still money in that area."

"Can you point us in the right direction to get there?" asked Bertie. "We'd appreciate it."

The old man thought for a minute or two, then gave them directions. They thanked Mordechai Asher, left his little sandwich shop, and headed straight to Benefit Street.

Decorative wrought-iron fences, elaborately detailed gates, and manicured green lawns separated the custom-designed mansions from each other and the rest of the lowly world. At least two acres apart, no two mansions shared the same stone or brickwork façade, nor did they have similar layouts. The only feature they had in common was that they all sat on hills of varying sizes, and their main entrances faced Benefit Street. Manned gatehouses held, or withheld, permission to enter these spheres of wealth. Bertie and Stan never got past the gatehouses. Most of their inquiries resulted in "Not hiring at this time" or "We are fully staffed at present." At several gatehouses they were shooed away like so many pesky flies.

Worn out after miles of walking, Bertie and Stan came upon an odd sight near the end of Benefit Street: a FOR SALE sign on a mansion lawn. What set the property apart from all the others was a hint of neglect. The lawn looked as if it hadn't been mowed for at least two weeks, and they could see a couple of windows boarded up. At one end of the wrought-iron fence, a bent vertical railing had been pulled out of the brick and concrete pillar, leaving a thin space a child could fit through. Stan tried the railing and was able to bend it a little farther, leaving a much larger opening.

"Now there's an invitation if I ever saw one," he said. "Shall we?"

"I don't know, Stan. We could be caught trespassing."

"You want to spend the night on the street where we risk being picked up by neighborhood security? Or do you want to be creative and adventurous? Or do you want to shell out some of our booty for an expensive hotel?" He held the bent railing away from the pillar and bowed with a comical flourish of one hand as an invitation for her to squeeze through.

"You're a very bad influence on me, Stan." Bertie squeezed through, and he followed before allowing the railing to spring back into place.

The two intruders made their way around to the rear of the house to lessen the chance of being seen from the street. At the rear service entrance, they discovered that a window pane had been broken and cleared of its shards. Surprised but unfazed, Stan brazenly reached through the empty window to the door latch and found that the door was actually unlocked. As he opened it, they heard a sharp clanging sound coming from the opposite wall. They'd set off a burglar alarm.

"Jeez, I told you so!" cried Bertie, wishing she'd obeyed her own instincts. "Now we're gonna be arrested for breaking and entering."

"*Clang! Clang! Clang!*" The alarm resounded as if it would never stop.

Chapter 9
Questionable Accommodations

THE ALARM CLANGED a few more times, then slacked off to a hum. The bell's external striker hammer continued to vibrate, but more slowly now, unable to reach the large dome-like metal gong that created its intolerable noise. Bertie and Stan were about to dash out the back door and hide among the trees when they realized the bell had stopped its clamor. They spun around to look at the bell—and a curious arrangement they hadn't seen before. On a shelf just below the alarm stood four wired, single-cell A-sized batteries, each cell a little over six inches high and about three inches across.

"Sounds like somebody's battery has run down," said Stan, with a smart-aleck grin. "It plum ran out of gas."

"Do you think anybody heard the alarm?" asked an anxious Bertie.

Stan shrugged. "I doubt it—the houses are set so far apart. Besides, it wasn't on all that long. I guess the real estate people neglected to get the batteries changed. Mounting it on an inside wall wasn't too smart either." He tried the wall switch. "Hey! No lights!"

"It's a good thing, too," said Bertie, as they moved from the delivery hall into the massive kitchen. "The lights could be seen from the street, and then we'd be discovered and arrested."

"You worry too much—get over it," said Stan, as he walked around the room checking out all the cabinets for food of any kind. He found a tin of teabags, two boxes of thick noodles, a can of mixed fruit, and a knocked-over, spilt bag of flour with tiny moving spots. "Ugh!" he said.

In the icebox she found unopened bottles of mustard, ketchup, and a number of discolored, smelly items, spoiled from the lack of ice for some time. She removed the ketchup and mustard and slammed the icebox door shut to contain the stench. "I guess I can boil some noodles and make pasta with ketchup for supper."

She took out a pot from a lower cabinet and tried the sink's water taps. The cold-water tap merely dripped, but the hot water ran into the pot with a tinge of brown from some hidden tank. After ten minutes, most of the coloring settled to the bottom, so she carefully poured the clearer water to a second pot and set it on the stove. A box of wooden matches sat on a rear corner of the stove. All Bertie needed now was some cooking gas in the large steel tank that sat outside the kitchen window. In another twenty minutes she had the noodles boiling. When they were soft, she drained and saved the water. That night they ate pasta-ala-ketchup for their supper.

Afterward, Bertie and Stan explored the lower reaches of the mansion. The lack of draperies on the tall windows let in what was left of the twilight. Most of the furniture had been removed. Only a few rejected or damaged pieces had been left behind. Rugs were gone, and brighter wallpaper squares indicated where paintings once hung. They explored the upstairs after climbing a marble staircase with gilded balusters and mahogany railings. As the twilight faded to mere shadows, their exploring eyes had to move about by moonlight. They discovered bedrooms, dressing rooms, sitting rooms, and additional rooms seemingly without any visible purpose.

Their greatest discovery proved to be twin-sized beds in some of the rooms on the third floor, the servants' quarters. Coil springs, thin mattresses, and a few holey blankets had been left behind. Bertie sat down on a bed and bounced up and down to stress the springs and test the comfort. "Well, I know where I'm spending the night."

"Does that mean I have to sleep elsewhere?" Stan asked.

"As long as we have the luxury of separate bedrooms—yeah," she replied. "So where're you gonna be?"

"Next door, I guess."

They retrieved their things from the first floor and returned to the third. After saying their goodnights in the hall, they tumbled, exhausted, into separate servants' rooms.

Just before daylight Bertie awoke from a sound sleep to persistent scraping and scurrying noises on the roof. Huddling in her half-wrapped, tattered blanket, she ran into the next room and stood over Stan in her bra, panties, and bare feet. Shivering from the morning cold, she shook him. "Stan! Stan! Wake up!"

His lids half-opened, his expression puzzled and annoyed. Bertie shrieked, "Do you hear that racket on the roof? How can you sleep? Maybe it's somebody trying to get in?"

Stan yawned. "Nothing to worry about, babe. Just squirrels playing around. They're not disturbing me. It's you shaking me that will do it every time."

"Squirrels? Oh." She felt silly. Wrapping the blanket more tightly around her shoulders, she whined, "Jeepers, it's freezing up here."

"Come on in," he said softly, "and warm your tootsies." He held up the end of his blanket as an invitation.

"Okay, but don't you go getting any ideas, buster."

She spread her blanket over the top of his and squeezed into the twin bed beside him. Despite the frolicking squirrels on the roof, they both fell asleep for another two hours. When Bertie opened her eyes, Stan's arm was draped over her waist. She could feel the full length of his body against her backside, and something more. Bertie liked the feel of him, every bit of him, but she'd never been this close to a man before, and that feeling made her extremely uneasy. She wasn't prepared to advance to that part of her life just yet. So many things to do and places to go first. She had to admit the sensation excited her and she certainly was curious. It wasn't that she didn't want to, she just wasn't ready for it.

His steady breathing on her neck told her that he slept on. She picked up his arm by the wrist and gently transferred it from her waist to his own hip. Bertie lifted the blankets, and slipped out of bed. She tiptoed out of the room and into her own without disturbing him. Quickly dressing to get warm, she headed downstairs to the kitchen and put up the kettle full of the pre-used water to make tea. Her colleague intruder joined her just as the kettle began to whistle. Neither mentioned their spontaneous intimacy. Not a word of it.

Bertie and Stan sat at the kitchen table on stools, sipping their tea. The table wobbled and the stools needed repainting or they wouldn't have been left behind. They contemplated what the new day held for them.

"We could hole up here for a few days before heading back to the trains," she said, taking a sip out of the chipped mug. "The cops will be done looking for the boxcar murderer by then, at least around Providence. But they have no idea where he got shot, nor where he even got on the train. I think that would open their search to include the entire route between New York and here."

"Hey, the sleeping's pretty good here," Stan said. "There's no reason to hurry away from this place."

"I agree," she said. "The beds *are* good, but the food and water are almost gone. Oh, by the way, I did find some potatoes and onions in bins under the sink, but even those few won't last long. Water is the scarce thing."

"We could buy water and groceries," said Stan. "Don't forget, I still have all this booty in the bag. It would pay for a lot of groceries over a long time."

"Don't you get it, Stan? It's not our money. We have to give it back."

"I thought you had gotten over all that righteous stuff."

"I haven't," she retorted. "And what are you planning to do to entertain yourself, hanging around here all day? We need to get jobs and pay our own way."

"Well, Miss Teacher, we could pick up some magazines and dime novels and do some serious reading," he replied with a lop-sided grin.

"You've got an answer for everything," she scolded. "Two days tops. No more."

They ate the remainder of the cooked naked noodles and drank tea for their breakfast. When Stan finished, he swung away from the table on his wooden stool and stood up. Rummaging through the little canvas bag, he drew out a wad of ten-dollar bills and stuck it in a pocket of his shirt.

"I'm going grocery shopping," he said. "You want to come?"

"No. I'll stay behind and clean up and look around a little more."

Stan left the house through the same delivery hall door they'd used the day before. While he skirted the right edge of the mansion to the street side, Bertie hurried to one of the windows at the front of the house to watch him cross the lawn and head to the opening in the wrought-iron fence they'd accessed to get in. Stan reappeared a moment later. A warm feeling enveloped her as she watched him. *I know I'm not in love with Stan, so it must be physical attraction. I've looked at boys and men before and admired some, but none have disturbed me like this. He does have a lean, athletic physique and he walks with some authority. And my God, his bush of red-brown hair. The beard I could do without.*

Stan disappeared through the fence. The stale, neglected house made Bertie feel the need to get outside in the fresh air. She followed the perimeter of the mansion in the opposite direction that Stan had taken and found a small brick outbuilding about ten feet from the main house.

On one side of the small building sat a concrete slab with a red hand pump emerging from it. A wooden bucket sat beside the pump. She took hold of the red cast-iron handle and gave it a few token shakes, which evoked a mere trickle of water spilling onto the concrete slab in a small puddle. Setting the bucket under the spout, she worked the handle up and down with a vengeance. The bucket began to fill, and when it was full, she had an idea. Knowing Stan wouldn't be back for a while, Bertie stripped to her bare skin and set her clothes aside. She upended the icy cold water over her whole body and shivered joyously. She filled the bucket twice more, and twice more doused herself.

When she had finished bathing, it suddenly dawned on her that she hadn't planned on how to get dry. At first, she used her hands to squeegee the water away from her skin. A bright, warm June sun and a cool breeze did the rest in another ten minutes. She dressed and pumped more water for use in the kitchen, at least three bucketsful that she transferred to cooking pots left behind. Straddling a kitchen stool, she peeled and sliced the remainder of the usable potatoes and onions and put them in a pot with water to boil on the stove. There weren't any seasonings except for a little salt left in the bottom of a shaker.

Stan hadn't returned after five hours of supposed shopping and Bertie began to worry. She went to the front window and sat down on a straight-back dining room chair with its arms broken to watch for his arrival. Finally, she saw him slip through the fence, toting two brown paper bags. She watched him come up the lawn hill and disappear around the side of the mansion. She rushed to the back door to greet him.

"What took you so long?"

"Well, I took a little sightseeing walk first and next I had to find a grocery store. When I came out of the store, I discovered I'd lost my way, how to get back here. It took me a while to get back on track. I'm here now, aren't I? And I came back with all the goodies, didn't I?"

Resisting the impulse to hug him, she asked, "What kind

of goodies?"

He called out the items as he took them out of the paper bags: "Six hot dogs, a half-pound of sliced bologna, a half-pound of butter, a loaf of white bread, two tins of soup, a half-dozen eggs, a bunch of carrots, a pound of sliced American cheese, a quart of milk, a quart of orange soda pop, two magazines, and a dime novel, a Western. I had to limit what I got because we don't have the ice to keep things from spoiling."

"How much did you spend, Stan?"

"Only thirteen dollars and eighty-six cents. Don't worry, Bertie, we still have most of the booty left."

The two had a luxurious supper and went to sleep as soon as night had left them in total darkness. They slept in their separate rooms. Bertie made sure of that. It wasn't that she didn't trust him. It was her own self-control that she questioned. They both slept well and daylight came quickly. But with it came all sorts of commotion outside. Bounding out of bed, Bertie rushed to the window and saw that the front gates were open.

"Oh my God! Stan, come quick!"

Stan joined her and peered out. There were stake trucks, mowers, and gardeners at work all over the grounds. "Jeezuz!" he said. "We're surrounded. We couldn't leave here even if we wanted to."

"Maybe when they finish their jobs they'll go home," said Bertie. "Maybe they won't even know we're up here."

"Sure, that's it," he said. "We'll hang out up here all day until they're gone."

They left the window and Stan returned to his room while they both dressed. He spent the time reading *Riders of the Purple Sage* by Zane Grey, while Bertie read and reread *Life* and *The Saturday Evening Post*. Just past noon they heard truck engines again.

"Sounds like they're leaving," said Bertie.

The two hopeful squatters ran to her window. "Oh no!" she said. Now other vehicles were lined up in the driveway with cleaning supplies sitting on the concrete beside them. And they noticed that the groundskeepers had left without finishing; only three-quarters of the lawn had been mowed. Then Bertie and Stan heard the massive front doors open, with clunking and clanking inside on the main level—pails and other implements being dropped on the marble floors.

"I assume the cleaners will scrub the first two floors," said Bertie, her voice quavering. "But what if they come all the way up here to clean the servants' quarters? They'll find us."

Stan shrugged. "Then our asses will be cooked, for sure."

Chapter 10
Housecleaning

THE MOPPING, SLOSHING, POLISHING, and scrubbing on both the first and second floors continued to resound up the staircase, telling Bertie and Stan that these workers were here for the day.

"If they come up here and find us, what will they do with us?" asked Bertie.

"What *can* they do?" asked Stan. "I'd say there are four possibilities. The worst is, they capture and physically hold on to us until the police arrive. Second, they throw us out on our bums. Next, they call the real estate people to report us. Finally, they ignore us as we walk past them out the door with all our stuff."

"I knew breaking in here was a really bad idea," scolded Bertie. "We're mansion squatters, and that's illegal in anybody's book."

"And stealing a ride on a train isn't illegal?" he reminded her.

"That's different," she argued, although knowing it really wasn't. "But now isn't the time to be debating legalities or ethics. We need an escape plan."

"The way I see it," said Stan, "if they discover us, it's *their* decision what to do. Let's take control of the situation ourselves. What if we calmly walk down three flights of stairs and out the front door as if we own the place? We'll take 'em by surprise and give 'em no time to react."

"What about all those nice groceries you bought?" she asked.

"They're expendable," he replied. "The booty bag can replace whatever we need, when we need it. That way we can travel light."

"You think it'll work?" she asked.

"You got a better plan up your sleeve?"

"Nope."

"Okay, then. Let's get our stuff together and march down the stairs like we own the place. Remember, keep on going no matter what. Don't stop for anything and say nothing."

The squatters gathered their belongings and started down the stairs. The usual din of so many people engaged in work muffled the sounds of their footsteps. At the second floor landing they saw the backsides of three hefty, diligent women—one with a dustmop, another pushing a carpet sweeper, and the third bent over, scrubbing a bathtub. The one with the dust mop sensed their motion and glanced in their direction, but only for a second. She had no interest in them.

Bertie followed Stan down to the first floor into the spacious reception hall. There they encountered a man on an eight-foot stepladder, dusting a yard-wide yard-tall crystal chandelier. His eyes locked onto them and followed them as they boldly strolled to the main entrance, a set of carved oak doors. He said and did nothing but watch them. Another worker, on a shorter stepladder, was washing a stained-glass front window. He paid them no attention. A woman on her knees was scrubbing spots from the marble floor near the double doors. She awkwardly stood up as if her joints hurt, and stared at them. A chill shot through Bertie. But the cleaning woman had stood not to confront them, but to allow their passage.

Just as the two walked through the doors they heard a bass voice of authority. "Hey, what the hell were you two doing in here?" The voice came from nowhere in particular. They knew better than to slow down to check it out.

"Maybe we should pick up the pace a little," said Bertie. Her first urge was to break into a run.

"No," said Stan. "Remember, act like we own the place. Just keep going toward the main gate and out of here. If someone gives chase, then we run like hell. Let's keep it together and stick to the plan."

They deliberately sauntered down the driveway to Benefit Street and turned to the right outside the gate. As they walked the length of the fence, they kept looking over their right shoulders through the wrought-iron railings to see if anybody had decided to chase them. No one did. A siren, heard in the distance, caught their attention, and Bertie wondered whether it was a police cruiser looking for them, or, if they were lucky, just a fire engine answering a call.

"Do you think any of those cleaning people called the cops on us?" she asked.

"No," Stan said. "We would have heard from the police by now. Besides, it was no skin off those people's noses. They had no stock and trade in that place. As far as they know, we didn't steal or harm anything or anybody."

"I hope you're right," she said.

"I'm thinking we could even go back there tonight when that cleaning crew clears out."

"You can stop thinking that way right now, Mr. Stan. The cleanup is for a reason. Either the place has already been sold, or the real estate people plan on showing it to potential renters or buyers real soon."

"Even if you're right, Bertie, it's doubtful there would be anything going on in the house after hours. Why should we pass up a perfectly good place to eat some of our own food and sleep and hang out for a few hours? And it would only be one night."

"Are you crazy?" she snapped. "What if someone did call the police on us, and the coppers keep an eye out on the place?"

"Aw, you worry too damn much. Stop sulking and enjoy our freedom. Within reason, we can do anything and go anywhere we like."

"Wishful thinking, Stan." She was close to tears.

"Hey, Bertie, I know how to cheer you up. Why don't I buy you lunch? I know this great place that has a swell bowl of matzoh-ball soup, and we can get a stacked, corned-beef sandwich there, too."

Bertie brightened. "Yes! I'm starving. Do you remember how to get there?" They had missed breakfast with their hasty morning retreat.

"I think so." He closed his eyes and called on his memory to retrace yesterday's steps. Within a few minutes, he spotted a few familiar landmarks and led her straight to Asher's Soup and Sandwich Shop. Upon entering, they sensed something amiss. Mordechai Asher sat by the rear door with his bald head in his hands.

"Mordechai, what's wrong?" Bertie asked.

He slowly looked up and raised his two bushy brows in surprise. The sight of the two friendly customers from the day before put a spark of hope in the elderly man's eyes. "Hello, my dears. I'm having a bad day. My wife, Ida, she's sick upstairs with a cold, sneezing and coughing. She always does the cooking while I wait and bus tables. It's nearly ten o'clock and there's not nearly enough chicken soup and no one to make sandwiches. I don't know what to do. You asked for jobs yesterday, but there's no way I can pay you anything."

"Maybe we can help you anyway," said Stan. "I can wait and bus tables while Bertie takes over in the kitchen. And you can run the register and supervise." He looked over at her anxiously to get her reaction. After all, he'd assigned her a job without her permission.

She nodded her head vigorously. "Of course."

"But we still can't pay you," whined a frustrated Mordechai. "We make so little profit we barely make ends meet."

"Tell you what, my friend," offered Stan. "You don't need to pay us any cash money. We will work today and tomorrow for leftover meals and a place to sleep on your floor tonight. We plan to be on our way by tomorrow evening. But if your Ida isn't on her feet by then, we might work another day or so. Right, Bertie?"

"Right!" she answered, unsure of what they were getting themselves into, but too hungry to care.

"You both are so generous—like two *malakh* (angels in Hebrew) sent down from heaven," said Mordechai.

The small deli's décor suited Bertie. Simple and friendly, seating no more than twenty-five. The front room, the dining area, had a floor of black and white linoleum squares and lemon-yellow walls. Wall sconces with triangular black metal shades. Square white Formica tables. Metal chairs with black-and-white checkered cushions tied to the frames.

"I guess I'd better get in the kitchen and get oriented," said Bertie.

"All of Ida's recipes are taped to the cabinet door over the sink," said Mordechai. "She did that for the hired help we once had. And the chicken stock is in those number-ten cans under the counter. There's corned-beefs, pastramis, and tongues in the refrigerator."

"Refrigerator?" repeated Stan. "What's that?"

"Like an icebox, but better," said Mordechai. "Come, I show you."

Stan and Bertie followed him into the kitchen and showed them the upright white box with the vibrating electric motor on top humming away. He opened the door for them to see inside.

"You see that motor up on top?" asked Mordechai. "It makes the cold inside the box." He put his fingers on the meat to test the cold as if to verify the science he didn't understand.

Stan stared in wonderment. "Wow!"

"That yellow and blue bowl with the cloth cover—is that

what I think it is?" asked Bertie.

"It's the leftover matzoh balls that Ida made yesterday," replied Mordechai. "Only five left. You will have to make more before lunchtime."

"Where do you keep the sharp knives for slicing the meat?" asked Bertie, as she began filling large stock pots with water for boiling.

"Slicing meat is done with that machine over there," he said, pointing to the side counter. "It's a miracle. Easy to use, but also quite dangerous if you get careless."

Bertie shuddered. "I'll leave the meat-cutting and sandwich-making to you, Mordechai. I can certainly handle the cooking part okay. With you back here to supervise, I feel pretty confident. Stan can take care of everything up front."

"I think I can take orders, serve food, and bus tables," said Stan. "After all, it's only a simple menu. Hey, can I use that apron on the hook there?"

"Sure, anything you need," replied Mordechai.

While the water boiled, Bertie assembled the box of matzoh meal, carton of eggs, a jar of *schmaltz* (chicken fat), and shakers of salt and pepper. She carefully mixed the ingredients, precisely according to Ida's recipes—afraid to deviate even a tiny bit. Scooping out measured amounts, she rolled them into small round balls and submerged them one by one gently into boiling water. The finished matzoh balls would be ready in forty-five minutes. While waiting for them to cook, Bertie opened a can of concentrated chicken soup stock and poured it into a four-quart stock pot. Then she scooped out an equal amount of boiling water from the matzoh-ball pot, and stirred it into the stock pot. She set the gas flame under the stock pot to allow the soup mixture to simmer.

At 11:30, Stan came into the kitchen with the first order of soup and a pastrami sandwich. Plucking the first matzoh ball out of the boiling water, Bertie hastily cut it in two to see if it was thoroughly cooked. It passed the test, so she put a second one in a bowl and smothered it with a ladling of chicken soup. She set the soup bowl on a saucer and placed it on Stan's serving tray.

Meanwhile, Mordechai removed the chunk of pastrami from the refrigerator, laid it on the slicing machine carriage, and turned the rotating slicer on. Pushing on the meat, he rocked the carriage back and forth and caught the uniform slices in the palm of his other hand. He stacked the meat an inch-and-a-half high on a slice of fresh rye bread, covered it with a second slice, and placed it on the tray next to the soup for Stan to convey to their first patron. Mordechai also rang up the mechanical cash register when each patron paid.

Stan soon came back with more orders, nearly always the soup, but the meats varied. The pace of orders quickly increased, and the tasks fell into a rhythm. When the dining area turned warm, Stan turned on the exhaust fan and the aroma of chicken soup wafted outdoors through the transom. They had an uptick of business during the noon hour, nineteen customers that day. Pleased with himself, Stan told Bertie, "Maybe it was the aroma outside that drew in the extra patrons."

They spent the next hour and a half cleaning up and handling two mid-afternoon customers. Mordechai brought soup upstairs to Ida and spent the rest of the afternoon with her, giving Bertie a chance to try her hand at the slicing machine. Having watched Mordechai pretty carefully, she managed the task without chopping off a finger.

At suppertime the same routine worked beautifully except there were only seven customers to deal with. By eight o'clock Mordechai had emptied the register and locked the front door for the day. Stan pulled a deck of playing cards out of his backpack. After a successful day, he and Bertie played gin rummy for a couple hours before turning out the lights and lying down on several blankets Asher had left out for them in the back hall behind the kitchen. Both slept soundly.

Stan's eyes popped open suddenly. He'd heard something, but what? He looked up at the clock. It was a little after one o'clock in the morning. There it was again. He sat up. It sounded like glass breaking. He looked over the tabletops and saw a hairy arm reaching in through the broken glass pane in the front door to undo the deadbolt lock. A second figure, silhouetted by moonlight, peered into the room's darkness from a larger storefront window pane.

Stan placed one hand over Bertie's mouth and brought a *shushing* finger to his own lips. She awoke ready to scream, but saw his finger in time and acknowledged it with a nod. The two sat there, watching in disbelief. Both felt the grip of fear. Were these burglars armed?

Chapter 11
Chaser and Chased

THE FRONT DOOR, with its smashed glass panel, edged open and two silhouetted figures stole into the shop. They scanned the room and located the cash register. While they busied themselves trying to force it open, Stan and Bertie, still on the floor in the back hall, crept quietly on hands and knees into the kitchen. The tables and stacked chairs in the dining area hid their strategic positions. In the kitchen they silently stood up and each grabbed one of Mordechai's carving knives.

"We'll rush them simultaneously with our knives and scream bloody murder as we go," Stan whispered in Bertie's ear. "Now!" he bellowed aloud a few seconds later.

The two intruders froze at the sight of two screaming crazies headed straight for them—with butcher knives slashing back and forth in the air. The self-preservation instinct quickly melted the frozen stances. With an about-face, the intruders fled the store and soon disappeared. Stan and Bertie never got within five feet of the robbers.

"Would you have actually stabbed one of them?" Bertie asked.

"I suppose not," Stan said, breathing heavily, "but I sure would have slashed at him. Maybe an arm or a hand—enough to get them to change their minds and get the hell out of here. How about you, Bertie, what would you have done?"

"I honestly don't know," she replied, "I probably would've followed your lead and bungled it."

They heard shuffling feet on the stairs and Mordechai burst into the room brandishing a baseball bat in his right hand. He stopped abruptly when he saw his two helpers standing there with knives in their hands.

"Good God, what's going on down here?" he cried. "What was the screaming and yelling all about?"

"We've just chased off two burglars," said Bertie. "We woke up when we heard them break in. When we got into the kitchen, we saw them trying to open the cash register. We scared them off by running at them screaming with knives in our hands. You should have seen the look on their faces."

"Unfortunately," said Stan, "they left you with a broken pane of glass in the front door. We'll patch it temporarily in the morning if you have a piece of wood, a few nails, and a hammer."

"That won't be necessary," said Mordechai. "I'll call my friend Marv Wollenski, the glazier. He'll come over and put in a new piece of glass—like new, even. Once again, you blessed angels have saved us from disaster. Thank you!"

Meanwhile, Stan walked over to the cash register. "I don't see any visible problems with it," he said, after examining the silver-colored, cast-iron machine for damage. "At least they never got into the cash drawer inside. And look, they even left their hammer and chisel behind."

"It wouldn't have done the *momzers* (bastards in Yiddish) any good," said Mordechai. "I took all the cash out last night. It's in the safe upstairs."

"Maybe we should all go back to bed now, or none of us will be worth anything in the morning," said Bertie.

Mordechai propped the baseball bat in the corner and disappeared up the stairs. Bertie and Stan flopped back down on their blankets. Sleep came slowly, only after their adrenaline and fear had sapped away. They awoke at six with someone pounding on the remaining glass pane in the front door. It was the first of the deli's breakfast customers. Before the two so-called angels could rise to the new day, they heard Mordechai on the stairs, then saw him rush past them to answer the door. He greeted the man and seated him at the opposite end of the dining area.

"Good morning, Meyer. I apologize for not being open already," said Mordechai. "We were all up last night with a break-in."

"A break-in, really?" said Meyer Levin. "What did the burglar take?"

"The two burglars took *bupkis*, absolutely nothing, thanks to my two helping angels over there."

Mordechai pointed in the direction of Stan, who had just scrambled to his feet in the back hall. And Bertie, folding blankets next to him, waved to Meyer and received a wave in return. Hurrying to the kitchen sink to wash up and get things organized, she also started the coffeepot that she'd loaded the night before.

"So, my friend, what will you have this fine morning?" asked Mordechai.

"I'd like some of that *gemish*, that mixture of eggs and meat scraps you always make for me. Oh, and coffee and a bagel, too. With a *bissel* cream cheese would be nice, my friend."

"Coming right up," Mordechai answered as he set the table.

He went to the kitchen to fetch the coffee and relay the order to Bertie. "There are some meat ends that won't go through the slicer in a mason jar at the back of the refrigerator. Second shelf. Grab a handful, chop them fine, fry them crisp, and toss them into three scrambled eggs. Can you do that, dear?"

"Sure thing," she replied.

Stan walked away from the kitchen sink, drying his hands on a dish towel. "Where are the bagels?" he asked.

"Out the back door," replied Mordechai. "They're delivered fresh every morning, along with the rye and pumpernickel breads." He unlocked the door and picked up a wicker basket containing three brown paper bags, still warm. He brought the delivery inside, pulled out one bagel, and handed it to Stan.

Stan put it on a small plate with a generous chunk of cream cheese, picked up the plate of *gemish* that Bertie had ready for him, and set it all before Mr. Levin. "I'll bring out your coffee in a jiffy, sir."

Meanwhile, other customers started to wander in and the sandwich shop trio fell right into cadence. Stan served fifteen breakfasts that morning and twenty-one lunches that noon, while Bertie and Mordechai manned the kitchen. Shortly before the supper trade began arriving, Mordechai came down the stairs.

"My Ida is so much better I feel certain that she can handle the whole kitchen in the morning. Of course, you both can stay as long as you like. It's been wonderful having you here."

"Thank you, said Stan. "But since you'll have your star teammate back, I think it's time for us to be on our way again."

"Yeah," agreed Bertie. "We should get going some time tomorrow morning. We need to shop around for more permanent employment."

"I only wish I had more business, enough to keep you here full time. You two have been so good to us—like our own children even. We had a son once—David Alan Asher. He died of rheumatic fever at the age of sixteen. That was eighteen years ago. David was smart as a whip and ambitious. He would have made something of himself—not dull shopkeepers like his parents. Stan, in some little ways you remind me of him."

"Thank you," acknowledged Stan. "I'd be honored to be your son, but you shouldn't belittle your profession. I think being a shopkeeper, especially owning a restaurant, is a respectable way to make a living. And more than that, you're providing a service!"

Bertie chimed in. "Your matzoh-ball soup and sandwiches are fabulous!"

"Thank you," said Mordechai, flashing a rare smile.

After the trio had served nineteen customers their evening meal and final cleanup had been started, Ida made her way down the stairs and sat down at the corner table. "I just had to meet the wonderful couple who have been such a big help to my Mordechai."

"We'll be leaving here in the morning, ma'am," said Bertie. "We're going to look around town a bit and then head for the railroad tracks."

"Are you two just travel companions, or have you a more romantic tie?" asked Ida.

"Oh, we're travel companions all right, and friends, too," replied Bertie. "Nothing more." *Although I wonder about that.* The tantalizing thought drifted through her mind.

"Yeah, we're just two grand buddies," confirmed Stan. "We only met a few days ago. I kinda like her, though."

Ida and Mordechai smiled as though they knew something the youngsters didn't.

The four of them teamed up to serve twenty-three breakfasts the next morning. The two helpers packed up as soon as the morning cleanup was done. The goodbyes were difficult; the four of them almost felt like family. Ida planted a kiss on the foreheads of both Stan and Bertie. She waved to them through the display window just before they stepped out of sight.

As they wandered through the city of Providence aimlessly, they found themselves in an upscale neighborhood. Not mansions, but well-to-do homes that nevertheless warranted police patrols. As they turned the corner, it was their bad luck to find a police cruiser parked on the near side of the street. A uniformed officer leaned against the open driver's door, talking to a man in front of one of the homes. He halted his conversation when he took notice of the two vagrants, who would have no good reason for being in this neighborhood. The big-bellied officer abruptly left his cruiser and started walking in their direction. With a scowl on his face and a hand resting on his billy club, he was bent on catching up with them.

"This doesn't look good," declared Bertie. The memory of Arnie being beaten was still fresh in her mind. "Maybe we should head in another direction."

"No maybe about it," shouted Stan. "He's coming faster now and it looks like we're meat for his dinner. Up in here!" Stan yanked Bertie through an open gate and up a driveway to a back-yard with a garage. A thick hedgerow paralleled the driveway all the way to the garage and beyond. "In here!" he yelled, pushing her into the narrow tunnel-like space between hedge and garage. They crawled to the rear of the garage before the officer turned into the driveway. Peeking out, Stan saw him trudge into the backyard. Too fat to be agile, he chugged left and right trying to locate his prey. Standing with feet apart, the officer scanned the spacious yard, but his pursuit was hampered by the abundance of blooming shrubs and flower beds.

Stan and Bertie silently followed the hedge to its end, cir-cled around it, and retraced their path back to the street. The two fugitives were about to pass the cruiser when Bertie stopped short. "Stan! That idiot of an officer left his driver's door open and the engine still running!" Gleefully, she reached in for the ignition key, turned off the engine, pulled out the key, and dropped it under the seat. Chuckling at her own ingenuity, she slammed the door shut, and the two took off racing down the block. At the corner half a block away, Bertie looked back and saw the officer standing next to the cruiser with the door open, shaking his head. She waved a friendly, or rather mocking, gesture to him, for she knew of two reasons why he was incapable of following them: the missing key and the beer belly overlapping his belt. Infuriated but helpless, he shook his billy club at them. Bertie and Stan ran for another four blocks, turning two more corners, hoping the hidden ignition key would also prevent the officer from radioing their escape to another cruiser. As they ran, Bertie couldn't help but ask herself where she'd gotten the moxie to sabotage a policeman's cruiser.

Tired and sweaty, they sought a grocery store where they

could purchase a cold soda pop, and learn their way to the railroad tracks. Ten more minutes brought them in sight of Papadopoulos's Drugstore. Making a beeline for it, they hurried inside, straight to the fountain, a long marble counter with three stainless steel stools topped by rubber cushions. They slid their fannies onto adjacent stools. The paper-hatted soda jerk, a youngster in his late teens, asked, "Hi, what'll you have?"

"I'll have a cabinet," said Stan.

"What's that?" she asked.

"It's a local name for a milkshake," replied Stan. "I'll have a chocolate cabinet."

"And you?" the soda jerk asked Bertie.

"A fountain Coke, please," she replied.

The soda jerk tossed two scoops of vanilla ice cream into a twelve-ounce stainless mixing beaker, added a dash of milk, gave it a shot of chocolate syrup, filled it to the mark with seltzer, and slipped it onto the spindle mixer/agitator. A whirring sound emanated as soon as the beaker was pressed against the machine. The soda jerk poured the foamy mixture into a tall metal glass and set it in front of Stan. Next, he placed a six-ounce glass under a fountain spigot and depressed the lever above it down twice, squirting Coca Cola syrup into the glass. Filling the glass with pressurized seltzer, he set it down in front of Bertie, then laid two paper-encased straws on the counter.

Initially, they paid no attention to another patron entering the drugstore and sliding onto the remaining stool. Two copper pennies rattled on the marble counter as they settled to stillness. Bertie turned and regarded the man on the stool next to her. Short and stocky, with a sullen face half-hidden under a tangled dirty beard. He wore a stained tan shirt and a wrinkled pair of dark trousers. She quickly turned away. The newcomer didn't say a word, yet the soda jerk understood and automatically poured the man a plain glass of pure seltzer.

The two thirsty ones nursed their drinks to the bottom. Bertie finished first and went to the magazine rack near the door.

Concerned that she would leave without paying, the soda jerk announced, "That will be fifteen cents for the cabinet and five cents for the fountain Coke."

"Sure thing. By the way, how do we get to the railroad station?" asked Stan.

"Go left out of here and left again at the corner and you'll be headed north to the station," the teen replied.

"Thanks." Stan reached into his pocket and came up with a roll of fives and tens. He peeled a five off the top, laid it on the counter, and waited for his change before joining Bertie at the magazine rack. What he didn't notice was the attention paid to the money roll by the stranger sitting on the third stool.

The two left the store and followed the soda jerk's instructions, but before they had gone far, Stan had this queer feeling that someone was watching them. He stopped and turned around to see a person walking a half-block behind them. The more he looked, the more the person resembled the grungy stranger in the drugstore.

"Why are you stopping?" asked Bertie.

"You know that guy who sat next to you at the counter?" asked Stan, noticing the stranger had stopped as well.

"Yeah, that creepy bum. I wonder what he's after?"

"It can't be anything good," said Stan. "Oh-oh!"

"What?"

"Maybe he saw the roll of bills I paid with."

"That's a no-no, Stan," retorted Bertie. "You should never show you have that much money in front of strangers. It's like giving them an invitation to rob you."

"You're right. I'm sure that's what the crumb-bum is after."

They started walking again. An anxious Stan glanced over his shoulder. Yup. The stranger had resumed tailing them.

Chapter 12
Confrontation

BERTIE AND STAN picked up the pace as they walked toward the railroad tracks. The persistent stranger lingered a half-block behind, making no effort to close the distance.

"What can we do about that guy?" asked Bertie, her gut tightening. Despite the June sun beginning to bake, goosebumps began covering her bare arms.

"We can try to outmaneuver the bum," replied Stan. "He's up to no good."

They tried a zig at one corner and a zag at the next corner, then two zigs and three zags, but the stranger doggedly reappeared on their tail. Cutting through a yard to the next street worked for a while, but twenty minutes later, there he was again. The two darted into another backyard and hid under the back porch of a two-story house for nearly an hour. Restful it wasn't—bent over, heads down, their knees ached from crouching on the dirt. Still, the ploy worked. They appeared to have lost the stranger and fled before the owner of the house discovered them.

As they ventured farther north, their surroundings became more metropolitan with additional traffic and pedestrians. They didn't see any recognizable landmarks to guide them back to where they had gotten off the train three days ago. A newsstand proprietor gave them directions to the station, but when they got there, they found that the tracks were underground, impossible to reach from the street.

"Let's see if we can get to the platforms inside via the station's gates," suggested Stan.

"You really think we can?" asked Bertie.

"We'll never know unless we try," he replied.

When they did try, they were met just outside the gate by a uniformed railroad employee checking for tickets. Stan had a plan. Weaving back through the crowd, he found a wire trash receptacle and retrieved a piece of cardboard roughly the color of a train ticket. He tore it into the approximate size of a ticket, and repeated with a second bogus ticket. He'd noticed that when a train was about to leave, people surged forward in bunches as they tried to catch a particular train. Stan and Bertie waited for just that moment and pushed their way through the gate between two other couples.

The ticket checker shouted, "Hey you!" Stan flashed the two bogus tickets and kept going, dragging Bertie along with him. The checker couldn't read them, but appeared to be satisfied that they were bona fide. He had other tickets to check.

"You're a genius," said Bertie, trotting alongside him.

"Not bad even if I do say so myself," said Stan, grinning.

That boarding crowd dwindled as they moved closer to the end of the platform. At the very end, the tracks began to converge. The fellow travelers needed to cross over to the workmen's path that paralleled the tracks—or face the danger of an express train overtaking them. Stan and Bertie soon realized they were still a long way from the freight sidings. After almost two miles of walking, Bertie began to recognize some of the surroundings where they'd gotten off the train four days earlier: a three-story tenement, a church steeple, and some ugly racial fence graffiti. She figured the freight cars of a similar train would stop in the same approximate location. A stack of spare rail ties convinced them that this was the best place to wait for a train going toward Boston.

The stack of ties, about two feet high and six feet across, became their bench. Stan sat while Bertie stretched out and laid her head in his lap. The evening advanced as two trains passed without stopping. A mixed train stopped, but all the freight cars were locked. Hours later, Bertie left Stan alone to pee in the nearby bushes. Near midnight, Stan heard footsteps in the adjacent gravel and traprock mix. He had been lulled into a false sense of security. He called out, "Bertie?"

No response. "Bertie?"

Silence, except for another crunch in the gravel and then another.

"Bertie?" he called a third time. His eyes strained to see into the dark shadow cast by the high border walls.

A form materialized out of the blackness into the moon-light—along with the face belonging to the same stranger who had dogged them all afternoon, He held a foot-and-a-half length of pipe in his left hand and wore a desperate look on his unshaven face. Looming over Stan, he raised the pipe to a threatening height, and growled: "Gimme your roll or I'll beat the crap out of you."

Stan tensed, leaned away, and said nothing while he hauled himself to his feet. Without warning, he leapt forward, butting his head straight for the stranger's solar plexus. Although he drove the stranger backward, the pipe glanced his own back with a sting-ing pain. Stan recoiled with the blow and fell backward onto the ground. The stranger took the opportunity to climb on top of him and batter his face, first with a left fist and then a right. The two battled for some minutes, exchanging punches, arm and leg twists, plus a good deal of rolling around on the ground. Stan took the worst of it with a bloody nose and blow to his left eye. He cried out, "Uncle!" as he held up his hands to protect his face.

"Your money," demanded the low-life, sitting on Stan's knees. He had recovered the pipe and held it threateningly over the vanquished one.

"Here, take it," said Stan. He reached into his pocket, retrieved a roll of bills, and passed it to the victor, who stuffed it into his own pocket. Stan watched the stranger's eyes, trying to determine whether the man intended to beat him to a pulp anyway, but another voice intervened.

"Who are you talking to, Stan?" cried Bertie, returning from her call to nature.

Before she arrived on the scene, the stranger got to his feet and ran off into the shadow of the below-ground border wall.

"Good God, Stan, what happened to you?"

"It was the son-of-a-bitch from the drugstore who was following us," he moaned.

"How the hell did he find us?"

"I don't know. He beat me up and got the money from my pocket."

"Never mind the money," she said. "Your face is a big mess. You're going to have quite a shiner in the morning. And hold your nose to stop the bleeding. What else did he do to you?"

Stan shrugged and squirmed. "I hurt all over, but at least he didn't get all the money. I'd put most of it in my backpack. He didn't take my guitar either."

Bertie removed a jar of water she'd packed at the deli and a clean sock from her own backpack. After pouring water over the sock, she proceeded to clean each of his facial wounds. Stan squirmed and sputtered "Ow" with each of her treatments. His nose eventually stopped bleeding, but he was in no condition to board any trains that night. Bertie thought they might be able to tackle one first thing in the morning. The two spent a restless night with Stan constantly fidgeting in her lap as she sat up cradling his beaten-up head.

At little after 5 a.m., with the sun still hiding below the horizon, Bertie heard the distant rumble of a train, the whistle first, then the locomotive's chugging as it slowed for the Providence passenger stop. They had camped in the right place; freight cars were sprawled to the right and left of them. Bertie looked over the boarding choices, knowing that her busted-up travel buddy couldn't hobble very far. There might have been unlocked cars with their doors open farther down the line, but each of the cars before them appeared to be secured by a padlock. Only one car seemed accessible: a lone flat car with wooden slats containing crates of live chickens—hundreds of them on their way to market, making a continuous racket.

With Stan's arm heavily draped across her shoulders, Bertie shuffled toward the noisy, smelly fowl. She lifted out the spike in the hasp, rolled back the door, and literally shoved Stan into the one aisle left free at the car's midpoint. She climbed in after him. Once she had Stan settled, she rearranged a few of the heavy crates so the two stowaways wouldn't be seen from outside the car. They laid their heads on their backpacks and tried to relax amid the surrounding chaos.

The train clanked and bumped into motion, disturbing the chickens into an even greater frenzy. The clucking and crowing eventually subsided, but the smell of chicken poop never did. Bertie felt nauseated on and off throughout the morning hours as the wafting stench hit, wave after wave. Finally, exhaustion and the rhythmic wheel-and-track beat lulled her to sleep.

Stan lay awake, staring mostly at sky and treetops. Each time he looked into one of the wooden crates beside him, he found a hen poking her head through the crate slats, staring back at him. It gave him a creepy feeling. Forty minutes later, he sensed that the train had stopped. He sat up, realizing the train had changed direction. Stan gave Bertie a shove.

"What's going on? Why'd you wake me?" she whined.

"We're backing into a siding," he replied. "I think we're going to be left behind in the boonies with the chickens."

She sprang to a sitting position. "Then we've got to get off and find a boxcar going our way," she said. "Are you fit enough to run after a moving car?"

"I don't think so," he replied.

The train came to a full squeaking stop after backing three

cars, including theirs, up to the loading and unloading pier at the end of the siding. These three cars were then decoupled and left behind, as the train rolled back onto the main-line track and continued on its way—without the chicken cars. It all happened so quickly that Bertie and Stan couldn't possibly transfer to a different boxcar. Once more Bertie helped her friend to his feet, and with his arm heavily draped across her shoulders, she steered him out of the chicken flatcar onto the unloading dock.

They were met by four men in rubber aprons ready to unpack the crates. One of them wisecracked, "What kind of chickens are these?" The others laughed and made clucking sounds.

"Don't say a thing," whispered Bertie. "You don't want to start anything, the shape you're in."

"Don't worry, I've learned my lesson."

"Cluck, cluck, and arruck," continued one of the wisecrackers.

The two stumbled to the end of the dock, down the stairs, and along the private gravel path toward the county road. With Stan's body aching and Bertie's strength draining, they ended up with no clue to where they were.

The county road proved to be sparsely traveled, and the traffic that did pass cared not a whit for two hitchhikers with their thumbs pointing uproad. At last, the driver of a bright, shiny, black LaSalle sedan noticed them and pulled to a screeching halt on the shoulder about fifty feet in front of them.

"Where you headed?" called the driver as they drew close.

"Boston," said Bertie. "Thanks for stopping for us."

"Climb in. The right-rear door is open."

"Thanks a whole lot," said Stan, as he followed his companion into the back seats. "We really appreciate the ride."

"My name's Emmet Perkins," said the chubby-cheeked driver with curly brown hair and brows to match.

"I'm Stan and this here is Bertie." Stan figured him to be in his fifties, perhaps a businessman, in a brown suit, yellow shirt, and brown-patterned tie.

Emmet Perkins released the hand brake, pulled away from the dusty shoulder, and accelerated onto the county road. They drove for a few minutes, and then he swiveled his head over his right shoulder to talk to his passengers. "I kin only take you as far as South Boston, Norwood, to be exact. That's where I live."

"That'll be great," said Bertie. "How far away is your place from Boston's railroad station?"

"Guess 'bout fifteen minutes by auto," he replied. "I don't know how many by walking, maybe forty-five minutes to an hour." He turned his head back to the road to correct his slightly left drift into the oncoming lane.

Stan ran his hands over the luxurious leather upholstery and took in the car's gleaming trim. "Wow," he exclaimed. "A fine car you have here, mister. I've never seen anything like her."

"A-yup," Emmet replied, turning his head to them again. "A beaut, ain't she?" He corrected his slight drift to the shoulder.

"Is she new?" asked Stan.

Bertie sat ramrod-straight, teeth clenched as she watched how easily Emmet got distracted.

"A-yup," Emmet replied, turning his head to them again. "Jes bought her a week ago." He swerved back in lane to miss an oncoming Pontiac.

"Can I ask what a car like this cost you?" asked Stan.

"Stan! Don't bother the man while he's driving," scolded Bertie, now cringing each time Emmet drifted across the road's center line.

"Spent over eleven hundred hard-earned on 'er," Emmet replied. While he looked over his shoulder to talk to them one more time, he missed seeing a large van marked Fancy Furniture Company entering the road in front of them. "My first new—"

"Look out, Emmet!" Bertie screamed. "The van!"

Chapter 13
Boston, Ever So Close

THE VAN, HEAVILY LOADED with furniture for deliveries, continued to creep onto the county road, its driver unaware that a brand-new 1936 LaSalle was bearing down on its rear end at fifty-two miles per hour.

"Look out, Emmet!" Bertie screamed a second time. "That truck is barely moving. We're gonna hit it. Oh God, no!"

Emmet Perkins snapped his head back around to the windshield, returning his attention to the imminent danger in the road in front of him. He slammed his foot down hard on the brake pedal. The brakes screamed as though they were mortally wounded, and the car began to slow. The calamitous gap toward the van continued to close. Bertie swallowed twice. She barely avoided throwing up.

With only split-seconds left, the van lumbered forward, away from Emmet's car. Two perilous feet of clearance, then three feet, then farther, to finally end the possibility of a collision.

But now the LaSalle's rear wheels fishtailed their own complaint—right, then left, then right again. Emmet swung the steering wheel an abrupt left to compensate, only to see high-speed oncoming traffic in the other lane. He steered a hard right over the road's shoulder, maintaining momentum, overcorrecting, carrying the car across a wide bumpy strip of wild grass. Narrowly missing a cinder-block outbuilding, he bump-stopped next to a hefty fence post that supported three rows of barbed wire. The driver and his passengers sat in silence for half a minute, stunned and breathing heavily. By the time they came to a complete stop, the furniture van had rumbled out of view. What they couldn't have known is that the driver had his radio on, blasting hillbilly music at explosive levels, and had no idea he'd been the unintended target of a potential tailgating accident.

Emmet spoke first. "My beautiful new LaSalle," he cried. In a state of despair, he placed his hands on his anguished face, then lowered his forehead to rest on the steering wheel.

"Hey, we're still alive, aren't we?" Bertie piped up.

"Thank God for that," offered Stan, as the two of them followed Emmet out of the car and around to the front to survey the damage done to his precious vehicle.

The three huddled at the hood where the car met the fence. The narrow-shouldered Emmet leaned over, crouched, and poked to assess all the damage. The engine was still running fine. The heavy steel bumper had absorbed and survived the brunt of the impact, driving the fence post completely out of the ground and distorting the barbed wire. The collision left a slightly bent grille, a major dent in the right fender, and a myriad of scratches in the car's shiny black paintwork.

"It'll cost me at least a hundred and change to fix this," complained Emmet as he brushed the grass stickers off the legs of his brown suit. All three settled back in the car. He put the transmission in reverse and tried to back the LaSalle out onto the road, but the rear wheels slipped, pulling grass and slicing into the muddy ground. He turned to face Stan and Bertie. They knew what the hangdog look meant. Climbing back out, they walked around to the front and leaned against the hood. It took all their strength pushing on the grille and hood to coax the heavy vehicle back onto the road.

A few miles later, the LaSalle pulled into a driveway next to a white clapboard cottage with two gabled windows and bounded by the idyllic white picket fence. There was even a vine-covered, arched trellis at the front gate.

"I guess this is where we part ways," said Bertie, while stepping out of the car. "We can't thank you enough for the ride this far. I'm just sorry you banged up your brand-new sedan on the way." She held out her hand for him to shake.

Emmet started to take her hand, but changed his mind. "I suppose the two of you could use a home-cooked meal. When is the last time either of you had one?"

"Well, our sandwiches ran out this morning while we waited for the train," replied Bertie. "And my last hot meal that wasn't a bowl of oatmeal was before I left home, weeks ago."

"You're forgetting the noodles and boiled veggies we had at the mansion," said Stan.

"Oh yeah. Especially the feast of noodles with ketchup," Bertie said wryly.

"Well, my wife wouldn't forgive me, if I let the two of you go without a hot meal," said Emmet. "So come on inside and meet my Addie."

"If you say we're not imposing, we'd be delighted to accept your hospitality and meet your wife," said Bertie.

When the three reached the front door, it was already open and Addie stood by it to greet them. His wife stood a full head shorter and quite a bit heavier than her husband. Most of the weight sat around her apron-covered waist. In her good-natured way, she welcomed each of the wayfarers with a hug. After the introductions, Bertie and Stan dropped their backpacks in the front hall and freshened up in the powder room. When they came out, Emmet ushered them into the spacious colonial kitchen. They sat down in captain's chairs around the maple table. Bertie noted the matching maple cabinets, the chandelier over the table with its frosted-glass bulbs, and brightly patterned linoleum. The kitchen décor, their new car. *He must make a decent living,* she thought.

Emmet carved up the chicken, while Addie set out bowls of roasted potatoes, gravy, and string beans. When she finally sat down to eat, she caught Stan staring at the empty chair and place setting. "Oh. that's for Elroy, our son. He's delivering the evening paper. He'll be along in a few minutes."

"Ah," said Stan. "I was wondering about the extra place."

"He's a good boy," said Emmet. "Always trying to help out any way he can. He gives us most all the money he earns."

Just then the front door opened. A teenager in a tan jacket, brown corduroy knickers, and knee-length argyle socks appeared in the archway between the dining room and living room. Everyone at the table looked aghast at the boy. One eye was reddened and puffy, and dried blood crusted below his nostrils. There were tears in his eyes, and his arms hung low against his lean body.

"What happened to you?" shouted Emmet.

"Oh my Lord. Oh my Lord," cried Addie, as she pushed back her chair and rushed to embrace her son.

"Tell us what happened?" repeated his father in a calmer tone.

In a faltering voice, Elroy explained. "I finished my deliveries and found that I had almost a dozen papers left. So, I went over to the corner of Ash and McCormick to sell off the rest. I wasn't there but fifteen minutes when Bob Ford came over and smacked me in the kisser." His hand went to his sore eye. "He's a whole lot bigger than me. He yelled at me to get off his corner—I was selling papers on the spot where he sells 'em. I guess I was too slow to answer him, and that made him still madder, so he took away the rest of my papers and beat me up good. Then he booted me off the corner. I fell down and he kicked me in the ribs."

"You poor dear," said Addie, slowly releasing her motherly embrace.

"Damn it," said Emmet, hovering over Elroy. "The Ford boy doesn't own that corner. By what right does he claim it? And he certainly didn't need to get violent with you, nor steal your extra papers. I'm going down there and teach him a lesson he won't forget in a hurry." He banged his fist down on the table.

"And maybe you won't!" said Addie, stamping her foot. "You've got more bull than brains, Emmet Perkins. Simmer down. We've had enough violence for one day. And Emmet—consider it a valuable lesson you've learned instead. These are hard times, and there are those who will guard what little they have with all their might. And Elroy? You stay away from that rotten kid's territory. Sit down, honey. I'm going to clean you up a bit." She hurried into the bathroom. Emerging with a wet washcloth and towel, she gently scraped the dried blood off her son's face.

A humiliated Emmet sat down and picked up his fork. Instead of feeding his face, he dallied, pushing the food around the plate. Despite his usually voracious appetite he was too upset to eat. A lengthy silence prevailed at the table until it was time for dessert. Addie sailed into the room with her homemade specialty, apple-rhubarb pie, almost a foot in diameter and three inches high. After seconds all around, the pie disappeared, the stomachs were satisfied, and the moods improved immeasurably.

"I'd like to apologize to our guests for my earlier outbursts," said a much-calmed Emmet. "I can't stand my son being taken advantage of. Of course, Addie's right. She always sees the bigger picture."

Addie tried to suppress a victory smile, as she carried a stack of dishes to the kitchen sink.

"I dry a mean dish," said Bertie. "Can I give you a hand with them?"

"Don't like to make the guests work for their meals," replied Addie, "but it would be nice for us to chat some. The men can talk in the living room. Here's a dish towel."

"Will Elroy be all right?" asked Bertie, as soon as they were alone.

"Sure," replied Addie. "He'll be fine. He's young, and the wounds will heal quickly. He'll get over it."

Suddenly, Bertie remarked, "I wish I had a nice caring family like yours."

"Now, it can't be as bad as all that," returned Addie, as she handed another washed plate to Bertie.

"An abusive stepdad and an alcoholic mom were the reason I left home," admitted Bertie.

"I'm so sorry. Where are you and your young man planning to stay tonight?"

"You and Emmet have been so gracious to us already, but we were hoping you'd let us sleep on your living room floor for one night," said Bertie.

Addie smiled. She was in her element. "Oh, I think we can do better than that, my dear. We have a guest room upstairs with a full-size bed. And there are twin beds in Elroy's room. I know you've been traveling together and doing God knows what, but in our house you'll sleep separately. Is that understood? Stan will bunk in with Elroy, and you, my dear, will stay in the guest room."

"Yes ma'am," murmured Bertie as the two women left the kitchen to join the men in the living room.

"And I'll have a nice warm breakfast for you before you leave."

"You are so kind," said Stan, seated on the burgundy horsehair sofa.

"It's almost eight o'clock, hon," said Emmet. "President Roosevelt is having another one of his fireside chats on social security and unemployment."

He sat in an overstuffed easy chair almost touching the four-foot-high radio in one corner of the room. That closeness wasn't accidental. It was meant for hearing and not missing a word over the airwaves. The antique finish to the radio matched the room's décor. An upright player piano with scrolls and foot pedals, and a wooden piano bench, stood on the wall opposite the sofa. Two matching upholstered chairs flanked the piano.

"I almost forgot," said Addie. "We wouldn't want to miss what the president has to say to the nation."

Elroy curled knees-up on the deep carpet in front of the

radio, with his back against the outside of the sofa's arm. Emmet adjusted the tuning dial, amid crackling static and background noise, until everyone heard "My fellow Americans …"

The president spoke for an hour, clearing up many details of his 1933 Social Security Act. He then expounded on the successes of his Civilian Conservation Corp (CCC)—solving unemployment by putting young men to work establishing parks, camps, and shelters, as well as planting trees to prevent flooding. His speech stimulated a lively discussion among the five listeners. Afterward, they retired to their rooms for the night.

Stan and Elroy were in their respective beds, with the lights just turned off, when Stan heard an unexpected request in the dark from his one-night buddy.

"Can I go along with you guys?" asked Elroy. "Please! I just know I can contribute somehow. I'm in good health, and riding the rails sounds like an exciting life. Nothing exciting ever happens around here."

"Why would you want to leave such a loving family?" asked Stan. "You have everything Bertie and I don't have. I have neither parents nor a home. Bertie has an alcoholic mom and an abusive stepdad. Besides, riding the rails is a precarious life, sometimes days without food, and never knowing where you're going to put your head down at night. It's not a decision we wanted to make. We were forced into it. You, Elroy, have too much to lose."

"I guess I didn't think about all that," replied the dejected boy.

"Goodnight, Elroy. Count your blessings, kid."

"G'night, guy, and thanks."

* * * *

The next morning Addie not only fed them breakfast, but packed them enough peanut-butter and jelly sandwiches for two days. Gratefully, Bertie and Stan hugged all three of their hosts. They left the Perkins house with a wealth of goodbyes and good wishes and headed off in the direction of downtown Boston and the railway connections. They thought they were following Emmet's instructions to a tee, but somehow veered off course in the northwesterly direction. Eventually, they came across a rail siding.

"Hey, this should lead into town," offered Stan. "Why don't we just follow the tracks into central Boston?"

"I kinda like that idea," said Bertie. "Railroad tracks usually make a beeline for wherever they're going. Let's do it."

The loose traprock made for difficult walking, as did the slanted grade beside the track. They picked their way along the path that paralleled the track for nearly six miles, under the punishing summer sun, until they came to several boxcars sitting adjacent to a loading platform. Hearing clatter and commotion, Stan and Bertie hid in a nearby dry culvert and watched eight workers in coveralls unload the full boxcars: wooden crates, corrugated boxes, and three waist-high wood barrels. All of this cargo was carted by hand truck inside a building that appeared to be a manufacturing facility. It took nearly an hour for the workers to empty the three boxcars. Leaving the freight doors wide open, they disappeared inside the building.

Noting that the platform was now empty. Stan and Bertie crawled out of their culvert and surveilled their surroundings. The building seemed isolated, sitting on land unsuited for farming.

"We could get aboard one of the cars now," said Stan, "and ride straight into town."

"But we don't know how long we'd have to wait before these cars actually go anywhere," said Bertie. "We could sit here for days, weeks even."

"We've been walking for hours," Stan complained. "Why don't we rest for a while and share one of Addie's sandwiches?"

"Sure, why not?" replied Bertie. "I've no idea how far we have to go now. I have a sneaking suspicion we've gotten off the beaten path somehow. I don't even know where we went wrong."

Bertie chose a shady elm tree on a gentle rise on the other side of the culvert, opposite the three boxcars. They shared the sandwich and rested for over two hours before they heard the distant familiar lumbering sound. As it got closer it, they recognized the tympanic beat of a steam locomotive engine.

"It's a work engine coming to move the boxcars," said Bertie, jumping up.

"If you're right," said Stan, "we'd better collect our things and get aboard one of those cars in a hurry."

They had already scurried up onto the platform and settled into the last car when the engine arrived and chugged to a bumping stop. Coupling took only a few minutes. The engine reversed itself and pulled the three cars away behind it. *We made the right choice*, Bertie thought. She stood by the door and watched the scenery fly by, while Stan tried to read a magazine he'd picked up a few days ago. The cars rumbled on for a number of miles and then, curiously, started to slow down. As the engine came to a stop, all Bertie could see was an abandoned whistle-stop shelter, hardly more than a hut with a small platform out front.

Suddenly, at least two dozen men in work clothes rushed onto the platform and scrambled to get on the three-car train, as though they thought they would be left behind. Most of them packed into the first two boxcars, but two agile young men leaped off the platform into the third, mostly empty, car where Bertie and Stan now crouched. Moments later, the short train jerked, then bumped, and began to move forward once more. As the train gathered speed, Bertie casually faced one of the newcomers, who looked to be about twenty.

"Where are all you guys going?" she asked, using her most male voice.

"To work at the camp. Aren't you signed up?" he asked.

"No. Signed up for what?" Stan responded.

"CCC, man, the Civilian Conservation Corps, of course. We're headed west to a place called Athol, Massachusetts, and we're gonna set up camp there and make a park out of a forest—build some roads and bridges there and plant some more trees, too."

Stan recalled listening to the radio in the Perkins' living room—President Roosevelt's fireside chat praising the CCC, but this guy's description turned him off. "Sounds like a whole lot of hard work," he replied. "More physical than I want to get involved with. You can count me out."

"Sounds pretty ambitious to me, Stan," Bertie countered in a brighter voice. "And a really good thing, too."

With an alarmed expression on his face, Stan turned and faced Bertie. "What are we going to do about this? Camp is definitely not where I want to go. It's like we're being shanghaied, or highjacked, or something."

"Not true, Stan," Bertie shot back. "You're letting your imagination run away with you. If we were being shanghaied, we'd be physically trapped into doing hard labor on a chain gang or crew on a smuggler's ship. Nobody's forcing us to do anything. Besides, we can't get off. The train's moving too fast."

Chapter 14

Conservation

THE LOCOMOTIVE and its three trailing boxcars soon left Boston's extended urban reaches for the Massachusetts countryside. Their car was free of cargo and the weather outside was warm and sunny. The two newcomers were dressed in fairly clean but wrinkled work clothes. One sat snoozing in a dark corner with his newsboy cap pulled down over his eyes. The younger-looking one, in a sweat-stained New York Yankees cap, chose to sit close to the open door near Stan. Up to now, Stan had been sulking, but his curiosity eventually shook off that mood. He spoke to the baseball cap. "I'm Stan, and this is my friend Bert, and as long as we're sharing the same stable, what can I call you guys?"

"I'm Lance and the guy over in the corner is Merwin." He nodded toward the man in denim bib coveralls.

"What do you get for all your efforts?" Stan asked. "Is there actually any pay involved?"

"We get thirty bucks a month plus some extras," said Lance.

"Extras? What kind of extras?" asked Stan.

"Meals, a place to sleep, and work clothes. And we even get

free medical and dental care,"

"Can anyone join up?" asked Bertie.

"Yeah," said Lance. "You can sign up as long as you're a man between eighteen and twenty-four."

"Don' forget, ya gotta be in top health, cuz the work is back-breakin' hard," added Merwin, now awake and sitting up.

"You're right, Merwin, you have to be in good shape, too," agreed Lance.

"How long do you have to sign up for? asked Bertie, cautiously. *The vague promise of a teaching job in the fall is just that—vague, no guarantees.*

"I think the minimum hitch is ten months," said Lance.

"Some guys kin stay longer, up to eighteen months, if'en their families are on Federal assistance like mine," added Merwin.

Bertie remained silent for several minutes, then said, "Hey, Stan, think about it this way. It's a government job with a real paycheck. Isn't that exactly what we're looking for?"

Stan made a scrunched-up face and then went back to reading his magazine. Lance broke out a deck of cards and dealt a hand of solitaire on the bare floor, while Merwin whittled away on a small rectangular block of wood with an apparent dog's head at one end. He hummed a familiar tune, softly, in a pleasing baritone. Bertie sat at the open door with her jeans-covered legs dangling outside. She watched more farms, forests, hills, and clouds slip by as they got farther from Boston. Almost two hours later, their short train slowed to a clunking stop at a small town in central Massachusetts. The wooden sign over the rudimentary wood station house declared the place as "ATHOL Station." And underneath it, "Property of Plymouth Railroad Co." There wasn't even a platform to assist in boarding and disembarking.

A tall broad-shouldered man in an Army uniform blew a shrill whistle and shouted to the men aboard the train, "I'm Sergeant Graham Kitchner. See these three stripes? Sergeant Kitchner to you." He pointed with exaggerated importance to the insignia on his left arm. "For the next ten months I'm your mother, father, confessor, and boss. Now, git yer arses offa that damn train and line up in three rows on the street out front of the freakin' station."

It took nearly twenty minutes to empty all three cars. The men surged around the station to the street and shuffled into the required rows. Bertie and Stan climbed down from the boxcar. Stan joined the tail end of the crowd. Bertie kept her distance—listening, straggling along.

"Now, ain't this a sorry-looking bunch, said Kitchner. "You, you, and you to the back column. You and you to the middle column." As soon as the men were distributed evenly, he shouted, "Put your right hand straight out so your fingers just touch the shoulder of the man to the right of you. Your right hand, stupid! Now you got it. When I say 'Left face' you simply turn left in the same spot."

Kitchner yelled the commands "Left face!" and "Forward march!" The men didn't actually march, they walked. The ragged bunch covered over two miles of a poorly paved roadway that took them past the edge of Athol and through a dense forest leading to their camp. The weary men emerged onto a sweep of cleared land. They were greeted by a sign reading "Camp Bearsden" and "The Lodge," a large, one-story, log-sided building. Two rows of six evenly spaced khaki tents flanked each side of it. On one end of the lodge, two chimneys coughed out dense black smoke; the opposite end held the offices and infirmary. Outside, behind the lodge, an attached wooden roof, supported by dozens of posts, sheltered row-on-row of long picnic tables with attached benches.

"Company halt!" shouted Kitchner when they were alongside the tents. "Two men to a tent. Choose your tentmate wisely, because it's the last decision you'll be making while you're at Camp Bearsden. I'll be making all the decisions from here on out. As soon as you pick out your cots, get in line at the table outside the office. If you want to get paid, you'll have to fill out the paperwork enrolling in the CCC. After that, you'll head down to the Miller River just behind these tents. Once there you'll strip to your skivvies and scrub the crud off your bodies, so the medics can examine your arses. If you're good to go, you'll be issued a work uniform."

Bertie heard all this and began to panic. *I can't strip in front of this bunch. And the medics are certain to find out I'm a woman. I don't know what to do, but there's no way I can get out of this now. Maybe I can confess at the enrollment desk. Maybe I can go back with the rejects if there are any. I have to talk to Stan and see what he's doing.* She trotted to Stan, pulled him out of the crowd and whispered, "What am I going to do? Any ideas?"

"I don't know, he replied. "Maybe if you confess, they might have a non-paying job for a woman. Or you could just walk back to that little town we passed through."

"What about you?" she asked. "Are you staying?"

"Yeah," he replied. "This is just what I've been looking for and didn't even know it. Maybe it's time I get serious about earning a living. The mooching life sure as hell isn't working out for me. Will you just walk out of here?"

"I haven't signed anything yet, so I think I'll just walk out the gate. They can't stop me, can they?"

"I don't think so," he said, his voice cracking. "Good luck. I'll miss you a whole bunch."

"Don't go getting all mushy on me, Stanford. We're friends. Good friends!" she corrected. "Damn it, I'll miss you, too." Bertie scanned the grounds to see if the sergeant was looking. He wasn't. She squeezed Stan's hand firmly and walked away toward the main gate.

About a third of the way to the gate, Bertie noticed another woman in the camp, an older woman, maybe fifty, lean, even bony. Her salt-and-pepper hair was tied in a haphazard bun. She was hanging clothes on a makeshift line stretched between two trees. Bertie shifted her path to connect with the woman. "Hello, ma'am, could you answer a few questions for me?"

"It depends," she replied. "I ain't had but a grammar school education, fifth grade to be exact."

"It's about the camp rules."

"Oh, Clara don't know nuthin' 'bout them."

"Clara?" asked Bertie.

"Yeah, that's m'name," said the woman, pinning an apron on the clothesline.

A bit startled, Bertie said, "Oh. Okay. Well, hi, Clara. So what's a woman doing in the middle of a CCC camp? I thought they didn't enroll women."

"They don't," replied Clara. "They hire us to do the cooking and stuff."

"Us?" echoed Bertie.

"Yeah, us. That lazy, no-good Eunice bitch, she quit on me. She never do anything I tell her. Now she's gone—flew the coop." Clara picked up a wet blouse. "Good riddance, I always say." She clipped the blouse to the line with wooden clothespins.

"Does this mean you have a job opening?" asked Bertie. "Who does the hiring, anyway?" She yanked off her newsboy cap and shook her thick hair free.

Clara chuckled. "I thought you might be a gal. Well, it's like this. I hired Eunice an' I suppose I could hire you, if'en yer askin'. It's a buck-twenty-five a day. Lots o' hard work—take it or leave it."

"Do I have to enroll for a long time or sign any papers?"

"Nuthin that I know about."

"Then I'll take the job. I'm Bertie. Bertie Patchet. And thank you!"

"Yer welcome, Bertie." Clara smiled with relief. "Yer 'bout Eunice's size so her white kitchen coveralls should fit you. Gimme a few minutes to finish here an' I'll take you 'round to the cookhouse, show you everything."

The cookhouse comprised the rear half of the lodge. It was divided into an enormous kitchen, a spacious pantry/storeroom, and an eight-by-ten-foot "bunkroom" that held one upper/lower bunk and hooks and shelves for the kitchen workers' things.

Bertie had expected to be living in a tent, so even the cramped bunkroom came as a pleasant surprise. She found herself relegated to the upper bunk, but she didn't mind that at all. Looking up at the split-log ceiling would be a lot nicer than looking up at a bulky sag in canvas and two-inch mattress. Sure, the lashed-branch ladder would be inconvenient and maybe even too flimsy to eventually hold her weight, but for now the whole arrangement looked like a godsend.

Clara made sure to tell her about the outhouse—outdoors, at the edge of the clearing. It had a partition and separate entrance at one end to accommodate the ladies. She described all of this to Bertie with her own words and unique syntax.

It was already twenty past one, when Clara said, "You got 'til two to settle in. Then you gotta come help me in the cookhouse kitchen. We gotta feed 'bout fifty mouths by six-o'clock."

Bertie dropped off her things in the bunkhouse and report-ed for duty early. She found Clara sitting on a wood box pulling feathers off a dead chicken. A crate with a dozen more fowl cadav-ers waiting to be plucked sat beside her.

"Here," said Clara. "You sit here and finish plucking the rest of 'em, while I take care of them pinfeathers."

Clara took the first undressed chicken to the firewood stove and singed the whole bird over the open fire for a few min-utes. Next she took it to a nearby table, where she sat down and captured each pinfeather between a knife edge and her thumb. A quick twisting-yanking motion of her wrist pulled the successive pinfeathers out. An hour later, with the two working serially, all thirteen fowl were ready for their spits. The spits laden with fowl were carried to an open-pit fireplace that stood a few feet outside the cookhouse entrance. A bent end with a wooden handle on each of the spits enabled Clara to rotate and evenly cook the birds. Meanwhile, she assigned Bertie to hand-peel a mountain of russet potatoes as her boss stood beside the stone barbeque fire, slowly turning the spit handles. The two women went from one chore to another for the remainder of the afternoon until they had a meal ready for the hard-working conservation crew.

At suppertime both women stood behind the table laden with huge pots and pans to dole out food to the line of young men.

When Stan appeared in front of Bertie with his divided metal tray extended, she asked how his day went. He silently smiled and put the tray on the table in front of them. He raised both hands and turned the palms up, showing Bertie the red blisters that would eventually turn to calluses. When the men behind him in line protested, she picked out the biggest quarter chicken on the pan and laid it on his tray along with a double portion of mashed potatoes and camp-grown carrots. She saw Stan three times a day at mealtimes. The work for both of them proved so demanding that any free time was spent resting.

And so it went for several weeks, well into the heart of summer. A frightening distraction occurred one dark evening when Bertie had finished all her cleanup chores. It happened while she was taking out the trash to the landfill ditch. The unusual brightness at the periphery of her sight attracted her attention toward one of the tents. Six-foot billowing flames leapt from the second tent in that row.

"Fire! Fire in the tents!" she yelled at the top of her lungs. Six young men rushed out of the flaming tent and started to form a bucket brigade line. More came from another tent to expand the bucket line. Bertie dropped the bag of trash and ran toward the well, where she was handed a nearly full bucket of water. She grabbed it and headed for the fire. By the time she arrived, the third tent was on fire and she noted that only four young men had evacuated. She threw the water on the third tent and handed off the bucket. She turned to them

"Anyone still inside?" she yelled.

"Jamey is," one of the men screamed back at her. "He's still asleep."

"He's hard of hearing and can't know of the danger he's in," said the second man.

"You can't just let him burn up in there," cried Bertie. "Help him!" she shouted.

When no one else made a move, she grabbed the next full bucket and doused herself with its contents. Then, she dove into the flaming tent to rescue the sleeping lad. She tried to wake him, but he had been overcome by inhaling the smoke.

Bertie rolled the lad out of his cot onto the ground, grabbed him under his armpits and dragged him toward the front flap. The central pole suddenly burned through, and the flaming canvas started to collapse around her. She shoved him through the flaps to the outside with all her strength, just as the flaming canvas draped across her body.

Chapter 15
Time to Move On

AS THE FLAMING CANVAS FELL, it disintegrated into sparks, burning flakes, and ash. The consumed canvas broke apart, opening and widening a hole that encircled Bertie. Just as it landed at her feet, at least two additional full buckets of water splashed across her body. She hopped and high-stepped her way to safety, incurring a few ember-burns on her cheeks and forearms. There were tiny holes all over her coveralls. Strands of her hair, flopping around her shoulders, were singed. The young man she'd rescued had emerged both unscathed and grateful. Once the fire had been tamed to mere smoke and water-logged residue, the group lifted up a soaked Bertie, placed her on Garth's broad shoulders, and paraded her about the campgrounds celebrating her heroism. Garth was six-foot-six and 270 pounds, a fully capable and willing conveyor.

Bertie's minor burns healed quickly, but her seared hair smelled terrible for days afterward, despite her repeated shampooing.

A new worry began to dog her. As the summer days wound down and autumn crept nearer, she began to think about that teaching position she might be offered. *The Connecticut Board of Education said I was only under consideration, but I had better call and follow up. I don't want them to give the job to somebody else. The camp has no phone, at least none available to me. I refuse to spend the rest of my life doing kitchen chores. Just look at my hands. I've got to get out of here before I become stuck in this miserable camp life. I guess I should tell Stan of my plans in case he wants to come along with me.*

As Stan came through the mess line at dinnertime, Bertie whispered, "We need to talk after I finish cleanup." They met a few paces beyond the old well and sat on a large log for her parting talk.

"I'm leaving camp tomorrow at daylight for parts unknown," she told him.

"I guess it was only a matter of time," he responded, his voice filled with resignation.

"I've got to find employment in my profession or I'll rot away in places like this. You want to come along for the ride?" she asked.

"No, my good buddy," he replied. "I've found solid employment here. Uncle Sam's pay isn't the greatest and the work is tough, but at least I've got three meals every day and a place to lay my head at night. Isn't that what I set out to find? It's a job, at least until something better comes along. And the work benefits everyone: clearing, building, planting, and making parks out of sheer wilderness."

"I kind of knew that would be your answer." She laid her hand on his bare arm. "I'll miss you, partner."

"Wait," said Stan. "How much cash do you have left out of your last pay?"

She reached into her pocket and pulled up a palmful of singles and coins. Poking them with the index finger of the opposite hand, she mumbled, "Exactly twelve dollars and thirty cents. I spend most of my pay at the post exchange. The pay for this job's barely over the break-even point."

"I still have over four hundred bucks left from the boxcar

victim," Stan replied. "You're entitled to some of it." He removed his shoe and extracted the two fifty-dollar bills lining the sole. "I hid the rest back at the tent."

"I can't take this," she answered. "You were the one who found it."

"You were there when I did," he said. "It wasn't doing the dead man any good. Besides, I'm getting a salary now, and you'll need mad money somewhere along the way."

Shrugging her shoulders, Bertie accepted the folded bills. She tucked them in her jeans pocket, leaned toward him, and left a kiss on his damp cheek. Then she rose from the log and headed for the bunkroom. He continued to sit there on the log, teary-eyed, watching until he could no longer see her.

She shed the coveralls and slept in shorts and a cotton shirt until 5:30 the next morning. Rising, she dressed, collected her few things into her backpack, and headed for the kitchen for the last time. She broke the news to Clara and helped her start the break-fast chores in return for a bowl of Wheaties and a few wrapped sandwiches to take along.

"I feel like I'm deserting you," said Bertie when she was ready to leave.

"Don't you worry about me, girl," said Clara. "I kinda liked havin' anutha female 'round, but I'll jes have ta draft one o' them lazy or limpin' young men out there to help me with the chores."

They said their goodbyes. Bertie shouldered her backpack and headed toward the camp gate. Once there, she turned around for one last look, started down the path, and began to retrace the long march from the rail stop two months earlier. The roadside view, blooming with early autumn wildflowers, made the forty-five-minute walk into Athol halfway pleasant. The burg-sized town was blessed with only a gas station and a country store that chose not to carry alcoholic beverages—discouraging the men at camp from seeking Athol for recreation.

Guesswork led Bertie to the tracks and the station house with the Athol sign. She didn't see a single boxcar, and the rails were rusty, attesting to their rare use. *No way are these currently used tracks to Boston.* At midmorning she desperately needed to use the restroom, but the door was padlocked. Upon closer examination, she discovered that the screws holding the hasp to the door were loose and turned halfway out. Bertie glanced about and saw no one. Using thumb and forefinger, she eased the four screws out the rest of the way, enabling her to enter the little restroom. Afterward, she quickly replaced the screws and refastened the hasp. Returning to the street, she tried to puzzle out her next move. She had no idea where she was except somewhere in north-central Massachusetts. Which way to go?

The Sinclair gas station sign caught her attention. Hurrying the two blocks to get there, she noted the clock high on the wall pointing to 9:50. A wire-frame stand outside the office door held maps of the region, the state, and the eastern U.S. The sign on the stand read "Take one." When Bertie reached for a Massachusetts state map, the old proprietor sitting inside on a stool stood up and gave her a dirty look because she wasn't a gas-consuming customer. She hurried away with the map. The owner, knowing he couldn't catch up with her, slumped down again with a scowl on his face. Around the corner, Bertie plopped down on a small patch of grass and spread out the map. It took ten minutes for her to find Athol, but when she did, she discovered that U.S. 202 passed just south of town on its way to the East Coast.

Bertie folded the map, and once on her feet, stuck the map in the beltline of her jeans for quick reference. She found Athol's Main Street, one block east of the gas station and followed it to Booker's General Store, straight ahead. She had determined east from the position of the sun and turned south on the west side of the road. Holding out her palm, she felt a few drops of glisten-ing rain. A glance up at the dark threatening clouds moving in from the south prompted another glance at the general store. Ber-tie could see clearer skies beyond them, so temporary shelter was called for. She broke into a run and reached the store's entrance just as the rain came down in torrents.

Not a customer inside. Only the middle-aged proprietor—Mr. Booker, she guessed—and one aproned clerk seemed to be manning the store. They kept a keen eye on her as she roamed the three aisles without showing any intention of making a purchase. Their suspicious glares weighed heavily on Bertie. Feeling guilty, she bought two long twists of black licorice candy for a nickel, and sat down on a barrelhead inside for forty minutes, until the summer storm passed. In a singsong voice, she called out, "Thank you," stepped out of the store, and continued her southerly trek to U.S. 202.

It was late afternoon by the time she arrived at the highway and grimly knew that her next move—hitchhiking—was a distasteful one, especially without Stan. The east-west traffic turned out to be extremely light. Only a couple dozen cars passed by in the next hour. Most ignored her extended thumb. One even slowed down to raise her hopes and then raced away when she approached it.

As the hitchhiker sat on a highway fence post munching on one of the peanut butter and jelly sandwiches, she thought, *Maybe I would appear less threatening, if I looked like a female.* Bertie pulled the checkered newsboy cap off, shook her head, and let her locks fall free. In the three months since she'd left home, her hair had grown substantially. *There! Now no one can mistake me for a boy.*

She finished the last of the sandwich and took a drink from her canteen. Standing up, she stretched before donning the backpack and adjusting both the canteen and hatchet so they didn't bounce when she walked. Moving closer to the edge of the highway, she stuck out her arm and thumb once more. Four more opportunities passed her by, but a fifth slowed past, then pulled off the road onto the shoulder to wait for her to catch up. Approaching the dark blue, two-door Buick, she saw the passenger door swing wide open to receive her. As she slipped off her backpack, climbed in, and placed the pack on her lap, she glanced over at the driver. He was fortyish, she guessed, with a slight five-o'clock shadow and meager mustache. Neither thin nor fat, he wore a bowler hat, plaid sport coat, and solid-blue tie. His smile, full of bright teeth, gave her an instant case of the willies, but she really needed the ride.

"I'm headed for Framingham," he said.

"That's good," said Bertie. "I'm headed east, too."

They drove off and rode for an hour and a half without saying another word. Then he turned sharply toward her and asked:

"What's your name, hon?"

"Bertie," she said automatically, but then regretted telling him. *Does this mean I'm befriending him? Giving him cause to make advances to me? That awful smile, it's almost like a leer. It is a damned leer.*

With the car moving at more than moderate speed and his head still turned toward her, he said, "My friends call me Phil." His gaze started at her legs, roved to her upper body, and lingered there.

He's looking at me like I'm his next meal. Did I make a mistake getting into this car with him? But how could I have known?

"Excuse me, shouldn't your eyes stay on the road ahead?" she asked.

His attention turned back to driving, although his smile melted into more of a frown. The second hour was just as silent as the first, but every so often he turned and ogled her from head to foot once more. Slowly, the leering smile returned, as though he'd settled on a new backup strategy.

Bertie felt a chill run through her body. *What's he planning to do with me, and what can I do to nip it in the bud? The ride's not all that important, but how am I going to get him to stop the car so I can get out and be rid of him?* Nature eventually answered her plea. She had to pee in the worst way.

"Sir, I'll need a restroom real soon," Bertie said. "We've been driving for over two hours." No response. She repeated her request and again he ignored her. Looking at the gas gauge, she saw that it was well below the quarter-tank mark. "If you don't stop soon, you're going to run out of gas pretty quick."

"I'll stop when I'm good and ready," he mumbled under his breath. "I know a good place where we can eat, gas up, and rest a bit."

"Good, because I have to pee real bad, sir." She secretly detached the hatchet from its sling and pushed it under the seat. *I may need it to threaten him to stop. The guy's a letch and a nut case.*

Phil drove another twenty minutes before they saw the neon signs announcing the Blue Haven Motel and Ben's Standard Gas. He surprised her by pulling up to the motel entrance and not the gas station. "They have much nicer restrooms here than in the gas station," he said.

Bertie didn't argue with him. Leaving her backpack behind, she bounded out of the car and entered the motel lobby. Avoiding the registration desk, she looked for a hint of where the ladies' room might be. She waited for the desk clerk to turn his back, and stole across the lobby to the hallway where the restroom sign pointed. Unaware that Phil had followed closely behind, she ducked into the ladies' room a few doors down the hall. He rushed into the men's room next door, finished in a hurry, and returned to the hall in record time to monitor her exit.

Upon finishing, Bertie opened the door slowly and peeked around it, hoping Phil wouldn't be there. But he was, and there was nothing she could do about it. They walked into the lobby. The registration desk was empty. No one was around. Phil matched her moves, step for step, as they walked through the lobby, out the front door, and into the parking lot. She bolted forward, raced to the car, and tried to open the passenger door, but couldn't—it was locked. *My stuff is still inside, my backpack, the hatchet, the money from Stan.* Bertie stood frozen, frustrated, not knowing what to do.

"I've decided to spend the night here, so I won't be going any farther with you," she said.

"Exactly what I had in mind," he said, his voice flat and controlled.

"Oh no!" she gasped. "I don't want anything to do with you. Let me get my things out of the car."

With an ugly grin, Phil unlocked the door, grabbed her

backpack, and stepped back from her. She reached out for it. He batted her hand away. Clutching the backpack, he strode to the trunk of the car and opened the lid. "You can have your things back in the morning," he sneered.

    Dear God, he's going to rape me.

Chapter 16
Heading East

BERTIE knew what she needed to survive this night with her virginity intact. A weapon of sorts. She immediately thought of the hatchet. Luckily, when Phil grabbed her backpack off the passenger seat, he had no idea she had stashed a hatchet underneath the seat. In his rush to get the backpack away from her and stow it out of her reach, he had also left the car door wide open.

He tossed the backpack in the trunk and was about to shut the trunk lid when Bertie lunged toward him with her hatchet in hand. "Don't shut that lid!" she yelled, raising her arm, brandishing the weapon back and forth in front of his face.

Phil foolishly reached out for the hatchet handle, misjudging her swift reflexes and determination. Her quick down-swing with the sharp blade caught his thumb, slicing it clear to the bone. He froze. Blood spurted out like a fountain. His eyes grew large, while his feet danced about to the tune of his great pain. He grabbed the parted flesh and tried to push the slices together to stop the flow of blood.

"No, no, no!" he screamed as she chased him away from the car's trunk. He ran in circles, yelping with every step. Whenever he looked back at her she raised the hatchet one more time.

Bertie reached into the open trunk, grabbed her backpack with her free hand, and raced across the parking lot toward the adjacent Standard gas station. Looking over her shoulder, she saw someone, probably a motel guest, attending to the bellowing bastard. Arriving at the pump island, she wiped the blood from the hatchet blade with a paper windshield towel and returned the trusty weapon to its backpack pocket. A blast resounded from a truck horn. She looked up to see a huge tractor-trailer roar to a hissing stop in front of the diesel pump. She had to jump to the opposite side of the fuel pumps to avoid being hit.

"Sorry, I didn't see you standing there," said the driver, a bruiser with chestnut-brown hair and beard as he stepped down from the semi's cab.

"You wouldn't be heading to the East Coast, would you?" asked Bertie.

"Boston's the destination for my load," boomed the driver. "But my company does not approve of riders."

"I guess I'll have to spend the night here then," said Bertie, with an expression of deep disappointment spreading across her face. *I'm not going anywhere near that motel as long as Phil is still around. Everything outside is wet from the rain. Maybe I can find an unlocked car to sleep in.*

"You look like you really need that ride," the driver said in a softer voice. "I s'pose no one would know if you rode along with me. Toss your stuff up in the cab and get yourself up there, too."

"Gee, thanks, mister." Bertie hustled around the front to the other side of the rig before he changed his mind.

"I'll join you as soon as I get gas and manage a pit stop," said the driver. He waved to a station attendant, who hustled over, fitted the hose nozzle to the fill hole, and pulled down the lever. He squeezed the pump handle and the diesel began to flow, taking many minutes for the big rig.

Bertie tossed her gear up onto the seat and climbed in after it. She set the backpack on her lap and wrapped both her arms around it. Looking back toward the motel from her new high-vantage point, she saw that the letch's car was gone and so was Phil. She'd never know nor care what happened to that creep.

It was nearly thirty minutes before the driver was ready to roll. He climbed aboard, slammed the door shut, dropped a brown paper bag on the seat between them, wrote something on a clip-board, and restarted the engine. Five minutes later they were on U.S. 202 heading east.

"I'm Sven, Sven Olsen What would you like me to call you?"

"I answer to Bertie." She looked over at him to be sure his eyes were still on the road ahead.

He detected an edgy tone. "You needn't be afraid of me, Bertie. I've got a daughter just about half your age. She's twelve now. Her name is Gwendolyn. Her mom and I call her Gwenny, a nickname I adore. She's the sunshine in my life."

"Sounds like you have a nice happy family, Sven."

"It would be if Gwenny didn't have polio. She walks on crutches now, but there was a time when we thought she was going to die. She's been through a lot and yet she still wakes up smiling and hopeful."

"That's a tough hand to be dealt," said Bertie. "From what you say, she's got a lot of courage."

"I gotta love her for that. I can't wait to finish this run and get home to Gwenny and my wife, Lilly."

"Where do you call home?" she asked.

"We live in Brooklyn, New York," he replied, "in a section that used to be called Pigtown. Our doctor thought Gwenny might have contracted polio from our neighbor's daughter, Maria Vincente, who caught it from Gina somebody, and so on. There's a lot of people living close together in the section. The disease is highly contagious, especially for children, and there's no cure for it. Strangely, some get better and others die or become crippled for life. I'm trying to find another place to live, but Brooklyn is the headquarters for the company that provides the loads I deliver. I'm not sure what to do anymore."

"I bet you'll figure it out," she offered.

"Lilly worked as a waitress until last April when she got laid off for taking too much time away from the job to care for Gwenny. My daughter is able to get to school and assist her mom around the house some. But Lilly can't seem to find a new job now that Gwenny is on her feet helping herself. There's a lot of that going on now."

"I know," said Bertie. "I'm looking for work, too."

"I can imagine," he said. "It's bad enough being a man looking for work, let alone a woman looking. There's only a few positions a woman can apply for—nursing and secretary."

"You forgot schoolteacher," she added.

"Oh yeah. Is that what you're applying for?"

"Yes," she replied, perking up. "I've been certified by the Central Connecticut State Normal School to become a teacher."

"So you've got real skills in your basket," he said. "But what are you doing in Massachusetts if you're certified in Connecticut?"

"There weren't any opportunities there, especially during the summer months when the schools are closed. I came north hoping to get a tutoring job with some rich family. I never found that dream job, so I wound up being a kitchen helper in a CCC camp in central Massachusetts, a tiny place called Athol. I spent the last two-and-a-half months there and that's where I'm coming from now."

"I see," said Sven. "And you're heading east to find what?"

"I was told that my application to the New Haven school system was near the top of the list and that I should contact them the first week in September in case any last-minute vacancies occur. I need to get to Boston for transportation back to New Haven—so I'm right there if the position is mine."

"Well, good luck," said Sven. "I had to join the Teamsters union and give up a good chunk of my pay to get these long-haul gigs. I consider myself pretty damn lucky at that."

"These days, I consider anybody who has a job lucky."

"When's the last time you had anything to eat or drink, young lady?"

"Early afternoon, I think."

"There's a couple of scrambled egg sandwiches in the brown bag between us if you would like one."

"No need," she replied. "I have a few peanut butter and jellies for the road in my backpack here." She unzipped a section, retrieved one, and began unraveling the wax paper wrapping.

"There's some hot coffee in the thermos bottle there," he said. Keeping his large left hand on the steering wheel and his eyes fixed on the road, he reached with his right hand into his brown bag for one of his own sandwiches.

"Thank you," Bertie murmured, almost overwhelmed by his kindness.

They silently munched away and shared sips of coffee for several minutes, when he said, "I heard a lot of yelling in the distance, and you seemed plenty disturbed when I picked you up back there. Do you feel like telling me what happened?"

"There isn't much to tell. I hitched a ride with a lecher. He tried to lock my belongings in the trunk of his car so he could force me to spend the night with him. He said he'd give them back in the morning."

"There's some pretty cruddy people in this world," Sven agreed. "So how'd you dump the crud and get away?"

"I threatened him with my hatchet," she replied, pulling out her tool to show him."

"Just threatened him?" he asked. "I thought I saw you tossing away a bloody paper towel when I pulled up to the pumps."

Bertie flushed and squirmed in the seat. "Well, maybe a little more than that," she admitted. "I swung it through the air in front of him and he tried to take it away from me. I accidentally caught his thumb with the blade. It's pretty sharp, you know. Maybe I scratched him some across his thumb."

"Scratched? He was still yelling bloody murder after I got down from the cab."

"Well, maybe I cut him a might deep, but he deserved it for what he was trying to do to me. If you thought I'd harmed him so wantonly, why did you agree to take me on?"

"I didn't figure it all out until just now."

"Are you sorry you did?" she asked.

"Nope." He wiped his beard with a paper towel.

The summer sky turned gray, then darker. Black clouds challenged the nightfall, racing to beat the heavy veil of darkness obstructing the visible road ahead. As the ominous clouds threatened, random droplets turned to sprinkles, then torrents pounding the cab and windshield, blurring Sven's vision. A swirling wind appeared out of nowhere. The rise and fall of the two-lane highway, cutting through rocky walled crests, forced Sven to halve his speed and double his attention. It was difficult—no, impossible—to see over the oncoming crests, testing and trusting his gut, one hill after another. As one particularly long hill loomed ahead, Sven took a deep breath and held it as he poured on the accelerator to make it over the top.

Cresting the top in a channel between two rock walls, the rig began moving fast, too fast on the down-slope. Out of the near-blinding rain, a large formless black shadow appeared on the down-slope across the road ahead. Sven applied the brakes, first in short pumps and then in a slowly increasing push. Bertie heard them hiss, squeal, and screech; then felt the trailer behind them vibrate and shift its weight sideways back and forth, rumbling and complaining. Its wheels sometimes left the ground, wanting to touch down again. The formless shadow rapidly took on the shape of a stranded car in the right lane, blocking the semi's passage. Closer and closer, the image sharpened and then it became apparent there were two figures waving their arms for them to stop and assist. A woman and a young girl stood in the left lane, unaware of either the danger they posed or the danger they faced.

If Sven jammed down on the brakes, the rig would jack-knife and the multi-ton trailer would sweep past them, taking the stranded car and standing figures alike down the far side of the hill.

The semi was still moving too fast to stop in time. If Sven swung the wheel hard right or left, he'd slam into the rock wall now enclosing them. There was no telling how the trailer would react—too many decisions for that final instant. His hands gripped the wheel with fingers of steel and he began reciting The Lord's Prayer.

Bertie bit her tongue, closed her eyes, and screamed.

Chapter 17

Recovery

BERTIE OPENED her eyes for an instant, and through the rain-swept windshield, stared at the offending car and the two people waving. Cringing, imagining the crash with all four lives lost, she squeezed her eyes shut once more and whimpered.

Sven swung the steering wheel a hard left. Now, the granite wall loomed large, close, and unavoidable—making utter destruction seem inevitable, when Sven pivoted the steering wheel a hard right. An instant later, the top of the cab tilted and scraped along the rough wall. He gunned the engine for a short burst that righted the cab and laid the trailer against the same surface—scraping, bumping, creating sparks. Sven jammed down on the brake and finally brought the entire rig to a halt, hugging the wall without so much as a foot to spare over the length of the huge rig.

The herculean maneuver and abrupt stop caused Bertie to slide forward off the leather seat. Had it not been for the backpack she held in her lap, her head would have slammed into the dashboard. Silence, punctuated by the idling diesel, reigned for several minutes. Bertie opened her eyes and regarded Sven from her crouch on the floor between the dashboard and the seat. She gasped. Sven's head lay across the steering wheel on his arms. His door had buckled and the glass in it had imploded and shattered. There were shards everywhere, even sprinkled in his hair.

As if a faucet had been turned off, the torrential rain lapsed into a quiet drizzle, then stopped.

Seconds later, Bertie saw Sven raise his head and begin to shake the glass shards from his hair and bushy beard. His whole body visibly trembled and his lips silently moved. She supposed he was finishing the prayer he'd recited during his heroic maneuver.

He looked over at her in her terribly awkward position and mumbled, "Bertie! You hurt?"

"I don't think so, no," she said, as she pushed the backpack onto the seat, then grabbed the door handle and the back of the seat cushion to pull herself up. Just as she landed on the seat, the door swung open because she had pulled down too hard on the handle. As soon as she righted herself on the seat, she found two faces staring into the cab: the woman and the young girl who had been waving them down.

"Are you two plumb crazy?" yelled Sven. "I came close to killing the both of you. Why were you standing in the only lane left open to me? I had nowhere else to go with the rig." His voice cracked and the words squeaked through.

"We wanted to be sure you'd stop for us," the woman replied.

"Take it easy, Sven," cautioned Bertie. "You'll have a heart attack yet."

"When the insurance investigators get through with me, I'll be lucky if I still have a job," he shouted. "If they suspend my license, I won't be able to get another one."

"Don't worry, Sven," Bertie said, "You were a hero. I'll speak up for you and tell them what really happened."

"Oh no you won't, my friend," he retorted. "They'll have my arse for breaking the company's no-rider rule. That's an excuse for the insurance company not to pay off. They're always looking for a way to weasel out of it."

125

"What's wrong with your car, ma'am?" asked Bertie.

"I don't know," answered the woman.

"Sure you do, Mom. Don't lie. We plain ran out of gas."

Bertie sized up the daughter. Probably about seventeen. Straw-colored hair in pigtails, and an impudent, adult manner.

"First things first," said a more calmed Sven, motioning for Bertie to climb down from the rig. There was no way for him to leave the cab with the rock wall on his left, so he slid over and followed her to the ground. "We have to push their car onto the right shoulder," he told Bertie, "or they won't be so lucky when the next vehicle comes along."

The daughter steered while the other three pushed the 1933 Chevy onto the gravel shoulder of the road. Sven announced, "I'm going to drive my damaged rig to the next service station and send back a can of gasoline for you. It's best that all three of you stay with the car until I send the fuel. I don't want the insurance people to know about Bertie riding along."

"Why can't we borrow a wee bit of gas from your tank, Mister?" asked the daughter.

"My rig runs on diesel, Miss," grunted Sven. "Your car runs on gasoline."

Bertie suddenly realized she would never see him again. "Sven! Thank you! You were wonderful. Good luck!"

"Good luck to you, Bertie. Hope you get that teaching job." He crossed the road, climbed into the rig from the passenger side, and slid over to the driver's position. He took off the emergency brake and goosed the engine twice before he edged the rig forward and onto the roadway, crossing into the correct lane. He tooted the deep-voiced truck horn three short blasts, as the rig picked up speed and disappeared down the long hill.

The mother invited Bertie to get in the back seat of the car while she took her place behind the wheel.

The daughter got in and sat sideways next to her mother, so she could face Bertie in the back seat. "My name is Elizabeth Mason. Liz. What's yours?"

"Bertie, Bertie Patchet. Glad to know you, Liz. You too, Mrs. Mason."

"Likewise," said her mother. "You can call me Velma. How did you happen to be riding in that big truck with Mr. Sven?"

"Just hitching a ride to the Boston area," said Bertie. "But you girls frightened the living daylights out of us by standing in the road like that. You should have been behind the protection of your car and in the headlights where we could have seen you better." She almost wished she hadn't lectured Velma, who had mousy brown hair laced with gray streaks and deep worry lines around her eyes and mouth.

"Sorry," said Liz, speaking up for her mother.

"Where were you headed when you ran out of gas?" asked Bertie.

Liz was eager to talk. "We were coming home from Grandpa Abner's up in Gardner, Massachusetts. We live on a farm just outside of Acton." Her mother, contrite and embarrassed, kept her eyes fixed on the road and let her daughter take charge of the conversation.

Without gas, they weren't going anywhere, so they settled in where they were parked for the night. Liz dropped off to sleep, and Bertie, with the whole rear seat to herself, stretched out and did the same.

It was morning before she awoke to the sound of a tow truck horn. Velma heard it as well and rolled down her window. She paid for the gas, and the tow truck driver poured it into the car's tank. He waved when he finished, headed back to his truck, made a U-turn, and drove off. Velma started the car after a few dry tries, and the three of them were on their way.

"Are you in a big hurry to get to Boston?" asked Velma.

Bertie wondered why she was asking. "I'm not sure. I won't really know until I contact the Connecticut Board of Education about a possible teaching position. I need to make a long-distance phone call to see if there are any openings for me. If there are, I'll have to get down to New Haven in a hurry. Otherwise, I'm a vagabond—again." She sighed. "Why do you ask?"

"How would you like to spend a few days on the farm with us? My husband is gone, passed away nearly two years ago, and we can always use an extra hand for chores. Grandpa Abner, my father, usually helps us out, but he's got a broken toe and can't walk. He's been disabled for some time now."

"I'd love to, but I won't know until I make that most important phone call," said Bertie. "If you wouldn't mind, I could make the call from your place. I know it's long-distance, but I'm willing to pay you for it."

"I thought you were strapped for cash," said Velma.

"Yes and no. I have my paychecks from my summer employment at the CCC camp. I have some leftover cash, too. I can even pay you in cash for the call, if you like."

"I'm not worried about repayment," said Velma. "If you're willing to help at all on the farm, that will be payment enough."

The Chevy drove eastward on Route 202 for another hour. A few miles short of Concord, Velma turned north onto a nameless country road. Ten minutes later, she entered a dirt driveway leading to the Masons' two-story, gray farmhouse. Bertie walked slowly inside and gazed around. The living room was furnished in a comfortable haphazard style with pictures of family gatherings on the walls. A large autumn landscape hung over the sofa.

Velma cocked her head to the left. "The phone's in the kitchen. C'mon, I'll show you. I know you're anxious to find out whether you have a job or not."

"Okay if I use your address and telephone number for them to respond?" Bertie asked, following her into the kitchen. She dropped her backpack onto the floor below the wall phone.

"Sure," said Velma. She wrote down her address and phone number on the pad next to the wall phone, including the county name, rural route, and box numbers.

While Velma and Liz climbed to the second floor to unpack, Bertie rummaged through her papers in a drawstring pocket of her pack and retrieved the letter containing the important phone number. She lifted the cylindrical receiver, put it to her ear, and wound the little hand crank. After giving the operator the long-distance number, she waited for the connection. A Mrs. Cora Eagan picked up the phone at the Board of Education.

"Hello, yes, this is Bertie L. Patchet. I'm on your waiting list for a fall teaching position anywhere in the state."

A minute passed while Cora Eagan shuffled a bunch of papers. "Yes, Miss Patchet, we have your application."

"Oh good! I'm calling to see if my employment status has changed. Are there any openings? None?" she repeated aloud. "Ah, but you expect two teachers to go on maternity leave—one in Bridgeport at the end of September and the other in New Haven in mid-October. Mrs. Eagan," Bertie said brightly, "I'll take either one, if you'll have me. Yes, I understand, no guarantees. Thank you, Mrs. Eagan, for penciling my name in for the New Haven position." She recited Velma's address and phone number, thanked the woman again, and hung up.

Breathing deeply with a tempered sigh of relief, Bertie picked up her backpack. walked to the staircase near the front door, and looked up to see Velma standing on the second-floor landing, hands on hips. "So what's the verdict?"

"It looks like I might get a teaching job in New Haven by mid-October. I'm available until then to help out—in exchange for free room and board. You okay with that arrangement?"

"That would be just fine," nodded Velma. "You're welcome to stay with us as long as you like. You'll have chores just like the rest of us, of course. Understood?"

"You bet," said Bertie. "I'm actually looking forward to them."

"You'll get a chance to see how much you like 'em after lunch," said Velma.

That afternoon, with experienced Liz as a teacher, Bertie spread hay and feed to the herd of six dairy cows, laid a fresh layer of straw in their shed spaces, and ran water into their trough.

Liz did the actual milking while Velma spent the day on

their old tractor hauling fence posts to the farm's perimeter. The milking was repeated twice daily, as early as five in the morning and as late as four in the afternoon. There were also pigs and chickens to be fed and the necessary mucking-out cleanup after them. The following day, all three of them bent to the task of replacing the weaker sections of the perimeter fencing. The next day, Velma drove the tractor alongside the flourishing vegetable field, hauling a flatbed trailer. Liz and Bertie picked the vegetables, filled baskets and cartons with them, and loaded them onto the trailer. Every Saturday they took the flatbed truck loaded with vegetables into Acton's market square for selling.

The physical work suited Bertie. Gone was her anxiety over where her next meal and bed would come from, and she got along famously with the Masons. And so it went for days and then weeks at a time with only minor variations.

But on Saturday, the third of October, everything went awry. It began that morning when the backyard water pump went dry and needed to be reprimed. On the way to market the right rear tire on the stake truck blew out.

"Oh no!" cried Velma.

They all climbed out to discover the truck bed sagging under the load of crated vegetables. Bertie managed to get a jack under the frame and crank it up to fit the tire's normal height. In wrestling the spare tire from under the rear of the truck bed, Liz and Velma had to do a lot of jostling—too much jostling. The jack began to slip away from under the truck frame. As the frame dropped to the ground, a number of stacked vegetable crates shifted, tilted, then tumbled off the open end of the truck bed, straight toward Bertie. She stood frozen to the spot, her mouth agape, waiting for her brain to kick in.

Chapter 18

More Tracks

THE HEAVIEST CRATE tumbled down so fast that a corner of it grazed the right side of Bertie's head. The second crate knocked her onto her backside. As that crate hit the ground, its sides buckled and burst open with scores of red-ripe tomatoes squashing, bouncing, and rolling helter-skelter. The third crate teetered, slid, and toppled down, rolling heavily over Bertie's right foot. She screamed as a protruding nail punctured her ankle. This crate landed battered but with its contents intact. The fourth crate slid to the edge of the truck bed, threatening to land with yet more impact. Bertie managed to slither onto her backside out of its range. Looking at her painful foot, there was no telling whether the sea of red she saw was blood or squashed tomato. That fourth crate never fell, yet teetered in wait.

Velma and Liz quickly dropped the spare tire on its side and rushed to find Bertie lying flat on her back in the roadside drainage ditch, partially covered in either the juice from squished tomatoes or blood. Her eyes were wide, glazed with shock and fright.

"Where are you hurt?" asked Velma, assuming the worst.

"My right foot caught the brunt of the falling crate," replied Bertie. "It's sore. I don't know if I'll be able to walk until I get on my feet." Her voice faltered as her hand flew to the tangled hair on her right temple and came away with the dampness of blood. "Ow!" she moaned.

"How bad is it?" asked Velma, examining the damp spot. "Should we get you to a doctor or a hospital?"

"No, no," pleaded Bertie. "It's just a scratch. I'm more interested in seeing if I can walk. Help me up, please."

Velma and Liz crouched on either side of Bertie. Placing their hands under her armpits, they lifted her upright and out onto the hard road. As they eased off, they remained close with their hands out to catch her if she started to fall. Bertie tested her right foot gingerly. Although it felt quite sore, she convinced herself that it was neither mangled nor broken.

"It's going to swell," Velma said, her voice anxious.

"Yeah," said Bertie. She expected it to swell greatly in the hours to come. It was that sort of wound; she'd had them before. Velma and Liz helped settle Bertie on the front bench seat of the truck.

"Go fix the tire," Bertie said. "And stop fussing over me. I'll be fine here. You're already late getting to market, so you need to get a move on."

Velma nodded, her face grim with feelings of guilt. This morning she and Liz had been in too much of a hurry to load the stake truck. They'd been sloppy, illogically loading the heaviest crates on top of the lighter ones.

Bertie sat alone for the next half-hour. She raised her leg and rested her foot on the dashboard, hoping to reduce the swelling. She washed both of her wounds with water from the bottle of drinking water they had brought along, and covered them with stick-on bandages from the first-aid kit she found in the truck's glove box.

Mother and daughter tackled the tire exchange. They also salvaged what they could of the runaway tomatoes and cleaned up the squishy mess left by the spill.

Because Bertie refused any further medical attention, they drove on to Acton's town square. Arriving late, Velma and Liz acquired a vending space at the edge of the farmer's market, a notably less desirable space, but they were grateful to find one at all. Mother and daughter arranged their wares in open-top wooden crates atop similar empty ones. Under sunny skies, the weekend market teemed with local merchants, restaurant owners, and villagers, all eager to purchase farm-fresh produce. Bertie stayed off her feet by alternating between a folding chair outside and the truck's front bench seat. By early afternoon the Masons had sold out most of their vegetables. They packed up all the crates and drove back to the farm.

Bertie found herself relegated to kitchen duties for most of the following week to give her ankle time to heal properly. By the time Thursday rolled around, she had already completed her share of the farming chores. That evening she informed the Masons that she wanted to start for New Haven on Monday.

"So soon?" burst out Liz. "I was hoping you'd want to stay for good. You're like my big sister."

"Yes," added Velma, "you're like one of the family. I guess we were getting too used to all the additional help and friendship you've provided. You realize I don't have much opportunity for adult conversation around here. It's almost like you've always been here. And the way you've pitched in is so amazing. I think I'm going to cry."

"Me too," said Liz.

"Please don't or we'll all get down in the mouth," said Bertie, offering Velma a hug. "It seems that my life is just full of good-byes."

Liz joined them in a three-way hug.

"What time do you want to leave?" asked Velma, separating abruptly and wiping away a tear.

"Right after breakfast."

"Would you like a ride into Boston?" asked Velma. "I'm

going into Concord for supplies anyway, so I might as well get them in Boston. What do you say?"

Bertie grinned. "How can I refuse an offer like that?"

As long as there was daylight, Bertie worked hard alongside Liz and Velma the entire weekend. When Monday rolled around, Velma prepared a full farm breakfast of eggs, sausage, and French toast as send-off fare. She also packed several portable meals into a shoulder pouch for her. As Bertie headed to the Chevy, Liz came running up to her.

"You weren't going to leave without saying goodbye, were you?"

"Of course not," said Bertie, "but you sort of disappeared right after breakfast. I thought you wanted to avoid saying it."

"I went to fetch this." Liz handed her a shapeless bundle covered in brown-bag paper and cross-tied with string. "You can open it during the ride."

"Thank you, Liz. You're so sweet. I'll miss you." Bertie kissed her on the cheek, squeezed her hand, and turned away toward the awaiting car.

Velma witnessed her daughter's act of kindness from the driver's seat. She smiled and started the car. As soon as her passenger shut the car door, Velma drove down the dirt driveway to the dusty secondary road.

Bertie spun about in her seat and waved to Liz through the rear window until the car turned at the end of the driveway and she lost sight of her. She swallowed the sadness of possibly never seeing them again. *Why are there so damn many permanent separations and disconnections in my life? Why am I not allowed to keep the friends I make?* The sense of loss settled in the pit of her stomach. She picked up Liz's gift and unraveled the brown paper wrapping to reveal a pair of royal-blue hand-knitted gloves. She held them up for Velma to see. "These are so beautifully made. Did Liz knit them herself?"

"She sure did," Velma answered tenderly.

"What a wonderful gift. And they're warm, too." Bertie said, almost choking up. She found a safe place for them in the backpack.

Velma drove for just short of an hour, still also feeling dejected, when a more practical idea surfaced. "You never did say where you wanted to be dropped off in the Boston area. At the railroad's North Station or one of the bus stations?"

"None of them," replied Bertie. "But I'd like to get out a block or two north of the railroad station."

"Aren't you going to take a train to New Haven?" asked Velma.

"I am, only I'm not taking a passenger seat," Bertie replied.

"What do you mean?"

"I'm going to hop a freight car south to New Haven."

"Oh my God, Bertie, you're a brave one. Don't you have enough for the fare?"

"I do, Velma, but it's going to be a while before I see any paycheck for teaching."

"I don't think either side of North or South Station would be the ideal place for that sort of thing. Why don't we try the Southampton rail yards? It'll take a little longer, but there should be more opportunities to access the freight facilities."

"You sound like an expert, Velma. Have you ever ridden in a boxcar?"

"No, but I've had to pick up parts for the tractor there a few times."

"So you don't mind the longer drive?"

"Not at all," replied Velma. "I really don't want to see you go, so I'm prolonging my time with you."

"Aww, thank you. I'll miss you both. Don't worry, I'll keep in touch."

Velma drove on, entered the Boston city limits, and maneuvered the major thoroughfares southward to the Southampton area. Once there, a number of side streets took them within sight of the rail yard tracks. Bertie had Velma drive close and parallel to the tracks until she said, "Here!" The car pulled up to the curb. The two friends climbed out and stood there staring at one another until they flew together in a tight embrace. Neither said another word. Velma got back in the car, and Bertie walked away—toward the tracks and the fence that separated her from her destination. She never looked back, but she heard the car drive off and listened until its motor's sound blended with the rest of the traffic din.

Bertie searched the wooden creosoted-black fence for an entry flaw. After walking and searching for a mile and a half, she encountered a small gate, but it was padlocked shut. Upon closer examination, she saw that the door's wood was significantly older than the rest of the fence. In fact, the screws in the rusty hinges were only half in place; she could twist them with her index finger and thumb. A couple minutes of turning, and the door hung only by its padlock and hasp. She slipped inside and reset the door so that it appeared closed to the passing eye. Inside the fence Bertie stood on a narrow concrete bulkhead that looked down on multiple tracks at least thirty feet below. There were neither stairs nor ladder nor sloping grade in sight to get to the track level. The bulkhead continued in both directions as far as the eye could see. She reasoned that the door was used only to access a few electrical boxes inside the fence.

Across the tracks she spotted loading docks situated behind several brick and concrete buildings. There were even two boxcars being loaded while she watched. *Somehow I have to get to the other side of the tracks.* Bertie continued walking on the near side without finding a way down. After a while she sat down on the edge of the bulkhead with her legs dangling to decide whether to go back to the door and find another access on the opposite side. But that meant she'd still have to find a street bridge to get to the other side and the direction she needed. She slipped out of the backpack and shoulder pouch and laid them beside her while she thought this dilemma through.

Bertie took a Swiss cheese and ham sandwich from the shoulder pouch Velma had given her, unwrapped it, and chomped down hard on it, trying to counter her sense of hopelessness. A flash of anger and frustration crept into her thinking. As if it were a buzzing fly, she shook her head right and left to cast it off. In the visual sweep to her left, her eye picked out a set of rusty metal rungs set into the concrete, one above the other about two feet apart. *It's a hidden ladder. My prayers have been answered.* Reaching as far down as possible, she let her backpack and pouch drop to the ground below. *A rope would have been helpful. I'm sure glad there's nothing breakable inside.*

Bertie slipped over the side of the bulkhead, grabbed the wide top rung with two hands, and tried to fit her right foot onto the next one vertically. That worked, so she tried the next, hand to foot, foot to hand, hand to foot, and several more successfully. It was hard work as either a hand or a foot carried the full weight of her body. About halfway to the bottom, the rung she was clutching began to move in its concrete setting. One end pulled out altogether and rotated, leaving her hanging in midair without another practical grip in reach. *I'm going to break every bone in my body!* She heard the remaining end of the rung creak in its hole. *This is it!* She squeezed her eyes shut in harsh anticipation of her ultimate fate. *There's nothing more I can dooooo!*

Chapter 19
Beyond the Fall

AGRATING SOUND warned Bertie of imminent disaster as the rusted, deteriorated iron rung separated completely from its crumbled concrete setting. With eyes squeezed shut, she dropped into a feet-first free-fall. Her right foot swiped a rung midway down, causing her body to bounce out and away from the wall. The bump slowed her fall slightly, but it had a major rotating effect. The spin slammed her head against the wall, knocking her unconscious. The horrifying free-fall drop finally ended with Bertie's stomach draped across the backpack that she'd deliberately dropped onto the ground. Three factors not only saved her life, but minimized her injuries. One, the lack of consciousness prevented her from stiffening her limbs upon impact. Two, she had rotated onto her soft stomach. Three, she had landed across the crushable backpack with her face turned aside.

Bertie had no idea how long she'd been unconscious. The first sensation she detected was a sloppy wet swipe across her left cheek. Forcing her eyes open, she discovered a muzzle of scruffy fur and smelly breath hovering just inches from her face. Stiffening with fear of the unknown, she jerked back and suddenly realized

how sore and racked with pain she'd become. Her quick withdraw-
al also caused the furry face to bolt back out of immediate sight,
but she could still hear its panting. She tried to turn quickly, but
wrenching pain restrained her. She turned more slowly to see a
German shepherd—of sorts. She rolled off the backpack in slow
motion.

The gray, brown, and black mongrel, a female, seemed to
be all alone. As far as Bertie could tell, there wasn't a single human
around. She held out her hand. The dog approached, sniffed first,
then licked it. She had made a friend. After two hopeless tries to
get to her feet, she scooted back against the wall and rested. *I'll try
again soon, but, first, did I break anything?* One by one she flexed all
her limbs and stretched her joints until she became satisfied that
she hadn't broken any bones. She pulled up her shirt and studied
the red bruises on her torso. They would soon turn black and blue.
No problem there. Looking up to the top of the wall, she couldn't
believe she'd survived such a fall without greater injury. The all-
enveloping ache she felt had to be from bruising and muscle strain.
At last Bertie made one extraordinary effort to stand and finally got
to her feet. She held onto the wall for the first few steps. *Ah, I can
still walk no matter how badly it hurts.*

When she trod a few steps to cross tracks to the industry
side, surprisingly, the dog made no attempt to follow. Instead, it
periodically barked and ran up and back parallel to the tracks. *I
think she wants me to follow her. I wonder why. Crossing the tracks
means a lot of high-stepping for me—following the dog could be a mite
easier and, after all, isn't this her home territory?* She made a quick
decision based on impulse, and returned to the wall to follow the
mutt.

Bertie's gingered steps soon became rickety as her new canine pal led her nearly half a mile, hugging the soot-covered bulkhead only a couple yards from the nearest track. Speeding trains
passed, one in each direction. *Scary!* Both made an ear-splitting
racket and roiled up gusts of soot-filled air that clogged her throat
and nostrils.

Their northerly trek seemed endless. *Where in hell is this animal taking me?* On and on she blindly followed, until the bulkhead began to curb the sun's rays, extending the great shadow over one track after another. Two trains passed. Bertie made a calculation. *That second track might be the main line south and the fifth track out might be the main line north.*

At last, the path between the soot-covered bulkhead and the first track broadened to five feet, then ten, and then a secluded acre of wasteland, protected by at least thirty feet of concrete wall on three sides. This was a tract isolated to prevent outside human interference.

At first Bertie was haunted by the formidable wall, but then she noted human movement near the wall. She hastily counted at least fifteen occupants. Another man climbed down an iron rung ladder from the top. As she cautiously came closer, she observed that none of the men in dark, haphazard clothing appeared to be workmen. The place seemed more like a community, although there wasn't a female among them. *I'm glad I remembered to tuck my hair into my cap. I don't think a female would fare too well down here.* She concluded that her new furry friend had brought her to a hidden hobo enclave. The dog made a beeline for a seated brawny man with a hawk-like nose. The friendly mutt leapt into his lap and curled up.

"Hey there, Lady. I see you brought us another stray," boomed the man. Although he smiled broadly, his words were embellished with a deep gravel quality. The man rubbed Lady behind the ears, and she laid her head back to receive more. Then he turned his attention toward Bertie.

"Hey you, the newcomer, I'm Brother Snipes. I run this establishment. What's your name?"

"Bert, Bert Patchet. I'm just looking for a place to put my head down for a couple hours, if it's okay with you."

"Sure, sure! Just pull up a patch of concrete and make yourself comfortable. We ain't got no room service here, pal. You obey the rules and you kin stay."

Bertie headed for the first available space she could find and plopped herself down in it. The last two hours had been arduous and she needed to rest some. She slipped out of her backpack, fluffed it up, and lay back on it. Sleep didn't come right away. Just when she was about to doze off, she sensed someone standing over her. She stared up at the dark figure and tried to see past the heavy beard. The eyes and shape of the face looked somewhat familiar.

"You don't recognize me, do you, Bertie?"

"Should I?" she asked.

"Yeah. Four months ago we were best of buddies. And you've forgotten me so soon?"

She stared up at him. Torn, faded jeans and checkered shirt. Mid-forties, balding, salt-and-pepper fringe. A thick beard and bushy brows matching the fringe. Brown eyes the color of late autumn in the rain.

"Oh my God," she screeched. "Arnie Folsome!"

For a second she worried that her female falsetto would betray her. She looked around to see if anyone had noticed. Apparently not. "Arnie, I thought the rail cops had killed you. You were being awfully brave to take that terrible beating so I could get away. What happened after I left?"

Arnie knelt down next to her, then rotated into a seated position. "I didn't realize that's what I was doing—trying to let you get away—until a lot later, so I guess I wasn't very brave after all. The sonofabitch cop beat the hell out of me with his billy club. You know somethin'? Those billy clubs should be called bully clubs. That's what they're used for. The cop broke my arm in two places and covered my body with bruises. When he finished, he rolled me off the loading platform like dead meat and left me for the crows. That night some decent guy found me and called an ambulance. They took me to a free clinic in Bridgeport. Those volunteer medics set my arm in a plaster cast. The clinic let me stay the night and threw me out the next morning without so much as a pain pill. I wore the damn clumsy thing for the next ten weeks. I couldn't work. I couldn't even walk very far. You were gone—God knows where. What was I supposed to do?"

"So what did you do?"

"I found this church in Bridgeport, the Good Shepherd Church. They had a soup kitchen and a place to sleep in their basement. A lot of churches did that, but I heard that Good Shepherd did it best. It seemed like I was standing in long lines, with a sorry bunch of unemployed guys, for one thing or another all day long. I hung around the church so much that Pastor Fred eventually gave me odd jobs to do. It was mostly lowly cleanup jobs, but I did get to help build a few tables for their bingo nights. Later on, when Pastor Fred trusted me more, I got to dish out food at mealtimes. All I had to do in return was become a good listener for all his sermons, which were proffered at least four times daily. I probably grumbled a whole lot, but I was certainly grateful for all he did for me."

Arnie fell silent, breathing heavily, as if talking in paragraphs was a huge effort. He looked at Bertie with a wry smile. "You sure you want to hear my four-month life story?"

She laid her hand on his arm. "Of course I do. You were such a good friend."

"Okay then," he said. "Finally, I went back to the clinic and convinced them to remove the itchy cast from my forearm. I felt like a free man for a change. I returned to the rail yards and caught a freight train north. Things were going pretty well for me, but I should've known better. I got chased off by the rail cops in New London. So I spent a few days there. Even snuck into Ocean Beach for a swim. I skinny-dipped at night to avoid their security—and didn't get caught! Afterward, I caught another empty freight in the same direction that ended up in Fall River, Mass. I had to hitch the rest of the way into Boston. Nobody's hiring anybody there either, so I wound up here with this bunch. Oh, occasionally, a truck will appear up at the top there." He pointed straight up. "Some boss or foreman guy points 'You, you, you, and you' for a day job. It's usually piddling poor pay for backbreaking labor, but at least it pays for our food and blankets. According to Brother Snipes, we're supposed to share everything for the right and privilege to stay here. Snipes is the self-appointed mayor of our little enclave. He has two thugs who do the enforcing for him, and he'll turn them loose on anyone he suspects of hoarding. No one here has ever contested his power.

"I suppose it's kinda fair," she said. To herself, she thought, *What if they discover the money in my pack that Stan and I recovered from the robbers? There's still a good lot of it left.*

"Yeah, it's a rough kind of policing nonetheless," said Arnie. "Say, you haven't told me about your travels since you got away from the rail cops that night in Bridgeport."

Bertie related her adventures with Stan in Newport, her employment as a cook in the CCC camp, and her stay at the Mason farm. "I'm on my way back to New Haven for a teaching job I've been promised, if I can get there in time. First, I need to recover from my fall, so I can get a move on. I'm so tired I can barely walk."

"Hey, I'll go back to my stuff now and let you get some sleep." Arnie got to his feet and disappeared among the sea of unwashed dozing bodies.

Bertie leaned back against her backpack once more and was blessed with sleep. She had a dream she was still on the Mason farm. A cow was standing on both her shoulders. She knew this couldn't be true and yet she felt the pressure of being held down. The pressure became so great that it tore her from the depths of sleep and the confusing dream. Her eyes popped open, but all she saw was the darkest night she could imagine. Then she realized there were two hairy hands holding her down against the concrete. A face appeared above her—a face she thought she knew.

"Go through his backpack while I check his pockets," Snipes whispered to his two cohorts. The brutality in his voice was unmistakable. Snipes was robbing her.

"What do you want from me?" Bertie cried out as she struggled to get out of the vise-like grips of the man holding her down.

No answer. Bertie wriggled about and kicked in the air. She felt the hands slipping in and out of one pocket after another. He rolled her to one side to get at the rear pockets and there he uncovered the wad of stolen money she'd been carrying. He rolled her on her back once more.

"Ah-ha, you've been holding out on me, young man. Naughty, naughty."

He punched her hard in the stomach, and she doubled up in speechless pain. He headed for her breast pockets to see if there was more loot. He found something there all right, but it wasn't loot. "Hey, he's a she! Well, isn't that a pleasant surprise? There's loot and pussy to boot, mates. I go first, and then she's yours for sloppy seconds." He began to unbutton her shirt. He was slow and taunting with each button.

Bertie screamed, kicked, and squirmed. Her screams fell on the deaf ears of those who slept and those who pretended to be asleep. None were brave enough to go against the mayor and his enforcers.

"Hold them friggin' legs down," commanded Snipes as he began to tug downward on her trousers.

Chapter 20
The Getaway

THE TWO HOODLUMS holding Bertie down heard the smack of a wood plank as it struck flesh and bone at the side of Snipes's head. The blow flung the would-be rapist from his kneeling position to the concrete a few feet away. Snipes lay sprawled out, unconscious.

The enforcer pinning her legs down saw the next smack coming. He released his grip and threw his hands up to protect himself, but too late. The board caught him deep in the midsection and sucked the breath out of him. He reeled away, howling, and retreated out of sight. The enforcer pinning her shoulders down let go and rose with elbows bent and fists clenched ready to take on anyone, but he couldn't see his attacker in the dark. The wood plank slammed against the back of his skull. He dropped to his knees and collapsed altogether on the unforgiving concrete.

"You saved me, whoever you are!" cried Bertie. "Thank you, thank you. But come out into the light where I can see you." She stood up on wobbly legs and turned slowly around, looking for her savior. "That bastard was going to rape me."

"I know. I'm here, Bertie," said Arnie, stepping out of the

shadows cast on the wall by a street lamp thirty feet above. He clutched a four-foot length of two-by-four at one end as if it were his cane. "Quick. Put on your backpack. We have to get the hell out of here before any of the three come to their senses. They'll be so pissed they'll kill us on sight."

"Okay, okay, I'm coming," she whispered. "But wait! Snipes stole my cash. I have to get it back." She shuffled over to his crumpled body. Touching him at all repulsed her, but she swallowed hard, and with a bit of a struggle, dug the wad out of one of his slash pockets and shoved it into her backpack.

"Good girl," Arnie said. He led Bertie across the jungle of tracks, high-stepping each pair as they came to them. For her, every track, every foot lift came with its own measure of pain. Hobbling along, her muscles and bones still remembered the fall, and especially the landing. Two-thirds of the way across, Arnie slipped his shoulder under hers to bolster her, lifting some of her burdensome weight. They made it to the other side, a distance approaching a quarter-mile. The loading platforms on this side looked to be connected and continuous as far as they could see in either direction. The nearest loading dock fronted a building that appeared to be a foundry. But better yet, just beyond it they saw a stretch of small factories where boxcars waited to be loaded.

All Bertie wanted to do was sit down someplace, anyplace. She was bushed and hadn't had a chance to recuperate. No amount of coaxing could get her to go any farther. She slumped down in front of the foundry's rear door with a stubborn, weird grin plastered on her face.

Arnie understood, left her there, and went exploring along the platform. At one loading dock he discovered a number of chest-high stacks of empty gunnysacks. He returned to Bertie with a half-dozen of them cradled in both arms. "Hey, lookie what I found."

"What?" she responded groggily, with half-open eyes and a disinterested mind to match.

"We'll sleep in comfort the rest of this night." He held up

the gunnysacks for her to see. "But first we've got to get out of sight. I don't know whether Brother Snipes and his goons are going to pursue us or not, but we can't take chances. That's got to be one pissed-off bunch, looking for revenge. So get off your cute little tail and let's move into one of these boxcars where they might not find us."

"I thought you killed at least two of them back there," Bertie said.

"No," Arnie replied. "Fortunately, they were both still breathing, and the other thug bolted."

"Should we try the first car?" she asked.

"Let's not make it too easy for the rail cops. How about the fourth car?"

"Make it the third car and you have a deal," she countered, hobbling next to him.

"You got it," he grinned. They tried to enter, but the sliding door was already closed, sealed with a wire-and-lead anti-tampering medallion instead of a padlock. Arnie bent the wire back and forth a dozen or so times until the fatigued wire cracked and separated. He then slid the door back to reveal a fully loaded boxcar. Rows of cartons stacked to shoulder height ran from one end of the car to the other. A three-foot-wide access path had been left for hand trucks. Most of the cartons were marked for addresses in New York City and New Jersey, so they knew the car was destined to head south at least as far as New Haven.

Arnie spread out the gunnysacks three-deep, head-to-foot, in the access path. While he arranged their beds, Bertie had another idea. She slipped the anti-tampering medallion's wiring through only one of the outside lock eyelets so that it would appear sealed to the naked eye from outside. Then she slid the door shut and lay down on her three layers of gunnysacks. During the few short hours of remaining night, the two slept soundly. That is, until bustling outside activity and workmen's chatter made them aware that morning had abruptly arrived.

They heard the adjacent cars being loaded, but their boxcar

remained untouched. Bertie could only guess whether it would be mere hours or many days before they would be underway. For now, they faced their usual tiresome challenges: food, water, and where to pee. The first of these Bertie solved by producing the bologna and two peanut butter and jelly sandwiches that Velma Mason had packed for her. They decided to share a sandwich twice a day, not knowing how long it would be until they reached their destination. Arnie still had two-thirds of a canteen of water. As for peeing, a carton or two shifted into the access corridor provided the necessary privacy to relieve themselves in an open corner, where Bertie chopped a foot-wide hole in the floor of the boxcar with her hatchet.

Arnie watched her with a mixture of admiration and alarm. *She's got chutzpah, all right. If a rail cop discovers her carpentry we'll be screwed big time.*

He wondered what precious items the cartons contained and even Bertie couldn't curb his curiosity. The lading slips glued to each carton bore addresses of hardware stores in several cities along their route. With Bertie's hatchet he carefully slit the sealing tape on one of the cartons. Fishing through the packing straw, he retrieved an electric registering device—a multimeter, apparently capable of measuring volts, ohms, and milliamperes.

"Wow," said Arnie. "I've never seen one of these gadgets before."

"Now put it back before we get arrested for theft," scolded Bertie.

"And before they find your hole in the corner," he retorted. He placed the meter back in the straw; folded the carton covers in an interlocking pattern so they'd stay shut; and placed another carton going to the same place on top of it.

They needn't have worried about the wait time; the loaded boxcar began to move late that same afternoon. A loud *clunk*, followed by a back-and-forth jarring motion, announced the good news. Other *clunking* and *clacking* sounds resounded as they were hauled from track to track to assemble the complex train configuration. Forty-five minutes later, the familiar *clickity-clack* assured them they were on their way at last. A long blast of the engine's whistle seconded the motion.

The minimal light from cracks in the imperfect wooden bulkheads left them with little to see or do. Seated on the folded gunnysacks, they played word and mind games as the freight train rattled along the tracks. All was well until one hour later, when the train began to slow as though it were planning to stop. It did come to a full stop and they heard activity outside, then angry voices on the other side of their boxcar door. Arnie and Bertie needed to hide. They scooped up the gunnysacks, grabbed their backpacks, and scrambled along the access path as far back in the car as they could. With barely seconds to spare, they ducked down behind stacks of cartons.

"Hey, somebody tampered with this lock," a voice growled. "The wire is only going through one of the loops."

"I see what you mean," said a second voice.

Arnie and Bertie heard the door slide back, flooding the car with sunlight.

"Nuthin' looks missing," said the growly voice. He rolled a hand truck up to a stack of cartons. "Here we go. These three are marked with New Bedford addresses."

He pushed against the stack, slid the hand truck under the bottom carton, and released the stack so it settled on the nose plate. Tilting back the hand truck, he rolled the stack of three cartons out of the boxcar onto the loading platform and out of sight. The door slid shut once more. Thirty minutes later, the train began to move again, and the two vagabonds crawled out from their hiding place into the access aisle.

After the freight train had reached and maintained its cruising speed for a quarter-hour, Bertie itched to find out whether the two men had secured the boxcar's door again. First she peeked through the crack, saw that it was free, and slid the door back to reveal the local countryside flying by her eyes. The fresh breeze and daylight exhilarated her.

Seeing Bertie smile, Arnie was prompted to challenge her. "What if they did seal us in? What would you do then?"

"I don't know," she said, with a sudden change of temperament and a sullen look.

"Then how would you get off in New Haven?"

"Damn it, Arnie. I just don't know," Bertie countered in a voice full of anxiety mixed with fear. "But that's not going to happen, is it?"

"It might. We could still stop in New London and Old Saybrook before we get to New Haven," he replied. "Maybe you should come up with a Plan B beforehand."

The train did stop in New London, and once more they crouched behind the stacks of cartons to hide. But the door slid open a little more quickly than they had anticipated—enough that Bertie's leg might have been in plain view just as she pulled it in. The two workmen went about removing a dozen or so cartons without acknowledging their presence. But she was certain at least one of them knew about the stowaways hiding behind the cartons. The door slid shut, but it was impossible to hear any more activity outside the boxcar. The train started to move, and when it reached cruising speed again, they made their way into the access aisle once more.

"Why didn't they report us?" asked Bertie. "They had to know I was hiding back there."

"Go figure," said Arnie. "Maybe we should check the door again."

Bertie went to the door and tried to slide it back and open, but it wouldn't budge more than an inch. "We're locked in," her voice squeaked. She tried to peak through the crack, as she had done before, but she didn't like what she saw. "This time it's a padlock. Now we're really screwed."

"I guess the only thing we can do is rush past the first person who unlocks and opens the door," said Arnie. "If we're lucky, we can get away from here without getting caught."

"If we're not lucky, then what?" she asked.

"Then, we're screwed like you said before," he replied. "Only I don't think I can take another beating like the guy in Bridgeport gave me."

"I do have one idea," said Bertie. "I'm not sure it's possible, but I could try to hack our way out of here with my trusty hatchet."

"For chrissake, no! That would be major property damage," said Arnie. "If they caught us doing stuff like that, it would be a prison term at the very least. It's bad enough that you hacked that hole in the corner floor."

"Hey, the train is slowing down again," said Bertie. "We'd better get ready to rush out of here."

They hustled into their backpacks and hunkered down ready to sprint out as soon as the door slid back. The train came to a full jerking stop. Although they heard activity outside, no one came to the door for at least ten minutes. Standing rock still, barely breathing, they heard someone tinkering with the padlock. The door started to slide back. They braced to leap. The door suddenly flew back and two hefty men with badges and shotguns completely filled the space.

The vagabonds had no way to execute either Plan A or B.

Chapter 21
Bars and More Bars

BERTIE AND ARNIE froze in their readied stances, afraid any move would trigger dire results. Both deputies lowered their guns as soon as they realized their captives were docile, unarmed, and nonresistant. In fact, they found the pair almost comical and had a problem suppressing smiles.

"Hey, Butch, look what we got," said the thinner deputy with the bulbous red nose. "Some honest-to-goodness trespassers."

"Please don't hit us," cried Arnie, whose body still remembered the pains of past brutalities. "We'll do anything you say. We're peaceful folk, harmless even."

"You're trespassing on railroad property," retorted bulbous nose. "We're arresting you for trespassing and vagrancy."

"We've got a nice jail cell for the two of you," said Gargantua, whose beer belly hung at least four inches over his belt. "Me 'n Oscar here, we're gonna escort you there."

Both deputies stepped back onto the loading platform, indicating with their guns that they wanted their prisoners to march ahead of them. Along the platform they marched, through an alley to the street, and out to a green and black paddy wagon. Bertie and

Arnie peacefully climbed into the rear compartment and sat down on bench seats.

Without the benefit of windows, the newly anointed jail-birds rode, with no idea where, through Old Saybrook and out to a suburb, where the town's lockup was situated. On arrival, they were deposited in the largest of four barred cells, along with five other prisoners, also trespassers or vagrants, awaiting similar legal action.

"Hey," called Bertie. "Don't we even get a trial?"

"You don't need a trial," said beer belly while locking the door on them. "By the way, I'm Butch. You were caught red-hand-ed. You'll get to see the justice of the peace in the morning."

"Morning?" asked Bertie.

"Yeah," said Oscar. "His Honor closed up shop and went home an hour ago. Old McAbee's entitled to a life of his own, ain't he?"

Both deputies exited the room knowing the cages and bars were sufficient to retain the prisoners. Bertie and Arnie took seats on the hard wooden benches that occupied most of the perimeter of the cell. Bertie looked around their cell. She saw sullen, despondent faces of subdued hobos just like themselves. But she didn't know there were other temperaments hidden among them.

"You mean we've got to spend the night in here?" asked Arnie aloud, but in a purely rhetorical manner.

"What's the matter, bub?" said a twentyish man, with a beefy, weight-lifter's frame. He rested, half-sitting, half-reclining, on the bench next to Arnie. "You don't like our company?" He jumped to his feet and faced Arnie with a steely stare that spelled a looking-for-trouble type of entertainment.

"Yeah, I didn't mean anything like that," replied Arnie, standing up and facing his accuser. "I just meant I didn't like the prospect of spending the night in jail. I'd rather be on my way. It had nothing to do with you or any of the rest of these nice guys."

"Honest, mister, he didn't mean anything by that," interrupted Bertie.

"Butt out, kid," said the beefy one. "This is between big mouth here and myself."

"I meant no offense, mister," protested Arnie, whose face had now bleached white with the fear of another senseless beating.

"Then why'd you open your big fat mouth?" asked beefy, while shoving two hands at Arnie's chest.

Arnie felt the shove lift him off his feet and send him back against the bars, where he slid down hard on his rear at the floor. His head hurt worse from the impact with the bars. One hand went to feel the back of his head, while the other thrust out in front of him, signaling a sign of unconditional surrender.

"Get up, you coward, and take your medicine," commanded beefy, standing directly over him.

A rallying cry and cheering arose from the majority of the prisoners, who were starved for any kind of distraction. They formed a grouping behind the beefy one to see better.

Arnie wisely stayed down. He was certainly no match for the beefy one. In fact, he curled into a fetal position, a defensive stance.

A frustrated and disgusted beefy returned to his bench seat, and the disappointed hoboes quieted down. Eventually, Arnie relaxed and stretched out his long legs. Bertie slid off her bench and stretched out next to Arnie on the floor. Several hours later, a different deputy showed up with a strange meat and potato hash drowned in watery gravy. Everyone ate off tin pie plates with popsicle sticks. A half-hour later he returned for the plates and sticks. They saw no outsider after that until morning. Bertie and Arnie spent a restless night, catching only minutes of precious sleep between patchy suspicions of their neighbors' possible intentions.

Morning started with a lukewarm creamed cereal and continued with orders to line up single file in the cell room while awaiting a turn in front of His Honor Cain McAbee, the Justice of the Peace, in the next room. Two at a time, the prisoners were allowed in his courtroom to stand before him. He sat behind a wooden desk at one end of a makeshift courtroom. A forty-eight-star American flag stood to the right of the desk. A deputy sat to the left of the desk alongside the Connecticut state flag. Bertie followed Arnie before the judge and they stood six feet from the desk. The judge looked up from his paperwork and pointed to Arnie.

"Next?"

Arnie took three steps closer to the desk and answered a barrage of questions the judge tossed at him.

"Name?"

"Arnold Folsome!"

"Age?"

"Thirty-three!"

"Occupation?"

Arnie hesitated and then whispered, "Financial adviser."

"What's that?" asked the justice. "Speak up, I can't hear you."

"Financial adviser. I used to work for a brokerage firm, Your Honor."

"I see. And where are you employed now?"

"I'm not."

"You're not what?"

"I'm not employed presently, Your Honor."

"Vagrancy! Fifteen-dollars or forty-eight hours in lockup," ruled the judge as he slammed down his gavel on the bare desk.

"But Your Honor, I don't have the fifteen dollars."

"Then it's the good old lockup for you," said His Honor with a self-pleasing grin on his jowly face. "You'll have to work hard for your meals, though. Our town has many useful projects for the likes of you."

"Wait!" called Bertie from her next-up position. "I'll pay his fine." She waved the two bills in front of her.

"Wait, wait indeed," said McAbee. "You wait your turn, young man. I'll get around to you next. But first, you'll remove your cap out of respect for this court."

As Bertie pulled off her cap, her glossy bobbed hair flopped down around her shoulders—now several inches longer than when she graduated months ago.

The judge did a double-take. "You're a freakin' woman," he said.

The deputy sheriff, standing at the door, guffawed.

"But I can still pay both our fines, Your Honor," Bertie piped up, hoping not to offend him.

When the judge regained his composure, with a suppressed smile, he said, "All right, then, Miss. I'll allow you to pay both fines. Step up and pay the deputy thirty-five."

"But twice fifteen is thirty dollars, Your Honor," murmured Bertie as she laid three tens and a five in the deputy's hands.

"The extra five is for the court's inconvenience," snapped the judge. "Besides, setting the fine is my prerogative. Now you two get the hell out of my damn sight before I set the fine even higher."

Needing no more incentive, Bertie and Arnie headed for the door that led to the street on the opposite side of the room. Just before stepping outside, she turned back and called, "Thank you, Your Honor."

Freedom found them breathing deeply with relief on a strange street. They stood on the sidewalk looking blankly at each other. What to do next? Could they hop on another freight train to New Haven without winding up back in the lockup? And where was the rail yard from here? There was no way to retrace their steps, having been driven blindly to the jail. A sign over an establishment a few doors away told them a cup of coffee could be had for one nickel.

"Let's try that place," said Bertie. "I bet they could tell us where the rail yard is."

"Good thinking," said Arnie.

The two entered the coffee shop and slipped onto stools at the counter. The counterman took a broad swipe at the surface in front of them with a wet rag. "What'll ya have, folks?"

"Two coffees, please," said Bertie as she pushed a dime in his direction.

"Coming right up!" He took two white porcelain mugs off the rear shelf and stuck them, one after the other, under the spigot of the large stainless urn until they were nearly full. After setting the mugs on the counter in front of them, he scooped up the dime. He slid two spoons, a sugar shaker, and a tiny pitcher of milk within reach and turned to walk away.

"Wait," said Arnie. "Can you tell us the way to the rail yard from here?"

"Ain't no rail yard, just tracks," the counterman replied.

"Can you point us in the right direction anyway?" asked Arnie.

"Sure. I figured you guys to be hoboes when you walked in. The tracks—it's simple. This shop is on Elm Street. Turn left when you walk out the door and follow Elm until you come across the tracks. Maybe a twenty-minute walk at most."

"Thank you," said Bertie. She doctored her mug with milk and sugar; Arnie only used sugar. Both sipped away at their coffees slowly, savoring not only the drink, but the comfortable stools with back supports.

They heard the front door jingle open behind them and turned to see who had walked in. The tall, shabbily dressed newcomer wore a newsboy cap, perched low, close to the eyes, and a black kerchief covering the lower half of his face.

He held a gun in his left hand.

"Everybody stay where you are," said the newcomer, "and nobody will get hurt. This is a holdup. You, behind the counter, open the register drawer."

The counterman did as he was told and hit the key that sent the cash drawer flying open with a *ca-ching*. Then he backed away, allowing the thief to move to the register. He watched the thief empty his hard-earned coins and bills from the till into the man's pockets.

As the thief backed away from the register, he continued toward the front door, facing them with the pointed-gun alternating among the other three occupants of the shop. "Anyone tries to follow me gets shot!" He reached behind himself for the door handle and pressed it open to back out to the street. He backed straight into a customer entering the shop.

Bertie recognized the customer as one of the deputies who had arrested them. She shouted, "Look out, Deputy, the man's got a gun!"

The surprised thief turned to face and point the gun directly at Deputy Butch, but the alerted officer grabbed the gun barrel and pointed it away from himself. Inside the coffee shop, the two men wrestled for control of it. The arms vying for the gun swung wildly about—firing several unintentional shots in unexpected directions. The two men banged up against one of the stools, tripped over the stool's base, and wound up on the floor. They rolled around, punching each other with their free hands while still contesting possession of the weapon with their other hands. The deputy rolled on top of the shooter and began slamming the back of the thief's hand against the floor until sore knuckles released the gun and it slid several feet away. The deputy dragged the thief to his feet and twisted the guy's arm tightly behind his back.

"Thanks for the warning, lady," said Butch as he started to march the thief out.

"Wait! My cash is in his pocket!" cried the counterman.

The deputy pushed the thief hard against a stool until he emptied the thief's pockets of both coins and bills and laid them on the top of the counter. "That everything?" he asked, pushing harder. Getting a nod from the thief, the deputy marched him out the door and up the street to the lockup.

Arnie had been so fascinated with the wrestling match that he failed to notice what had happened to his companion. When he finally spun his stool around to face her, she wasn't there. He looked down and saw her lying on the floor in front of him in a still and silent heap. He slid off his stool, knelt, and searched her body for any injuries. He found no blood anywhere. The most he found was a bright red mark on one of her temples.

"Bertie! Bertie!" he pleaded, while tapping her cheeks.

"Wake up! Please, Bertie."

But Bertie didn't answer him. She remained in the comatose state. Arnie rose and turned toward the counterman. The first words caught in his throat, then he bellowed, "Quick, call her an ambulance!"

Chapter 22

Concussion

THE AMBULANCE ARRIVED and carried the unconscious Bertie to the Old Saybrook Medical Center. After convincing the driver that he was the patient's stepfather, Arnie was allowed to ride along up front. He used the stepfather lie again at the hospital while describing the crisis in the coffee shop to the admissions person. He remained with Bertie in the emergency room until a stern nurse redirected him to the waiting room. He was able to learn the gruesome facts. Bertie was in a coma. She had been grazed by a bullet in the temple and struck the back of her head on the floor when she fell off her stool, Either of these impacts could have caused her coma.

As Arnie sat in the waiting room, he began to examine his actual relationship with Bertie. He was practically twice her age, so the stepfather lie became a viable description for the hospital to inform him of her condition. *But how do I really feel about Bertie Patchet? I've already demonstrated that she means a great deal to me when I sacrificed my body as a diversion for her escape during the Bridgeport beating. She must mean an awful lot to me. I love her, but how? There couldn't be any sexual attraction—hell, she's been* dressed

160

like a boy ever since I met her. I enjoy being around her, for sure, but is that anything but friendship? Certainly not a romance. Our age difference has never come up before, but maybe I do look on her as a daughter. I'm more than fond of her.

An hour later, Arnie saw the same stern nurse coming down the hall and he caught her eye. She shook her head and wanted to continue on her way, but he pursued her and pressed for more information. "Please, can't you tell me anything at all?" he pleaded.

"I'm only the nurse and I'm not supposed to say anything, but your daughter's been down to X-ray. The doctor says there seems to be some swelling at the back of the brain. He wants to wait and see if the swelling goes down and relieves the pressure there. He thinks there's a good chance of that happening."

"What about the coma?" Arnie asked. "When will she come out of it?"

The nurse shrugged. "That depends on relieving the pressure. I think I've already told you more than I should. I really must get back to work now."

"Can I see Bertie and wait in the room for her to come around?"

"I don't see any harm in that," the nurse said. "Doctor Jamison hasn't prohibited any visitors in her case. At least not yet. She's in room 232. Maybe if you talk to her, it will speed things up a bit. Take the elevator to the second floor. It's the sixth room on your right."

Arnie followed her directions and entered the private room quietly, as though his presence might disturb the comatose patient. He stowed her backpack and his own in a corner of the room. Then he turned to regard his friend. She lay in the center of stiff white bedding like a stick figure—a fixture, not a living person. Her hair had been combed out, and her face bore no expression. He sat down in a visitor's chair after shuffling it closer to the bed, and stared directly at her for twenty minutes until tears started to flow down his cheeks. Then he tried to stare at anything in the room but her. It hurt too much. He wound up looking out the window most of the time, paying attention to two gray squirrels, a dog chasing them, a cluster of evergreen trees, and streams of passing traffic.

At 8:00 p.m. an intercom announced that visiting hours were over, staggering Arnie. He had not looked ahead. Where would he spend the night? He didn't think they would toss him out of the ER waiting room, so that became his next destination. Before he left Bertie's room, he transferred the sandwiches from her backpack to his own and shoved her backpack into the tiny closet. In the ER waiting room, he slumped into a hard chair and dozed off as best he could all night. The next morning, as soon as the hospital intercom announced the start of visiting hours, he headed back to Bertie's room. He wondered how many days he could pull off this routine without revealing that he was living in their hospital. Each night he'd switch to a different jacket or shirt and sit in a different part of the waiting room to implement his ruse.

Two days passed without any change in Arnie's routine. On the third morning he noticed that Bertie's left leg, outlined under the thin sheet and blanket, was in a different position. *Maybe a nurse had something to do with that,* he thought, so he disregarded it as a positive sign. But later in the day the same leg had moved to another position, and he thought he heard a low-level moaning coming from her. Arnie called the nurse. She agreed that it was encouraging news. It was evening before Bertie opened her eyes.

"Bertie, you're awake!" declared Arnie.

"What? Where am I? Why am I in bed?"

"You're in the hospital," he answered. "Old Saybrook Medical Center." He leaned over and pressed the nurse call button.

"Hospital?" she questioned. "Why am I in the hospital? I feel fine."

"You've been in a coma for several days."

"Several days? What's today's date? I've got to get to New Haven or I won't get that teaching job. I've got to get out of here. Now."

"Whoa!" said Arnie. "It's October third. Don't you remember anything that happened?"

Weakly, she said, "All I remember is suggesting we go for coffee in that nice little shop down the street."

"Well, Bertie, that nice little coffee shop was held up while we were there. Then one of the deputies from the jail walked in on the thief. You yelled out to him that the thief had a gun. They wrestled around for it. Some shots were fired. A stray bullet grazed your temple and you fell off your stool onto the floor. You lost consciousness. We couldn't wake you, so we called an ambulance to take you to the hospital. You've been in that coma for almost three days."

Just then, the nurse came rushing into the room. "Yes, a coma," said Nurse Gail upon overhearing their conversation. "Doctor Jamison believes it wasn't the stray bullet that caused your coma. It was the swelling from when you hit the back of your head falling on the floor. The swelling from that impact put undue pressure on your brain. The swelling went down enough for you to wake up. Thank goodness!"

Bertie tried to reach for the bedside water glass. "When can I leave here?" she asked, now with her normal strong voice. "I have a teaching position waiting for me in New Haven. It's terribly important that I get there on time, or someone else will get my place."

Nurse Gail listened while she fluffed up the pillow and tidied the bedding. "You are not going anywhere, young lady, until the doctor says so. He'll want to run tests. You've had a very traumatic experience, and that, my dear, will require a good deal of rest and recuperation."

"When can I see the doctor?" asked Bertie.

"Let's see, you've missed the morning rounds," said Nurse Gail. "You'll see him this evening. He makes rounds then."

"Why can't I see him sooner?"

"Because Doctor Jamison is seeing patients all day at his own clinic. Old Saybrook is a small medical center, part of the Grace-New Haven Hospital system. As a result, we have a limited number of full-time doctors."

Doctor Jamison didn't arrive in Bertie's room until Arnie was forced to retreat to the ER waiting room and Nurse Gail had finished her shift. The doctor and an intern ran a battery of tests and concluded that the result of the impact was a short lapse of memory, covering the period just prior to the shop's entry, right up to the impact and coma. "This type of temporary memory loss is quite common in these cases," the doctor assured her. "I'm prescribing rest and relaxation for the next four days so I can observe any further signs of concussion."

But Bertie wasn't having any part of this. Four days were far too many—enough to put her teaching position in jeopardy. The doctor was still talking when she began scheming, concocting an escape plan in her head. She needed to coordinate it with Arnie. In her mind the getaway had to be in the wee hours of the following night. Returning to her room after the doctor left, Arnie listened to the plan and reluctantly agreed, although he worried greatly over the effect on her health and well-being.

Late the next evening, Bertie removed her backpack from the closet. What the nurses didn't know was that she had worn her street clothes to bed for her "flight," careful to stay hidden under the sheets. Around 4:00 a.m., she stole out of her room, down the hall to the fire stairs, and out the fire exit into the dead of night, where Arnie waited patiently for her. Insisting they walk slowly, he located Elm Street for them, and they followed Elm to the tracks, arriving just as the new day broke. Bertie discovered a *New Haven Register* in a tall trash can. Arnie spread the newspaper out on the ground on the far side of the open tracks, and they had a place to sit while they waited for the right westbound freight train to come their way.

The first two trains were eastbound, one a freight, the other a passengers-only train. Neither one stopped or even slowed down. The first westbound train, a mixed passenger and freight train, didn't stop either. In the next hour four more trains passed in both directions. The only westbound freight in that lot had all of its boxcars padlocked. Nearly three hours later, a freight train stopped with open doors. There were no rail yard cops in sight, so they took advantage of the situation and boarded the nearest one. Arnie started to slip out of his backpack with an eye toward using it as a pillow.

"Don't get too comfortable, pal," said Bertie. "It's only a twenty-minute ride to New Haven."

"You're right," he agreed, as he slipped into the straps once more.

They sat beside the open door watching the scenery become more and more familiar as the train eased into the New Haven rail yard. As soon as it came to a full stop, Arnie leaped down from the boxcar, and tried mightily, with little success, to keep Bertie from overexerting.

They plodded along one edge of the rail yard, across the outer passenger platform, and to the fence breach she'd used months earlier. Climbing through it, they sat down on the grass to rest. When it was time to move on, Arnie's protective instincts proved right.

"I feel dizzy," Bertie whimpered. She tried to stand, teetered, and collapsed as her legs buckled under her. "I've got to close my eyes," she whispered. Just as her lids fluttered shut, she passed out, fell on her left side, and rolled onto her back.

"Bertie! Bertie! Wake up!" cried Arnie. He shook her shoulders, then resorted to gentle taps on her cheeks. Despairing thoughts flooded his mind. *She's had a relapse. Is she in another coma? Should I call an ambulance? If I do, will she blame me for losing her teaching job? Should I let her sleep and hope enough sleep will restore her to consciousness? How long should I wait? I feel guilty, responsible for conspiring with her to escape from the medical center when she wasn't healthy enough for such a dangerous, taxing trip.*

"Oh God!" he yelled.

Chapter 23
An Awakening

ARNIE KNELT ON THE GROUND next to the inert Bertie for some time—pondering his options, absorbing his punishing guilt, and just plain sulking without coming to any sensible conclusions. His thirst caught up with him and he took a drink from his water bottle. As he pulled the bottle from his lips, an idea came to him. *Hey, I'll dribble some water on her face. Maybe it'll wake her up.* A few sprinkles later, she stirred. A few more drops brought about a soft moan, and a third time caused an eyelid to flutter. He stopped when both eyes suddenly popped open.

"What? Where am I?" she asked. Fright filled her hazel eyes, as though she'd awakened from a nightmare. She struggled to a sitting position, surveyed her surroundings, and the anguished look on her boyish freckled face calmed down within a few minutes.

"You passed out on me, and I couldn't wake you up," said Arnie, his heart beating faster with relief. "I thought you had relapsed into a coma again. I thought I was losing you. I felt guilty that I helped you get away from the hospital too soon."

"If it's anyone's fault, it's mine, so stop feeling so damn guilty," replied Bertie. "Remember, I did it to myself."

"I almost called an ambulance," he told her. "But they would have locked you up in some hospital bed. I don't think you would have gotten to your interview on time if I had called one."

"Thank you for not calling," she said, hoisting her five-foot-ten body to her feet and trying out her legs.

"Are you sure you're okay to be moving around again?" he asked. "We could still get medical help, you know."

"I'm fine, Arnie. Really I am. I've got to get to a telephone and tell them I'm back in town and still interested in a teaching position."

"There's a pay-phone booth on that corner next to the gas station," he pointed out. "Do you have any change on you?"

She fished in her pants pocket and held up two Indian-head nickels as they crossed the street to get to the phone booth. She stepped inside and closed the door. The last sound he understood was the *ping* of the nickel's passage in the coin slot. The rest was mumbles as the traffic din blended with Bertie's words. He could hear her talk some and listen a bit in an animated, six-minute conversation. When it was finished, she slid the folding door back and bolted out of the phone booth in an elevated mood.

"Well?" he asked. "Have you got the position or not?"

"I don't know yet," she replied, "but I do have an interview with a Mrs. Iris Sellers at two o'clock today. I have to go to 53 Meadow Street, room 204. It's like I'm auditioning for the role of teacher."

"Do we even know where Meadow Street is?" he asked.

"I do. It's only a few blocks from here," said Bertie. "We're on Union Avenue. We stay on it a couple blocks and turn left onto Meadow."

"You can't go looking like that," said Arnie. "You'll flunk first-grade cleanliness. When's the last time either of us had a bath, miss? You'll need a change of clothes, too. Do you even own a dress? I think you'll need one for this interview."

"For your information, I had a shower in the hospital, Mr. Smartie Pants. Granted, I should wash my hands and face and brush my hair. I do have a dress and some nice shoes in the bottom of my backpack. I only hope the dress isn't too wrinkled from being folded up so long. What I really need is a washroom where I can clean up and change."

"I see a men's restroom on this side of the gas station," said Arnie. "There should be one for the ladies on the other side. Maybe they're not locked. I could distract the attendant by asking for directions to somewhere while you try the door."

"Sounds like a plan," said Bertie.

Arnie strolled in the direction of the attendant, eventually catching his attention. Bertie, taking advantage of the distraction, walked a circuitous route around to the ladies' restroom. Once inside, she locked the door, stripped down, and began to wash using the soap dispenser. The paper towel dispenser was empty; she patted dry using toilet paper. Retrieving the brown paper package from the bottom of her backpack, she undid the string. Holding up the dress, it unfolded to reveal few wrinkles, but definite creases where the folds had been. She slipped into the dress, tied the waistband, and tried to smooth the more prominent creases with the flat of her hand. A glance in the shoulder-high sink mirror told her it would have to do.

Still looking in the mirror, she saw that her thick loose hair had grown in the last months. Soon she wouldn't be able to hide her femininity under her hat, but if she got the teaching position, hiding it would no longer be necessary. She vigorously combed her hair, wincing at tangles and snarls, but fighting through them and adding a red ribbon. She had to look her very best today. As Bertie returned her loose belongings to the backpack, she heard a knock on the restroom door.

"One minute please," she sang out as she hurriedly slid into her backpack straps. When she opened the door, she found a young woman holding a child, waiting for her to exit. They exchanged stern looks as they passed one another. She excused herself anyway, stepped around the impatient woman, and spotted Arnie on the corner near the phone booth.

"Wow, don't you look spiffy," he said, as she approached. "You sure do clean up nicely, ma'am."

"Why, thank you, kind sir." She curtsied for him.

They began walking north on Union Avenue. Turning the corner, the found that Meadow Street was only a block long. The gray concrete Board of Education building stood on their left, and the large clock above the front door told them they had arrived forty-five minutes too early for the interview. Standing in front, they made idle conversation for half an hour until Bertie asked a medley of key questions.

"Arnie, if I do get this teaching position, what do you plan on doing? Where will you go? How will you survive?"

He captured his scruffy beard between thumb and forefinger in a pondering gesture. "I haven't given it all that much thought. I admit I'm tired of going nowhere on the rails. I guess I'll have to stay here and look for work. Don't worry. I can take care of myself. Yeah, I'll miss traveling with you. Believe it or not, I did learn a few things from you."

"And me from you," she replied. "Will you be here when I come out?"

The question struck him so hard he felt a large lump forming in his throat and a sinking feeling deep down in his stomach. *I want to see the look on her face when she comes out and says she got the job. But that would only make the goodbyes more difficult.* Arnie looked at her with solemn eyes He pressed his lips together and said nothing.

She knew what he was thinking. Although there hadn't been any romantic link with him, Bertie felt he'd been like family, and she didn't want to lose him. She reached out and threw her arms around him for a great big goodbye squeeze. After starting up the stone steps, she reached the top and turned back for one last look and a wave. He had already turned away and started walking toward downtown.

With Arnie gone, she looked up at the sky as though only God could watch over her now, but all she saw were charcoal-gray clouds gathering swiftly. Was this a bad omen? She shook her head to thrust out the notion and reached for the brass door handle.

Bertie entered the high-ceilinged hall and approached a young woman seated at a reception desk. "Hello. I have an appointment with Mrs. Iris Sellers."

"And you are?"

"Miss Bertie Patchet."

The woman reached for a clipboard and perused a list of names. "Ah, here it is. That would be room 204, on the second floor. The stairs are on the right in the rear of the building."

"Thank you," said Bertie. She climbed the steps in a rush, and at the second floor, spoke to her inner self as though she were a third-person adviser. *Now calm down, Bertie. You can handle this. You're a trained teacher. You know your stuff. You will not be intimidated.* She took a deep breath and continued slowly down the hall, stopping before the door to room 204 marked PERSONNEL." The office revealed a large space painted in a pale pea green with five floor-to-ceiling windows. There were three desks, two of them occupied by a woman and a man. The man was reading a book.

"You must be Miss Patchet," said the prim-looking woman standing before her. "I'm Mrs. Sellers. Won't you please have a seat?" She pointed to the chair next to her desk. Mrs. Iris Sellers, her hair severely tied in a bun, wore a navy-blue, ankle-length dress with a Peter-Pan collar. Once she and Bertie were seated, the questions began.

"Have you ever been employed as a teacher?"

"No. I'm a recent graduate of Connecticut State Normal School. But I did some student teaching in various school systems in New Britain, New Haven, and Hartford."

"Ah, yes, I see that now in your application," said Mrs. Sellers.

Most of the remaining questions and answers dealt with teaching skills and behavior management in the schoolroom—a battery of all sorts of classroom tribulations. The last few questions were more personal, some hard for Bertie to answer.

"This is October, and you graduated in May. What have you done with that much time, young lady?"

I can hardly tell the woman I've been hopping freight trains all over New England. She thought quickly and responded, "I've been taking advantage of the time and spent it traveling."

"Sounds interesting. Where did you go?"

Whoops, how do I answer that one? "Oh, I spent some time in Newport, Rhode Island, the Bearsden Forest, and on a farm in central Massachusetts." *Oh God, I hope she doesn't want details.*

"So you like the great outdoors," offered Mrs. Sellers.

"Yes, ma'am." *I wonder what that's all about.*

"Do you think you'll have a problem being cooped up in a classroom almost ten months of the year, year after year?"

Oh-oh! "No, ma'am, I adapt very easily to my environment. My school years should attest to that," claimed Bertie.

A strained silence ensued for several minutes while Iris Sellers, her head down, wrote first on the back of Bertie's application, then in what appeared to be a log book of sorts. When she finished, she looked up and said, "Well, that should cover the interview. Do you have any more questions?"

"Yes, ma'am," Bertie replied. "Do I have a teaching position or not? And if I do, may I know where and when I start?"

Mrs. Sellers eyed her sternly. "I won't know anything until I take your application and my comments to the Personnel Committee. The final decision is up to them. They won't meet until Friday morning. That's the day after tomorrow. We'll just have to be patient, won't we?"

Bertie mentally recoiled. *The condescending "we" as if the woman's talking to a child.* "Of course, I can be real patient, but how will I find out the committee's decision and get my employment instructions?"

"We do have your contact information, Miss Patchet. We'll notify you when our decision is made."

"But I left the address and phone part blank," Bertie answered. "I'm a new arrival in New Haven. In fact, I just arrived in town this noon. I don't have an address or phone number yet."

"Where are you staying tomorrow night?"

"I don't even know where I'm staying tonight," Bertie answered. "I'll begin to look for a place to stay as soon as I leave here. Can I come back here Friday afternoon to find out the committee's decision?"

Iris Sellers made a pouting face, turned over her application, and wrote at least two more sentences on the back. "It's a rather unusual request for us," she grumbled, "but I suppose I could make an exception for you."

"Thank you, ma'am. Can you at least tell me if your comments are favorable—whether you recommend me or not?"

"I'm sorry, my comments are confidential. It's our strict policy here."

"I see," replied Bertie, careful not to show her disappointment.

"Good day, Miss Patchet."

"Good day," murmured Bertie.

She left the office and slunk down the hall to the stairwell. Down the stairs and across the lobby, she shuffled toward the exit in a daze. Peering outside, Bertie encountered two more hurdles to her floundering confidence. Arnie wasn't there to comfort her, and black clouds were unleashing a heavy downpour. If she ventured out, she would surely catch a terrible cold in her weakened condition, but she was too embarrassed to hide inside the building. Without benefit of either raincoat or umbrella, she stumbled down the slippery concrete steps and into the storm.

Chapter 24
The Howling Storm

THE RAIN POUNDED DOWN on Bertie's uncovered head like drums rolling to an execution. In just the few seconds on her way down the Board of Education steps, her only dress got drenched, flattening against her bare skin. Her thick hair hung heavy, clinging to her cheeks and neck like a sopping shroud. Hesitating on the sidewalk, her mind grappled with the complexity of her situation. The wind was driving the rain from the south, so she turned north to keep it from battering her face. Rivers were forming in the streets and the whipping wind began to nudge her along. North meant going toward downtown. She trudged in that direction until she encountered a string of awnings fronting a strip of retail stores.

Without an iron, my clothes are ruined. I need a whole new teaching wardrobe, a place to stay, and an address to furnish to that Mrs. Sellers. I could get a place and buy clothes with what's left of the money in the bottom of my backpack, but what if Sellers or that hokey committee of hers nixes my hiring? Then all that money's wasted. I can't even think about it anymore. I've got to get out of this weather. It's beating me up. What am I going to do?

173

Bertie found shelter in a store entrance, partial protection between two display windows. She stamped her feet, and the squishing sound of her shoes told her that now even they had a questionable future. The display windows featured smartly dressed male mannequins; hats propped on stands; and bright ties draped over metal racks. She read the sign on the transom over the door, Ted's Menswear. If that message had been "Dotty's Ladieswear, perhaps she would have seen it as an inducement to buy herself new clothes.

The store's lights were on inside. Pressing her nose to the glass door and peeking in, she noticed a very tall, gangly man in a gray suit and tie approaching the front of the store. *Is he coming to chase me away? I'm not harming anything, am I?* She backed away as he came nearer. He opened and held the door for her. He had a clean-shaven face with wavy dark-brown hair carefully combed back from his high forehead. As he motioned for her to step inside, she listened to his soft, considerate voice.

"Young lady, come in out of the rain. You'll catch your death out there."

Although the offer caught her by surprise, she quickly stepped inside and turned to face her benefactor.

"Oh, I'm dripping all over your nice carpeting," said Bertie. "I don't know where to stand."

"Don't worry about the carpeting," he reassured her. "It's not the first time, nor will it be the last time it's been soaked. But what's more important is your health, young lady. We have to get you dried off. Follow me."

Bertie stood there without moving. *What's this guy up to? Is he trying to take advantage of me? I'd better be careful.*

Seeing her hesitation, he said, "Not to worry, young lady. All I had in mind was to show you the washroom in the back of the store. You'll find a bunch of towels and even an electric hair dryer there."

"A man with a hair dryer?" she asked.

"Yeah, I've got all this bush of hair up top," he explained

174

while running his fingers through it.

Bertie saw a sparkle in his brown eyes, then a warm smile emerge, and she felt a little more at ease with him.

"The washroom is small, but you'll have complete privacy. There's a lock on the door. If you like, there's even a terry robe hanging on the back of the door, should you choose to use it while drying your dress and things."

"May I ask why you're being so nice to me?"

"I was brought up to do the decent thing, and to respect the female of the species," he replied with a wink. He led her first through a small office containing a steel desk and chair, a typewriter, and one steel file cabinet. Next he opened the door to the storeroom at the rear of the office, where they were surrounded by shelves of merchandise from floor to ceiling. An ironing board and iron stood propped up next to a small table and chair. The washroom appeared to be at the far end of this busy utility space. The rain beating on the roof was even louder in this room.

"You are indeed a rare one, and I mean that as a compliment," said Bertie. "Do you often take in strays like me?"

"Strays? Only if they're soaking wet and standing in front of my store looking helpless," he replied. "Of course, a couple of cats and a dog preceded you." He grinned at his own humor. "By the way, my full name is Theodore Freemont. But it's too formal for me. I answer to Ted, and I'm the proprietor and owner of Ted's Menwear. It's a little awkward for me to keep calling you *young lady*, so if it's not too impertinent of me, what *can* I call you?"

"I'm Bertie, Bertie Patchet."

By this time, they had reached the washroom. Ted took a key hanging on a hook next to the door, and unlocked it. Bertie stepped inside, closed it, and pressed the button in the knob to lock the door. Peering into the mirror over the sink, she discovered a miserable-looking ragamuffin looking back at her. By now her clammy undies were sticking to her, so she decided to strip down to the altogether and pile everything on the sink. It took four hand towels from the stack on the shelf to dry her body. Another look in

175

the mirror gave her chills. Having never really been at ease in just her own skin, she reached for the terry robe hanging on the back of the door. Slipping into the arms and wrapping the folds tightly about her naked self, she secured them in place with a knotting of the sash. The robe's hem settled about her ankles, and she decided Ted was certainly tall.

With index finger and thumb, she dangled her clammy bra by one strap. *Thank heaven I don't have to bind myself with an Ace bandage anymore to hide my femininity.* She wrung out her bra and panties over the sink before turning the electric hair dryer on them for a few minutes, and then on her tousled auburn hair, more ruddy red than brown. That took longer. Wringing out her sopping-wet dress, she decided, *This is hopeless. I could put on dry jeans and a shirt from my backpack, but maybe Mr. Ted Freemont wouldn't be so taken with me in that outfit. But why should I care what he thinks?* Another thought struck her. She opened the washroom door. "Okay to use your iron on my dress?" she yelled out to Ted.

"Feel free," he called from the front of the shop.

After ten minutes of careful ironing the way her mom had taught her, she slipped her only dress over her head. Admiring her fresh self in the mirror, she left the washroom and slowly walked toward the front room. Ted stood at one of the display windows looking out at the swirling rain. Some of the rage had gone out of the storm, but the rain water was running rivulets down the glass and rivers still ran through the streets.

Ted spun about when he heard her. She couldn't quite place the curious expression on his face when he first perceived her across the room. *Neither Arnie nor Stan ever looked at me like that. Then again they never saw me as a woman. Am I imagining this? Is it possible that he's actually interested in me?*

Ted smiled broadly. "My oh my, you clean up nicely. I had no idea you were such an attractive young lady"

"Wow," she exclaimed.

"I'm sorry," he apologized, "I had no right to say that to

you."

"That's okay," she replied. "Let's just say you got a little ahead of yourself. Everyone can always use a new friend, but I'm not really looking for any romance. Not just yet, anyway. At least not until I actually get my teaching job and find some reasonable lodgings."

"Oh, so you're a teacher. Ah, I should have known."

"Why is that?" she asked.

"I noticed the intelligent look right away."

"Now I know you're trying to flatter me. Is that because you're ready to toss me out, so you can close up and go home?"

"I'm not going anywhere in this damnable weather," said Ted. "I figured to stay here tonight on the folding cot in the storeroom. But what about you? You must have planned to stay somewhere tonight."

"Everyone has to be somewhere, but I hadn't planned on anywhere in particular for tonight," she admitted with a silly grin. "I just arrived in New Haven this morning for an interview with the Board of Education."

"Did you get the job?" he asked.

"I won't know until Friday."

"What happens if you don't get it?"

"I don't want to think about that. I suppose I could go back to the farm in Massachusetts."

"Are you from Massachusetts?"

"No, I was born and raised here in New Haven," she replied.

"What about family here?" he asked.

"None that I would have anything to do with." She sat down in one of his folding chairs.

"You don't have a place to go? There's no one expecting you?" He pulled a second chair closer and eased his lanky frame into it. He was interested in what she had to say.

"Nowhere, no one," she emphasized, trying not to sound too tragic. "I'm still the little lost waif you rescued earlier—only drier."

"You could spend the night here with me," Ted suggested. "You could even have my folding army surplus cot."

Anxiety crossed her face, making her freckles jump. "Oh, I couldn't possibly. That's your only bed! Where will you sleep tonight?"

"Oh, don't worry about me," he replied. "I've got extra mattresses in the storeroom. I can throw one on the floor. Quite comfortable. I've done it before when my dad was alive. You see, the store was his. I inherited it from him."

"Was he a Ted, too?"

"Yup."

"That makes you a junior," she commented.

"Only I don't like being called junior. It makes me feel inferior."

She smiled. "Hardly. I think you're superior."

Just then the lights blinked a few times, then extinguished altogether. Even the street lights had lost their power. They were completely in the dark.

"Stay where you are," he said. "I know my way around. I know where I can find some candles."

She heard his footsteps on the carpet as he went to search for them. A short time later, he returned from the storeroom gripping a quaint brass candle holder with a lit candle in place. In his other hand he held a second holder with a candle propped up, ready. The glow cast by the candle grew as Ted approached. She watched him light the second one from the first. He set them both on the glass counter near where they sat.

"It's smart of you to keep candles in the store," she remarked.

"Power outages happen fairly often in this neighborhood. Unfortunately."

"What time is it?" she asked.

Ted checked his watch. "Six-fifteen. Are you as hungry as I am?"

"Starving," Bertie said.

"Normally, I'd suggest the diner down the block," he said, "but with the storm and the power out it'll most likely be closed. I've got a bag on the shelf next to my coat. Half a dozen dinner rolls with poppyseeds and two apples. It's no banquet, but they'll hold us till morning."

"Sounds like a banquet to me," Bertie piped up. "Thank you. And I do have a bottle of water in my backpack. I can share it with you."

"No need." He grinned and went to fetch their feast.

While munching gratefully, their small talk came easily and continued for hours until it was time for bed. They each carried a candle into the storeroom. Ted unfolded the cot and set it down for her. He pulled two rolled-up mattresses down from a high shelf. Untying the cords, he laid one out flat on the cot. The second one he carried out to the front of the shop and laid it on the carpet behind one display window, well out of sight of the street. When he returned to deliver a few beach towels to cover Bertie, she had already lain down on the cot. As he leaned over to cover her, she reached up and pulled his head close for a firm peck on his clean-shaven cheek. She couldn't clearly see his face in the dim candlelight, but she just knew it had turned red.

"What was that for," he asked.

"That was for being especially generous to your rain-soaked waif."

She heard him clear his throat and saw the candlelight fade toward the door as he retreated. She closed her eyes. Despite so much of her life in turmoil, she fell into a cavernous sleep full of wandering, happy dreams, a complete reversal of her current life's fortunes.

In the midst of all this joy, she was awakened by a thunderous bang and a crashing of glass. It seemed close, too close. She bounded off the cot to her feet, bolted to the storeroom door, and flung it open. She could hardly believe what she saw. A massive tree had fallen, crashing into one of the plate-glass display windows.

The sound of crumpling shards followed as the weight of the tree bore down on the glass.

"My God! Ted!" she shrieked. Bertie saw him trapped under all the glass with the tree on top.

Chapter 25
Consequences

IN THE BLACK NIGHT thick as tar, Bertie stared in horror. The plate-glass had collapsed under the weight of a stately but aged elm tree that fell into the right-hand display window. When the weight of the tree trunk hit the seven-foot-high window, the glass surrendered with an explosive boom. Three of the tree's main branches lay bent against the building outside. Two more had torn through the destroyed display window. Inside the shop, small leaf-covered branches swept through the display area like a bulldozer. The multi-pointed edges of shattered glass dangled like holiday decorations. Shards with spear-like edges lay everywhere.

The scene inside the shop was fraught with danger: huge glass shards and tree branches. The tree's upper trunk had landed precariously at an angular perch on a thick marble slab—one of two slabs that created the platforms for the seven-foot-tall display windows.

All Bertie could think of was Ted's immediate safety, but where was he? She couldn't find him anywhere. Where should she start looking? Suddenly, she screamed. "Ted! Oh my God!" The bulldozing action of the tree had dislodged him and his mattress from the rear space of the platform, depositing him under the mattress onto the floor in front of her.

When the mattress began to stir, Bertie reached down and flipped it away. Ted lay flat on his back, squirming. His eyes watered with tears and his face twisted with excruciating pain. She searched for the source of his misery. Although minor scratches covered his face and arms, she saw none so critical as to cause that amount of pain.

Moaning softly, he pointed weakly with his left hand to his right shoulder. Bertie located the culprit. A long narrow shard protruded vertically from his upper arm to his shoulder. Gently, she steadied his arm with her left hand, and with her right hand, gripped the slippery, bloody flat surface of the glass shard. Counting to three in her head, she pulled it out with one swift, determined movement.

Bertie never expected the gush of blood that ensued. She immediately threw one palm over the spurting blood and held it there firmly while she made a quick scan of the limited resources around her. On a nearby table, she spotted an arrangement of silk ties fanned out in a flamboyant array. Leaping up, she grabbed one and swiftly sank back down on her knees. Slapping the broad part of the tie over the wound, she wrapped it tightly around Ted's gashed arm. It seemed to stem the flow. Around and around she wrapped, with a final tuck of the tie's tail to hold the rudimentary bandage in place.

The storm howled even louder. The display window was now a huge gaping hole. A swirling horizontal wind inconsiderately chose that moment to shower them with cold rain. Both Ted and Bertie were now soaked and chilled to the bone.

"Can you walk?" she asked. She held out a hand to help him up.

"I think so. Thanks for the nursing." He got to his feet, using his good arm to propel himself upward. "All this merchandise going to waste. I wonder how much I'll be able to salvage in the morning."

"We've got to get everything out of this weather," she said.

"The storeroom has a long empty table," Ted responded. He tried to pick up a pile of expensive shirts in both hands, but winced from the pain in his shoulder.

"Don't, dear," said Bertie, surprising herself with the flush of affection surging through her. "I'll give you a few to carry in your good arm. Let me do the rest."

"You're a doll," Ted murmured. Balancing three shirts in the crook of his left arm, he slowly made his way through the door to the storeroom and set them down on the table. Bertie tackled first things first. She followed him, dragging his still-dry mattress behind her. She pulled it through the door, then tossed it down on the floor of the storeroom next to her cot. As an afterthought, she flipped the cot's mattress onto the floor beside his.

Trip after trip they carted merchandise from the front of the shop to the storeroom. When the table could hold no more, they found either shelf space or floor space for merchandise in boxes. In the front room, well back beyond the likely wet zone, they tucked heavy brown wrapping paper around the merchandise laid out attractively on tables. They draped more heavy paper around the racks of hanging shirts, jackets, and suits.

"That ought to do it for tonight," Ted said.

Bertie glanced at her emergency bandage and saw red blotches on the silk tie. "Oh God, you're bleeding again!" she cried out. She took a closer look at his wound. "We have to get you to a doctor and make sure you don't have an infection."

"No one in their right mind is going anywhere in the middle of the night," said Ted. "Besides, there's a first aid kit on the top shelf in the washroom. I'll let you disinfect and put on a real bandage in the morning."

"Oh Ted, why didn't you tell me that in the first place?" she scolded.

"I just remembered it, damn it."

"I have to change your bandage now."

"Naw, it'll keep 'til morning."

"Now, Ted," Bertie said in her ready-to-be-a-teacher voice.

Returning from the washroom with the kit and a roll of paper towels, she unwound the silk tie, then proceeded to clean, disinfect, and redress the wound—this time with sterile gauze and a large bandage. She attended to his various other scratches as well. They both tried to get back to sleep. Bertie left one candle burning on a little table nearby, a minimal nightlight in the utter blackness of the windowless room. Sleep did not choose to visit either one of them. The traumatic events of the evening had assaulted their minds and emotions too much for reasonable sleep, so they simply lay next to each other. Still anxious about her benefactor's well-being, Bertie kept bouncing up to examine his bandage—to make sure the wound wasn't bleeding again. *Apparently not*, she decided with relief.

Although Ted lay still, his eyes followed Bertie's every move-ment. Once, when she sat up to examine her bandaging handiwork, she bent close to him and noticed his expression, especially how his eyes followed her. She felt compelled to actually kiss him. Not on the cheek out of friendship, pity, or mere relief, but an impulsive kiss on the lips that startled even her. *I just met this guy. I can't go around kissing a man I hardly know. What's happening to me?*

"Thank you," he said.

"I did what I could to stop the bleeding," she said.

"No, the other thing."

"What other thing?" she asked.

"The kiss. I've been wondering what that would be like ever since I met you. I just didn't have the courage."

"And were you disappointed?" she asked, a tinge of color flushing her cheeks.

"Not in the least," he answered. "It's a good way to heal. And you'd make a great nurse. In fact, you'd make me a wonderful wife."

"You can't be hurting all that bad if you're making fun of me," she said.

"But I'm not making fun of you," he protested. "I'm serious, dead serious. I'll even marry you to prove it."

"That's ridiculous. You and I just met," she blurted out while thinking, *I don't want to hurt his feelings. He's cute, he's honest, and the real thing, but is he my real thing?* "We don't know anything about each other. Maybe marriage *is* possible. But these things take time, and you're rushing me."

"I'm sorry, I didn't mean to, but I don't want to lose you."

"You won't unless it's not meant to be," she consoled him. As an afterthought, she leaned over and kissed him on the lips once more. "See! Now let's try to get some sleep."

Wholly different thoughts led to an uncertain on and off dozing for the rest of the night. Sometime in the tail of the night, the storm passed, and quiet reigned until dawn. Daylight gave way to busy streets; vehicle noises stirred the two into an awakening. The storeroom was crowded with merchandise in every space around them. They hadn't viewed it in the light of day.

"Good morning, Bertie," said Ted, propping himself up awkwardly on his good arm. Standing up with a sense of dread, he opened the storeroom door, shuffled through the office to the front room, and stood amid the chaos, shaking his head. Back in the storeroom, he stood over her mattress.

His looming presence woke her. She sat up. "Good morning, Ted. What's it looking like out there?"

"The front room's impossible. The tree has to literally be demolished before a glazier can be called to replace the display window. And, I can't move any merchandise in there until the window is sealed. So that means I can't sell anything in the meantime. The store is effectively closed."

"Well," said Bertie, her voice matter-of-fact. "I'll be waiting around for my answer from the Board of Educations until mid-morning tomorrow, so if there's anything I can help you with, I'm at your service."

"Thank you, but I don't even know what *I* can do. By the way did you happen to notice? There's a whole lot of blood on the left side of your dress. Since it's my blood, I'd be happy to pay for

185

a new dress. In fact, five dresses for your new teaching wardrobe."

"I can't let you do that, especially since I don't have a job yet," she said, grabbing her backpack and stepping into the washroom.

"Not to worry, my dear," he called to her disappearing form.

Bertie emerged twenty minutes later in a flannel shirt and dungarees. "These are my work clothes. What do you think of the real me?"

Ted gave her a hug for his answer and she responded heartily, but pushed him away gently when he wanted more. "We'll go shopping this afternoon," he said.

"We'll see. By the way, do you have any tools?" she asked.

"Not a whole lot. A hammer, screwdriver, and a pair of pliers, and maybe a saw or two at home," he replied.

"Didn't I see a painter's drop cloth out back?" she asked.

"Yeah. The painter I hired last year left it and never came back for it," replied Ted.

"On the brighter side," she started, "I have an idea. The tree trunk occupies most of the display window opening, so there isn't much of a threat as far as theft is concerned. If we can get rid of the smaller tree stuff inside the store, maybe we can nail up the drop cloth against the elements. Then we can bring the merchandise out again. But—" She hesitated. "We will need those saws." After saying it, she wished she hadn't.

"Good thinking," he replied. "First thing I'm going to do is go down the block to Woolworth's and get us coffee and donuts for breakfast. Then I'll head home for the saws. It's only six blocks away. It shouldn't take but fifteen minutes each way."

"Wait a minute, Ted! I should've kept my mouth shut!" Bertie faced him with legs apart and hands on hips, all five-feet-ten of her in a stance of authority not to be denied. "Your wound! If you overdo, if you try to carry anything in your right arm, you might start it bleeding again. I knew I should've taken you to the Emergency Room for stitches."

As tall as she was, he towered over her. His intelligent brown eyes looked at her with curiosity, and his lips curled up slightly in a wry smile. "Hey, girl, you sound like my mother. It's okay. I'll carry everything in my left hand and just use my right for balancing. Besides, the saws are lightweight." Without waiting for a response, he headed out the door.

His reaction startled her. *I'm that bossy? I guess I am. Oh well.* She turned her attention to her next chore, rummaging through her backpack for her hatchet. Bertie had been carrying it inside the pack lately, because visible—hanging from its loop—it would appear as a threatening weapon to most people. She climbed up on the window platform and began to trim away leaves, twigs, and small branches. She had a considerable pile dispatched when he returned with a most welcome breakfast. They sat cross-legged on the carpet in the office to consume it—without talking. Bertie was unsure how to break the silence.

She stood up, brushed donut crumbs off her pants, and said, "Thank you, Ted. Just what I needed. Now be careful."

"Sure will, hon." He nodded and left for home.

In the front room Bertie continued trimming branches. When Ted returned with the saws, the hard work really began for her. She wouldn't let him help. She chopped and shortened the three larger branches protruding inside the window up to the display window platform. "Hey, Ted! Now we can nail up the drop cloth." She allowed him to feed it up to her, little by little.

Five hours later, they were both were exhausted and hungry all over again. They washed up, and put on fresh shirts. Bertie also cleaned his wound and applied new bandages before leaving the store.

It was 3:30 in the afternoon. Despite the storm, all the merchants on the street were open, Ted steered Bertie into a nearby dress shop and convinced her he was paying for everything. "Consider it a day's pay for hard work well done," he'd told her. She tried on a number of conservative dresses, and when it came time to choose among them, Ted encouraged her to take all four of her

187

undecided favorites. After another weak protest, Bertie also gave in for a pair of sensible shoes, a nightie, and some undies.

When he'd finished paying for all their purchases, she tucked her hand into his left forearm, and they strolled out, with Bertie feeling a new excitement and happiness she hadn't known for some time. *He looks so handsome in his fresh white shirt.* A few blocks away, they found an inviting Italian restaurant. The menu featured *abeetza*, a local Italian word for pizza pie. They agreed on a medium-size pie with mushrooms and sausage and washed it down with glasses of beer, a delicious reward for a whole day of hard work.

Outside on the sidewalk, Bertie asked, "Okay, Mr. Fremont, where to now?"

"Homeward!" he announced, as he took the first steps in the right direction, assuming she would naturally tag along.

She withdrew her hand from his arm and remained standing in front of the restaurant. "But where will I stay tonight?" she asked. "Can I stay in your storeroom one more night? Really, Ted, I promise I'll look for a place to live tomorrow."

Now it was his turn to look parental. He eyed her sternly. "You're coming home with me, of course," he said. "I thought that was understood." He held out his hand to her.

"I can't do that," Bertie answered, neglecting his gesture. "How would that look to your neighbors—two unmarried young people living together in one apartment? And think of the stink it would make at the Board of Education if they found out. Teachers have to keep up appearances, you know."

A wide grin suffused his face. "Good news. My parents left me their three-story house when they passed away. I rent out the whole first floor to the Swift family. Marty and Sue Anne. You'll like them. I live on the second floor, and there's a very livable separate apartment on the third floor that I could rent to you. I must warn you, the ceiling slopes at the edge of the house. Hon, the arrangement is all very proper, I can assure you." He held out his large hand once more and this time she took it without hesitation.

She was beginning to feel a new sense of comfort with him, and struck up a lively conversation until they arrived at his house.

Ted's home was tall and stately—white clapboard, with screened-in verandas fronting the first two floors. He unlocked the one front door set back from the other and they walked up to the second floor. Turning on the lights, he showed her around, stopping at a linen closet. With his left hand, one by one, he removed sheets, a blanket, and pillow, and handed them all to her to carry. Then they set about climbing to the third floor, to where he told her she would live.

"This is so perfect," Bertie exclaimed as she set all the bedding down on the single but quite wide bed. Roaming through the fully equipped four-room apartment, she said, "I can hardly believe my eyes. It's a palace! Oh Ted, I have no idea what I'll be paid as a teacher, so I don't know if I can afford your rent. Besides, I don't know if I even have a job."

"That's easy," he said. "If you get the position, you'll pay me whatever you can. If you don't, it's free until you do. The place lies empty otherwise. Now, just relax, get settled in, then come on downstairs and we'll listen to the radio together. If you want something to read, there's a bookcase in the front hall overflowing with books." He gave her a soft kiss on the cheek and left for his apartment downstairs.

In one of the closets Bertie found a few cleaning supplies. She made the bed, dusted the furniture, and swept the messy accumulations of a long-unused apartment. When she finished, she went downstairs just to bid him goodnight. She craved sleep. Back upstairs, she shed her clothes, kicked off her shoes, and slid into bed. She hadn't bothered to close the bedroom door. Reveling in the luxury of the plentiful space and thick mattress, she slipped into a heavy slumber.

A few hours later, her pleasant sleep was disrupted by a bad dream. A nightmare, actually, about her stepfather's lecherous advances and fighting him off. She awoke in a sweat, facing the wall. Suddenly, she sensed something moving in the dark room.

Oh no. I didn't think Ted would stoop to this. I had high hopes for him. Now what? Next, she heard heavy breathing. *More like an animal's panting,* she thought. *Good God, I'm afraid to turn over.* Not having a weapon handy, she cringed, gripping the pillow, poised to toss it, waiting for the next bad thing to happen before she made her move.

Chapter 26
Revelation

BERTIE STIFFENED as she listened to soft growls close to her right ear, and felt the hot breath of the panting creature on the back of her neck. She sprung her trap quickly, flipping her whole body a half-turn to the right, swinging the pillow hard where she imagined the creature's face would be. The impact brought confusion on both sides of the pillow. Bertie screamed. triggering a loud yelp and the clicking of paw claws on the linoleum as the creature raced from the room and scrambled down the hall stairs.

The retreating animal was a large shaggy dog. Bertie felt ridiculous and embarrassed. *Why did I mistrust Ted after all he's done for me? Why did I think it was him trying to take advantage of me? Wow, do I feel guilty! Now that I think about it, he wouldn't harm a fly. And why didn't Ted tell me he had a dog?*

Just then, Ted called up the stairwell. "I heard you scream. Are you okay? Should I come up?"

"No, no, no. I'm fine. I had an unexpected furry visitor. You didn't tell me you had a dog—a rather large nosy dog at that."

"That's only Max. He's a harmless mutt, very sociable and

191

curious. When you're decent, come on down. I've got scrambled eggs and ham going in the kitchen."

"Sounds wonderful. Give me ten minutes to shower and dress." *Yes, a shower! What a luxury.* Bertie had never had one. Her own house and the farm had only bathtubs. The hot water beating down on her body washed away not just grime, but the very real accumulated fears: Where would the next meal and place to sleep come from? How would she deal with the ugly physical threats and assaults? She stood under the hot water luxuriating, scrubbing with a washcloth and fresh bar of soap.

When Bertie finally arrived in the kitchen, Ted was spooning diced ham and eggs from a frying pan onto a plate for her and another for himself. He turned away to deposit the empty pan at the sink. When he looked back, he was visibly taken by the sight of her in one of her brand-new dresses.

"You sure look nice this morning," he said sitting down. "Quite pretty, in fact."

"I'd better look my best today," Bertie replied, as she sat down in a chair across from him. "I've got to get that teaching position. Oh Ted, I don't know how to thank you for making all this possible."

"You don't have to thank me. You've been my helper, and besides, you're one special gal."

"I want to thank you anyway, Ted Freemont, for everything—for all you've done for me. It's beyond my repaying."

"Forget this payment business. I'm in love with you." A silly grin beamed across his face, a touch of honesty in his look.

His declaration hit her like a thunderbolt. "Oh, Ted, how can you say such a thing? We've known each other for less than thirty-six hours. I won't hear any more talk about loving. I'd say we're very good friends for now. Let's just see how things work out. I must say I am fond of you. Extremely fond."

Hearing a new voice in the house, Max came trotting into the kitchen, regarded Bertie for a few seconds, then marched over to Ted for a scratching behind the ears. When the scratching stopped,

Max bent his head back, craving more. When that didn't happen, he circled once and sprawled out next to his master's chair.

"Meet Maxwell Freemont," said Ted. "Early this morning I fed him and put him out in the backyard. He loves it there and I don't have to walk him quite so often."

"But what did you do about him when you spent the night in the store with me?"

"Oh, I called my tenants to take care of him. He's family."

Bertie looked down at the shaggy bundle. His round head was yellow-white. Thick strands drooped around his muzzle like a handlebar mustache. "The fur on his head looks combed and neat, like it's been coiffed," she said.

Ted laughed. "Yeah. Whenever I get a chance, I brush his head to look groomed. Not the rest of him, though. I don't have time, and he wouldn't sit still anyway."

Bertie studied Max. His large black ears curled around his head. His body fur was a combination of tan, pale yellow, black, and white, looking perpetually disheveled and almost damp, even though it wasn't. Bertie gingerly tickled him under the chin. He lifted his head at her greeting and his two soulful black eyes fixed on her. Tilting his head, he clearly questioned her sincerity. He wasn't ready to trust anyone who would hit him with a pillow.

Bertie knew she'd have to woo Max a bit. Maybe later. Right now she was starving. "Ham and eggs on my first day here. Do you eat this elegantly every morning, Ted?" she asked, while chasing a scrap of egg around the rim of her plate.

"Most mornings I have a bowl of cereal," he replied as he attacked a chunk of ham with his knife. Usually, I'm too lazy to cook before going to work. Today I wanted to impress my new tenant."

"You certainly have, Ted," she said, spooning a mouthful of egg. "I haven't eaten this well since I left the farm."

"The farm?" he asked after swallowing. "You haven't mentioned a farm before."

Bertie told him all about the farm up in Massachusetts, the

Mason family, and how she pitched in with their chores. How the beauty and expanse of the countryside, the crisp, fresh air, and the honesty of the hard work captured her. "If I could have been born into any family, I'd have picked the Masons. I'd love to go back there someday." She sighed deeply.

Ted listened, but felt a need to focus. "Today's Friday. When do you find out about your job?"

"Mrs. Sellers told me the new employee selection committee meets this morning, so I should be able to find out this afternoon."

"Any particular time?" he asked, while carrying the dishes to the sink. He started washing, rinsing, and setting them in the rack.

Picking up the dishtowel to help dry, she shrugged. "I thought I'd drop in there about two o'clock and see what's what."

"Any plans before that?" he asked.

"I was hoping I could come down to the store with you, if that's okay."

"Fine, we'll leave in ten minutes," he said.

"But how about you, Ted? Have you done anything about the tree and window yet?"

"I can't do anything about the glass until that tree trunk is gone," he said.

"And what about the tree trunk?"

"Two blocks from the store there's a truck that picks up day laborers. Maybe I can find someone there who has the necessary equipment. If not, I'll see who I can find in the Yellow Pages."

Ted locked up the house, and they retraced their path back to the store. Sure enough, the truck was parked at the same spot as the day before. A few dozen men of all shapes, sizes, and ethnicities, milled about, waiting for luck and opportunity to come together— that rare chance for a day's work at a day's pay, even though the pay would be less than decent. Any pay would be better than none.

Bertie waited under the awning of a nearby store while Ted set out for the truck.

194

A stocky, bull-shaped man in a plaid newsboy cap slid out of the cab just as Ted approached. *The boss*, Ted guessed.

"Hey, man," the guy barked. "Get to the rear of the truck with the rest of the laborers."

"Mister Boss-man, that's no way to treat a customer," retorted Ted. "I'm not one of your laborers. However, I do need to procure a couple of strong men with saws and axes to dismantle a tree that crashed into my store's display window."

"Twenty-five dollars a day fer each man," said the boss-man. "Fifteen dollars fer the equipment, and thirty more fer the truck to haul the wood away. You got the dough fer all that?"

"You bet. Ninety-five dollars and your guys clean up afterward," countered Ted.

The boss shoved a hairy hand in Ted's direction and said, "Deal." Ted shook it to close their arrangement.

The boss climbed up on the bed of the stake truck and started shouting what he wanted to the day laborers surrounding the rear of the truck. Every hand went up. There was "Me, Me, Me" on the lips of each of those men and pained disappointment in the eyes of the ones not chosen. The boss selected two hefty workers and retrieved a two-man saw and a long-handled ax from a wooden box in the truck bed. He handed this equipment to the chosen men. Then he turned to Ted and held out his own hand for payment.

Ted laid two twenties and a ten down on the boss's palm and said, "The rest when the job's done."

The boss-man started to shake his head, but fear of queering the deal made him say, "Put another twenty there and I'll trust yah more."

Ted laid down the next twenty. He and Bertie followed the two workers as they walked the two blocks to the menswear shop. While they tackled the tree outside, Bertie and Ted set about bringing all of the merchandise they'd carried to safety the day before to the front room once more. She still anxiously warned Ted about overstressing his right arm and shoulder and disturbing the wound.

195

He promised to be careful.

Although the nailed-up drop cloth protected the merchandise from flying sawdust and debris, there was no protection from the incessant back-and-forth scratching of the two-man saw or the continual chopping of the ax. Bertie vigorously dusted shelves and counters. It was lunchtime when Ted felt they had restored order to his shop's merchandise. They had lunch at Woolworth's counter, and brought back a tuna sandwich and coffee for each of the laborers.

The clock was approaching two. Bertie used the washroom to freshen up and check out her appearance. As she left, Ted gave her a thumbs-up and wished her good luck. She walked the distance to the Board of Education building, climbed to the second floor, and stopped outside the door to take a deep breath before opening it and entering the room.

Inside, she had the feeling *All eyes are on me. There's even a momentary silence. Or did I imagine it?* As she neared Mrs. Sellers' desk, the woman did not even crack a welcoming smile, but kept shuffling papers in front of her.

Standing opposite her, Bertie saw her name on the outside of a sealed envelope. Mrs. Sellers picked up the envelope and solemnly extended it toward her.

Reading the woman's stern look, Bertie thought, *Oh God, bad news.* When she fingered the envelope and hesitated, Mrs. Sellers ordered, "Open it, my dear."

Bertie tore off the end, pulled out the letter, and read, "Congratulations!" *Now there's a good start.* "You have been accepted as an entry-level teacher at Horace Day School at a salary of $1,200.00 per annum beginning Monday, October 19, 1936. You will be teaching third grade. First you will report to Principal Reginald Davies at 8:00 a.m. for orientation and curriculum preparation." There were additional paragraphs to be read, but Bertie joyously glanced up at the ceiling in a gesture of gratitude to The Almighty. When her eyes focused again, she discovered a broad smile on the secretary's face. She read to the end and looked up one more time.

"I hope you find the terms satisfactory," said Mrs. Sellers.

"I do, I do, and thank you for all your help," said Bertie. As she left the room, the woman called out, "Best of luck in your new position."

Bertie skipped down the steps all the way to the street. *I feel like I have wings and I can fly away any minute like a bird. I've got to tell someone, shout it to the world. I'm now a teacher. I did it all by myself.* Her pace was more of a trot than a walk, touching the ground only in short taps as she went.

At the shop, she noted that the remains of the tree trunk no longer rested on the marble window ledge, but on the sidewalk. The protruding branches and a sizeable chunk of that trunk had already been reduced to firewood size. The trunk became smaller every few minutes as the two hard-working laborers chopped and sawed away. Both men stopped to watch as Bertie sidestepped the debris to access the store entrance.

Inside, she wanted to shout out her news, but Ted was attending to the lone customer, who was trying on a camel-hair sport coat. Ted patted the shoulders and smoothed the coat on the back of the middle-aged man as he stood in front of a full-length mirror. Without turning, he acknowledged her arrival with a raised hand and a wave. The customer posed one way, then another, and tried on a blue blazer next. He shook his head and asked for the camel-hair again. Checking himself in the mirror, he nodded and smiled at his choice. Ted packaged the coat in a box and rang up the sale, escorted the customer to the door, and wished him a good day.

Ted now turned his full attention to Bertie and extended his arms out to her. It seemed so natural for her to rush into them that she did so without forethought. His embrace felt so good, she couldn't reproach herself for being so bold with a man she'd only met two days ago. *There's something special about this man, something stirring my feelings for him. I'd better take control of my emotions before I completely surrender to him. He's already spoken of loving me. Is he the one?*

"I take it you got your teaching position," said Ted, grinning.

"How could you tell?" she asked.

"It's written all over your face, dear."

Bertie pulled out the letter from her purse. He read through it, absorbing all the details. When she'd put it away and set her purse on the counter, she took hold of both his hands and danced him around in several circles.

"I feel like celebrating, but I have no idea how," she said.

"I'd like to help you celebrate," he said, "but it looks like I'll be spending the next five nights in the store. With only a drop cloth between all my merchandise and the whole outside world, the store would make an excellent target for thieves. I contacted the glazier, and he can't deliver a window to us before Tuesday. Wait! I've got an idea. If you'll watch the store for me, I'll go out and pick up a few things and we can celebrate right here."

"If you're sure that's what you're willing to do for me," said Bertie. "A celebration isn't required. I don't even know why I said that."

"Sure it's required. One of life's special moments. We can't let it pass unnoticed."

"Okay then, I'll guard the fortress."

Ted stepped outside and saw the two laborers loading the last of the firewood onto the pickup truck parked curbside. The driver's door swung open. The boss-man stepped out and approached Ted.

"The job's done, my man," he said. "Time to pay up in full. That will be thirty bucks now."

Ted reached into his pocket and pulled out his wallet. He extracted a twenty and a five. "I believe we settled on ninety-five, sir. That's all I owe you." He laid the bills in the man's outstretched palm.

"Oh, yeah, I guess yer right," the boss-man grumbled, pocketing the bills.

His laborers swept the remaining sawdust and twig debris

into piles and shoveled it all into a bin at the rear of the truck bed. Throwing their hefty brush-brooms up into the truck, they stepped onto the running-boards on either side of the cab. The truck drove away with the men hanging onto the windowless doors.

Ted returned an hour later about seven o'clock with two bottles of rosé wine, a wedge of Jarlsberg cheese, a round rye bread, and an apple/raisin pound cake. He deposited them on a small round table in the office. At closing time, he locked the front door, and they sat down for their celebration. They toasted, wolfed down the delicious food, and conversed for hours. After finishing the second bottle of rosé, they managed to drowsily lie down on one mattress and snuggle. Ted's lips left hers to explore Bertie's neck and shoulder while his hands began to roam freely. She completely soaked up every morsel of his attention, exhilarating in sensations she'd never felt before. How could she tell him what she was feeling? When his touch finally wandered farther than it should, she broke off his expanding explorations and sat up.

"I think itsh time for me to head back to the house," she slurred. The rosé was taking its toll.

"You could spend the night here with me," he whispered. "I don't think you're in any shape to walk back to the house alone tonight."

"Waz wrong with my shape?" She awkwardly rose to her feet and swiveled her hips in a provocative way like a beginner belly dancer.

"Sweetie, you've got a fabulous shape. But I'm not sure you can find your way home safely after all that wine."

"I'm fine, but what about Max? Doesn't the poor dog have to be fed tonight?"

Ted looked crestfallen. "Oh hell, you're right. My tenants are away, but I can't leave this place empty tonight."

"Of coursh, you can go home," she slurred once more. "I'll shtay here and guard the fort like before. Max needs you, darlin."

"You called me darling."

"I did? Yesh, I did." She giggled.

"What will you do if someone breaks in?" he asked.

Bertie rummaged through her backpack until she came up with her trusty hatchet. "I'll show him thish, the Patchet hatchet." She waved it back and forth for effect. "He'll go running or elsh." Bertie began pulling the second mattress into the front room, close to the drop cloth. She set the hatchet down on the floor next to it, then stretched herself out on top of it. "Jush let 'em try shomethin."

Against his better judgment, a worried Ted left the store in her charge. He guessed she'd never drunk that much wine before.

An hour after he left, Bertie heard a peculiar grating noise. Her head had cleared by now. She sat up, identifying a muffled sawing sound. In the dim light of the candle at the other end of the room, she stared in horror. A knife blade was protruding and sawing vertically through the heavy canvas of the drop cloth. She sprang to her feet. With hatchet in her shaking hand, she aimed for a spot just above the moving blade.

Chapter 27
The Proposal

GRIPPING THE HANDLE WITH BOTH HANDS, Bertie swung the hatchet in a wide arc. The nailed-up drop cloth tore open, and a bellowing scream issued from the other side of it. A clumsy, shuffling noise on the display platform beyond told her the thief was retreating. She peered through the glass of the other display window to catch him flashing by. In the coincidence of light from a passing auto, she recognized the escaping culprit as one of the laborers who had worked on the tree that day. Looking back at the ten-inch hole in the drop cloth, she saw it had a half-ring of blood at the bottom— she had cut the thief after all. The rosé had worked its magic, giving her the courage to strike out. But now that it was all over, she trembled with distress and started to sob. Only once before had she ever intentionally harmed anyone and that was to protect her maidenhood from the lecherous Phil in front of the Blue Haven Motel.

Ted came through the door and saw Bertie sitting cross-legged on the mattress. As soon as she looked up at him, he saw her red eyes and tear-stained cheeks. He knew something had happened. He knelt down on the mattress and took her in his arms for a much-welcomed hug. Several dabs of his handkerchief soaked up the tears.

In gasping bursts, she told him exactly what had happened and what she had done to the thief. He sat with her for half an hour before she began to calm down. Eventually, she felt a cold, wet nose nuzzling its way between them. Ted had brought Max with him, along with a bag of Purina. Even the dog sought to console her with a lick on her damp cheeks. Bertie slowly diverted her attention toward petting him and chucking him under his chin. He had obviously forgiven her for the pillow business. Both Max and Bertie found it therapeutic. He sprawled out his shaggy self a few inches away from her mattress.

"Why did you bring Max with you?" she asked.

"He's an excellent watchdog," replied Ted. "Besides, it's easier to feed him here than running to and from the house."

That sounded okay to Bertie. But she'd had it with talking. She rolled onto her right side and curled up in a fetal position, desperate for sleep, desperate to free her mind from the attempted break-in.

Ted brought the second mattress out from the storeroom and laid it flat up against hers. He stretched out his six-foot-four frame, and also turned on his right side. As evening rolled into night, the fully clothed couple grew closer, literally. Snuggling up behind Bertie, he molded his body to hers, spoon-style, with his left arm encircling her waist. When Bertie awoke around six o'clock on Saturday morning, she felt enveloped by Ted's strong, comforting body. All she could think of was *This is heaven.*

The morning brought Ted another inspired idea. He didn't want to spend four more days with only a thin mattress between himself and the hard floor. And he was sure Bertie didn't want to either. After bringing back breakfast from his house, he called a local carpenter-cabinetmaker to install and nail up two four-by-eight sheets of three-quarter-inch plywood, instead of the vulnerable drop cloth. By early afternoon the plywood had been delivered, fitted, and nailed in place.

Sales had been slow that morning, most likely due to all the sawing and hammering. Bertie used that time to step out and purchase additional undies, stockings, and even two frilly nighties. She stopped at Liggett's Drugstore on the corner of Church and Chapel streets for more personal items.

In the afternoon Bertie became an unexpected, quite skilled, saleslady. While Ted was busy with one shopper, a second customer came in. Bertie sold the smartly dressed woman three dress shirts and helped her pick out three go-with ties for her husband. Later on, she made sales in handkerchiefs, underwear, socks, and a newsboy cap. Even Max, with his cordial tail-wagging, proved to be an attraction for the customers, inviting pats on the head and conversations, especially with pet owners.

That evening, Ted locked up, and the three of them trudged home. They were free to sleep at the house once more now that the store was secure. It was closed on Sunday, and that meant they could sleep in the next morning. That is, until Max decided at 7:30 that it was time for him to be fed and walked.

On that sunny morning, Ted made pancakes for breakfast. *Slighty leaden*, she thought as she chewed vigorously and doused them with maple syrup. *But hey, I didn't have to make 'em.* Afterward, they put together sandwiches, pickles, and Dr. Brown's Cel-Ray soda for a picnic lunch. They rode an electric trolley on tracks all the way from downtown to a park near the Yale Bowl. The trolley could hold at least fifty riders and had a pole that reached an overhead electric cable for its power. The open sides made for a pleasant scenic ride. The seats, in long rows, were made of vinyl with the backs designed to move forward or backward. As the end of the line, when the conductor was ready to retrace his route, he would walk through the car, flipping each seatback to the other direction. It was a brilliant invention.

They got off at Edgewood Park and strolled along several wooded paths, dazzled by the trees in their autumn finery of oranges, reds, and yellows. Bertie and Ted spread a blanket on a hill overlooking a placid duck pond, and watched the mallard ducks glide along: the mommies with their chicks paddling behind; the males with their iridescent heads gleaming in the sunlight. Near the picknickers' blanket, squirrels entertained them with their antics and busy searches for winter food.

Bertie broke out the lunch. After they were stuffed, the two lay on their backs, looked up at the sky, and conjured up images in the cloud formations. Bertie had stowed away the prior night's horrifying incident. "I'm happier than I've ever been in my whole life," she murmured to Ted. He responded with an attempted kiss on her cheek. She met him with her lips instead. Ted rose up on his left elbow and extended the kiss for many seconds—that is, until he felt passion moving through his whole being. Twisting the upper part of his body to hover directly above her, they came face to face. His expression became serious as he considered what to say next.

"I'm going to marry you, Bertie Patchet."

"Oh really? Don't I have anything to say about it?" She smiled coquettishly.

"As long as it's a yes," he replied. "Can't you see that I'm in love with you? Now that I've found you, I can't imagine my life without you."

"I admit there's some sort of magic between us, but it's unveiling a bit too fast for me to digest." She leaned up to meet his lips for a quick kiss.

"Take and waste all the time you want, but in the end, you'll marry me, Bertie. I swear it."

"I don't know what to say except that I do enjoy being with you. You're so likeable and easy to get along with."

"I'm young, healthy as far as I know, and financially secure. The business has taken a financial hit this week, but the insurance will cover a good part of that. Don't forget, I do have a house and a number of years of savings to boot."

"When and if I do marry you, Ted, it won't be for your money. I intend to marry for love. There hasn't been much love in my life, but I'm looking forward to finding it. I have to admit I'm extremely attracted to you. I don't know if that's love or not."

"Then marry me, Bertie, and I promise you'll have all the love I have in me." His face came closer and their lips met for the longest duration yet.

She felt the stirring inside herself and quickly squirmed her legs together. *Oh God*, she thought, *I'm more than attracted to him. Do I want to spend the rest of my life with him? What would be so bad about that? He's fun to be with.* Putting both hands on his cheeks, she studied his features for several minutes: his wide-set, kind eyes, strong straight nose, high forehead, and look of keen intelligence. *I like what I see. Can I imagine walking away from his proposal? Can I imagine my life without him?* She felt a sudden sinking feeling. *Maybe I do love him already, but how does one tell these things? All I know is I don't want to lose him.*

"Marry me, Bertie," he repeated. "I'll always be good to you. I'll always love you."

"I love you too," escaped from Bertie's lips without her knowing how the words managed it.

"What did you say?" he sat up in disbelief.

"I said I love you too." This time the words conveyed the force of her newfound conviction. *Oh God*, she thought, *I hope I know what I'm doing.*

"Then you'll marry me?" He crossed his fingers behind him.

"Yes," she said quietly, as the tears streamed down her cheeks.

The love birds cooed and kissed and wooed for the rest of the afternoon. A line of rain clouds arrived just as the sun began to set. They gathered their things and caught a trolley back to town, but this time one with the sides closed, as the open-sided ones ran only during the daytime. They'd had enough scenery for one day. A short walk from downtown brought them back to the house.

Max greeted them with plumed tail wagging furiously, pestering to be fed. He watched, as if supervising, while Ted poured dog food from the bag and Bertie filled the water bowl. The dog sensed there would be changes in the Freemont household. He now had a mistress as well.

Bertie the non-cook took over the hasty preparation of supper, boiling franks and heating up canned baked beans. While they ate, they talked of wedding plans. She hadn't seen the inside of a church in over a year. Ted also had a spotty record as a churchgoer. They concluded that a civil ceremony with the county clerk would suffice for now. Neither one had anyone they wanted to invite, and that eliminated any need for special preparations. They decided their wedding would take place three Saturdays from that day. Ted would close the store for the whole day. Instead of a honeymoon, they agreed to use the money to pick up a few things for the house, especially a queen-size bed.

They shared in picnic cleanup, and because it was nine o'clock already, and the next day was a workday for the both of them, they each retired to their own apartments.

Bertie prepared for bed. She picked up the alarm clock with the double bells atop, set it for 6 a.m., and twist-wound the springs for both the time and alarm functions. *Setting the alarm for the morning is important,* she thought. *After all, I'm employed now.* She started to put on a plain cotton night shift, but in the last minute, chose instead one of her new frilly nighties. Bertie stood in front of the full-length mirror on the back of the bedroom door and turned slowly around. The room's backlighting outlined the shape of her body in the image she saw there. *Oh my. Will Ted find me desirable?* Just then she had an inspiration. *There's only one way to find out.*

Bertie tiptoed out of the room, down the stairs, and along the hall toward the open door where Ted slept. Just before reaching the bedroom, she stopped to gather the last wisp of courage she needed for the bold deed. *Call me a hussy*, she thought, making the decisive move. Entering the room, she found that he'd been reading, but had fallen asleep with the light on and book in hand. Rescuing the book from his fingers, she placed it on the nightstand and turned off the bedside lamp before slipping under the covers next to him. There wasn't an awful lot of extra room, so a gentle nudge moved him in the right direction without wakening him. Next, she curled her form close to his and fell sound asleep until he discovered he had company.

Bertie did find out the answers to all the questions she had posed to herself that night. Around 2:00 a.m. she found bliss. The two awoke on Monday morning to the sound of Ted's alarm, which he'd set for eight o'clock. One look at the face of his clock spelled doom for Bertie. Her clock upstairs had rung itself out, well out of earshot. *Oh no, I'm late already. Will I be fired on my first day of employment?*

Chapter 28

The Classroom

THE MENACING FACE OF THE SILENCED ALARM CLOCK pushed Bertie to dress at top speed. She was supposed to meet the principal at eight o'clock. That was now impossible. She succeeded in getting out the door in less than twenty minutes—not exactly ideal, since it left no time for breakfast and minimal time for hair brushing. The thought of losing her teaching job on the first day of school was terrifying. She ran the three blocks to the trolley stop only to see the latest one already a block past. She punctuated her wait for the next one by shifting from foot to foot in frustration.

Nine minutes later, the next trolley car rolled into sight. Its extended arm intermittently sparked, breaking contact from the source of its electromotive energy. This overhead cable defined the car's route and guided its steel wheels on the tracks. The massive yellow and black trolley car stopped long enough for her to board. She exchanged cash coins for tokens and deposited one in the open-top glass box up front. She could see the token rattle around its tiny maze until it came to a flat stop at the bottom. The driver pressed a lever and the token disappeared through a trapdoor to its safe box underneath. Ready to leave for his next stop, the driver rotated a large handle, moving it across a series of contacts that controlled the trolley's motion and speed. It lurched forward as Bertie swung into one of the vinyl seats. She stewed over the many stops along the way; each one seemed to scold her for her tardiness. The trip took twenty-five minutes, a good thing to know for future planning to get to work on time.

Stepping down from the trolley car, she held onto her skirt, ran the last few blocks to the school, and stopped at the front steps to collect herself. She climbed the stairs and stepped into the high-ceiling grand hall. There were no students milling about. Glancing down the corridors right and left, she saw that all the classroom doors were closed. Classes were already in session.

Across the grand hall she saw the door marked "Principal, Dr. Reginald Davies, Ed.D.," emblazoned in gold letters across its rippled glass window. Bertie hesitated outside the office, feeling another stab of anxiety. *Oh God, when am I ever going to get to teach? Can they fire a person before she even starts her first day?* She took a deep breath, knocked twice, and stepped inside. A gray-haired woman in a black dress with a white Peter Pan collar sat behind a wooden desk with tiny cubby holes. Apparently, she was the principal's secretary.

"May I help you?" she asked in a matter-of-fact voice.

Bertie cleared her throat. "I had an appointment with Mr. Davies at eight this morning. I guess I missed it."

"Luckily, you are not late. *Doctor* Davies had an important conflicting appointment elsewhere this morning. I'm Mrs. Worth and you must be Miss Patchet. Dr. Davies tried to send you word of his postponed meeting, but didn't know how to get in touch with you. However, he will be available at ten o'clock this morning."

"Oh, thank you, I'm Bertie Patchet, and I now have a permanent address and telephone number for you." She reached across the desk, removed a pencil from a cylinder holder, and wrote on a pad of her own at an empty corner of the desk. All the while she was thinking, *What a relief, I'm not tardy after all. I get a well-*

deserved reprieve, even if I do say so myself.

"Ahem," mumbled Mrs. Worth, looking disturbed over Bertie's reaching so close to her.

"Oh, excuse me, I'm sorry," said Bertie, while thinking, *Wow, what a priss.* "Would it be okay if I wait here for him?"

"As you wish," intoned the secretary, pointing to a row of wooden chairs along one wall. She turned toward a typing table on her left and let her fingers assault the Underwood's keys at an impressive rate.

Bertie took a chair near a window. The view encompassed the school's empty playground in the near field and neighborhood homes beyond. It was a twiddle-your-thumbs wait for another hour before Dr. Davies came through the door. Bertie gave him the once-over: an elfin man in a black vested suit and elevated shoes. A mustache and tiny goatee didn't quite alter his baby face.

"And a good, good morning to you, ladies," said Dr. Davies as he entered the room. "You must be our new teacher, Miss Bertie Patchet. Are you not?"

"I am, sir." His authoritative but soft, friendly voice quite disarmed her. So in contrast to stern Mrs. Worth.

"Well, I'm glad to have you on board, Miss Patchet. The good news is that we sorely need another teacher. The bad news is that we need you right now. So there's really no time for a proper orientation. I'm assigning you to a third-grade class this morn-ing—throwing you into the tiger's cage without a chair, if you don't mind the metaphor. One of the mothers is kindly babysitting the class in anticipation of your arrival. Now, if you'll come along with me, we'll head on over to the room and save Mrs. Hornaby further dismay."

Bertie followed in the principal's footsteps and stopped at the third closed door. To the right of it she noted an open door to a dimly lit cloakroom with coats and jackets on hooks. Dr. Davies held the classroom door for her, and she stepped inside. He stepped in after her and waited until Mrs. Hornaby had finished what she'd been saying to the class. Smiling, he leaned over and whispered in her ear.

"Well, now, class, your new teacher has arrived," began Mrs. Hornaby, who then launched into a mini speech combining thank you and goodbye, before slipping out of the room.

These few moments gave Bertie the opportunity to take in her new surroundings. The room was spacious with three tall, wide windows on each of two walls and gray slate blackboards on the remaining two. The children sat in five rows, six deep, on wooden seats, each one fastened to the fold-top desk behind it. The seats and desks, supported by scrolled wrought-iron legwork, expanded in size from the front row to the rear row to accommodate a diversity of children's heights and weights. *A typical Connecticut classroom, just what I expected. I've had enough surprises for one day.*

Ushering her to the large wooden desk at the front of the room, Dr. Davies offered wishes for her success and left. Bertie Patchet was about to take on the third grade as a working teacher. She walked to the center of the room and greeted the children.

"Good morning, everyone. I'm Miss Bertie Patchet, but I prefer to be addressed as Miss Bertie. Turning to the blackboard, she picked up a stick of chalk and wrote her name in large letters. Facing the class once more, she asked, "Is there anything you want to say to me?"

"Good morning, Miss Bertie," chimed the children in unison.

"Thank you," said Bertie, thinking, *I like them already.* "I'm as new to you as you are to me. To be fair, I will treat each of you as if you had no past—only a present and a future. That way you will all start fresh as equals. I have not been given a seating chart, nor any curriculum to guide your studies. As a result, I would like to find out a little more about who you all are and what you've been studying." Bertie smiled and paused to let them absorb what she'd said.

"I'd like to play a little game with you. You will not be graded on either your participation or your success. I will ask you some questions on a variety of subjects. If you know the answer, raise your hand high and remain silent. If I call on you, please stand up, tell me your first name, state your answer, and be seated again. If you abide by my rules, we will learn quite a lot about each other. Are there any questions?"

Apparently not. Bertie started with the multiplication tables, calling out random two-element combinations. No hands were raised. The brand-new teacher tried a few word problems. No hands. Then she asked about punctuation, how and why each mark was used. No hands. Next, she tried subject and verb agreements, and the choice of a proper or poorly constructed sentence. No hands.

She was primed to move on to spelling, foreign countries, state capitals, and dates in history, but stopped herself. Silence reigned. Little bodies were growing restless in their seats. A lightning flash of recognition hit her. She was talking to eight-year-olds as if they were thirteen, in eighth grade.

"Okay, boys and girls, let's start over." She began slowly, with arithmetic: adding and subtracting single numbers. Hands shot up. "Do you know what state we live in?" Hands. "Good. Do you know what the capital of Connecticut is?" Only two students raised their hands.

"Hartford," Bertie told them and explained what the capital of a state meant.

After an hour of the game, Bertie learned to put names to faces and seat positions. From the number of hands raised, she had a good idea whether a particular subject had been taught yet. Even the students who didn't raise their hands eventually heard the right answers. She figured they were learning, too.

The lunch bell rang. The children had brought their own lunches and kept them in their fold-top desks. In good weather they ate outside on the playground benches. Today was dark and rainy, so they stayed in the classroom. Bertie noticed that nearly a quarter of them had no lunch; others had scarcely enough. Late to rise that morning, Bertie missed making her lunch. She was deeply distressed by the children's poverty, but she shied away from asking why. The matter of a child's dignity stood in the way of asking. But she resolved to find out how the school could help feed these poor children.

The student bathrooms were on the first floor close to the youngest student classrooms. The faculty facilities were on the second floor. On her way to use them, Bertie passed the open doors to the fourth- and fifth-grade rooms. Peering inside as she walked by, she saw many children on folding chairs in the aisles, indicating the extreme overcrowding—another agonizing sign of the Depression. Too many students. Not enough schools.

The afternoon session began with another half-hour of the game. Having gathered as much information as she could about the class, Bertie switched to a penmanship lesson. Finding inkwells, pens, and paper in the corner supply closet, she enlisted the help of two students to distribute these items to each desk in the room.

The top right corner of each desk held an inkwell—a three-inch hole designed for an ink bottle. A large upper ridge on the bottle prevented it from sliding inside the hole. The ink was a mix of blackened powder and water. The dip pens had six-inch stems, tapered from a half-inch at the nib end to a quarter-inch at the opposite end. The nib fitted into a groove at the larger end of the pen and held the supply of ink between dippings. One could write a few words from a single dip, but penmanship was a dreaded and messy affair for most third-graders.

Bertie instructed the children in writing the upper-case alphabet three times and the same with the lower case. Next, she tried a few short sentences with them. She continually walked around the room, gently checking and correcting technique. She noted that the girls were generally neater and more artful than the boys. She wondered why so many of the boys were responsible for spills, blots, scratches, and inconsistencies in their writing. It struck her that the girls seemed to have better skills with their fingers than the boys at that age. But did the boys have other skills, maybe physical? She'd ask Ted if he had any ideas.

Before the students had a chance to return the supplies to

the closet, they heard the clanging of a loud bell coming from the hall. It wasn't the dismissal bell, nor was it the inter-period bell, for those rang rapidly rather than clanged. Bertie wondered whether it was a routine fire drill or a real fire. The newest teacher had been caught by surprise. She fought down her anxieties and tried to think of ways to get all her students out of the building safely. But what if it isn't the right way, the way all the other classes are taught?

Chapter 29
Challenge

THE FIRE BELL CONTINUED TO CLANG AWAY as though it were running a marathon and couldn't stop until the finish. Bertie sniffed around for smoke and smelled none. But she knew that wasn't the conclusive test for danger. Her training and responsibility for thirty youngsters suddenly snapped into place.

In a calming voice, she began to issue commands like an experienced drill sergeant. "Stand up beside your seats and wait for me to call your row." She stood by the open door and called on the first row to walk single-file out the door and down the nearest staircase. "Do not attempt to pass students from another class. Follow them outside instead." The first row began to move, and the others followed as soon as she called on them. As the last row filed through the door, she checked the empty room. *No one's left behind.* Bertie shut her classroom door and followed her students downstairs and outside—but not before noting smoke coming from the boys' bathroom on the first floor.

About five minutes after their exodus, they heard sirens screaming as the fire trucks approached. A team of four firemen rushed into the building to size up the danger. Two of them carried red extinguisher tanks. When they had doused the fire and there was nothing left but smoke, the firemen learned that a rubbish bin had been set afire by one of the older students—experimenting with cigarettes, they speculated. Actually, it turned out not to have been an accident. The sixth-grade teacher blamed one of her students. That morning she had banished this boy from her classroom; the boy had slapped another kid for swearing at him. But the teacher hadn't learned that there were two sides to the altercation. The more aggressive youngster was dispatched to the principal's office for reprimand, but he disobeyed and snuck into the boys' bathroom instead. He vented his anger by setting the fire. A two-week suspension from school ensued.

As for the students witnessing the event from the schoolyard, most were happy to miss the class work even for the short while. Because of the lingering smoke and the clockwork ringing of the dismissal bell, the students were sent home.

But Bertie remembered thirty inkwells, pens, and paper left out on desks. She returned to the classroom to restore tidiness, a task that took her nearly an hour. This wasn't the end of her first day of school. She would need to do lesson plans! In the top drawer of the teacher's desk, she found a five-page third-grade syllabus with vague outlines covering the subjects over the next seven months. She took the syllabus with her, knowing she'd have to prepare as many lesson plans for the coming days as she could.

At home Bertie climbed the stairs to the third floor, tossed her hat and coat on the bed, and sat down at the versatile desk, a roll-top type, which she'd never had the luxury of owning. She slid the top up and out of her way and searched through all the cubbies. She found what she needed, including a dry fountain pen. Another cubby hole yielded a small covered jar full of ink. She opened the jar, pulled down a lever on the pen's side that collapsed an internal bladder, immersed the pen's nib in the ink, and finally released the lever so that the bladder would suck in the ink supply. She began to write.

By the time Ted came home from the store that evening,

Bertie had completed her lesson plan for tomorrow, and a good start written for the next day. She stopped to help him prepare dinner and resumed her work after they had tackled the dishes. She washed, he dried—a good sign. They had begun their engagement by sharing the chores.

* * * *

And so, Bertie Patchet was prepared to teach that next day and for many school days thereafter. Principal Davies sat in on a few of her early class days, then at least once a month, as he did with all his teachers. Although he said very little after monitoring her class, he always gave her a nod of approval and a smile upon leaving. She enjoyed teaching, and in a matter of days, Miss Bertie had earned the enthusiastic approval of her students. Months passed. They carried their newfound energy and interest in their schoolwork home to their parents, who were pleased that even their marginal students had begun to learn.

* * * *

At Ted's Menswear, once all the repairs were finished, the store began to prosper again. Bertie and Ted said their nuptials on the third Saturday as they originally planned. Also as planned, they postponed any honeymoon so they might enjoy a few new pieces of furniture.

* * * *

But when life runs so smoothly for any length of time, one can usually expect a bump in the road to come along and spoil things. Two years of teaching passed quickly for Bertie. It was the second week in April, a Wednesday, when eight-year-old Pasquale Gramaldi mumbled something uncalled-for during class. At first, Bertie didn't hear him clearly. "Will you please repeat what you said, Pasquale?"

"Miss Boxcar Bertie, ma'am." Pasquale had blond hair neatly combed to one side and wore a white shirt, dark pants, and blue suspenders. He shifted uncomfortably in his chair.

"Can you explain yourself, young man?" asked Bertie.

217

"Where did you ever get such an idea?"

"From my uncle, ma'am," said Pasquale. "My Uncle Butch Bonardi. He's a sheriff's deputy over at the Old Saybrook county jail. When I told him my teacher's name, Uncle Butch asked what you looked like. He said he remembered you from a couple years ago. He recalled arresting you off a train, charging you with truancy, and throwing you in jail overnight. He couldn't understand why the judge let you go the next morning."

The small boy's surprisingly articulate report stunned her. She had no idea how to respond, so she tried to deflect it. "Pasquale, truancy is when a student skips school. I think you mean vagrancy. Vagrancy happens when a person has no way to earn a living."

"Is it true, Miss Bertie?" asked Pasquale. "Did you actually go to jail?"

A chorus of excited high-pitched titters arose in the classroom, along with a shuffling of papers and books. Bertie looked from face to face—wide-eyed, innocent, and astonished—and saw that she was about to be defamed and condemned. Her heart skipped a beat and a sourness curdled deep in her stomach. *I'm trapped now and I have to give Pasquale an answer. Maybe if I tell the whole story, maybe I can regain my students' trust. Of course, my story will follow the kids home. Oh my God, the parents! They'll surely pass judgment on me, and I'll become a pariah in their eyes. I might even lose my job here—maybe everywhere.*

"Yes, class, I'm afraid there's some truth to it, but that's not all of it. At the time, I was a college graduate, a teacher without a job and without money. I had to travel to a place where I could find work. Boxcars are on freight trains. They're used to carry goods from markets and stores to many cities. Sometimes there are empty ones because all their cargo has been delivered. For a few months I rode in empty boxcars because I couldn't afford the fare on a passenger train. That was when I was going to different cities trying to find a job. I knew that it was cheating the railroad and I knew I did wrong. I spent one night in jail and paid a fine to make things square. Although your uncle arrested me, the judge let me go free the very next morning. He knew that I was basically an honest citizen who would make a good teacher someday. But, Pasquale, why did you call me Miss Boxcar Bertie?"

"My uncle kept saying 'Boxcar Bertie' when he was talking about you. He was laughing. He thought it was downright funny—you being a girl and all, riding them trains. You being a girl and all was why he remembered you."

"Those trains," Bertie corrected. "Pasquale, do you know what it is to be poor and not know where your next meal is coming from?"

"No, ma'am," murmured the boy, lowering his eyes.

Most of the children understood what she had to say.

"I wouldn't mind being called that as long as it's said with respect. But it doesn't belong in the classroom. Everyone here will continue to address me as Miss Bertie. Is that clear?"

"Yes, Miss Bertie," repeated the class in chorus.

But that was not the end of the Miss Boxcar Bertie incident. The students did carry that classroom exchange home to their parents, and there were anxious calls to Principal Davies. He thought long and hard about it, weighing his options. She was an excellent teacher. His school, all Connecticut public schools, were facing a desperate teacher shortage. He decided that the students needed her far more than two or three sets of agitated, prissy parents demanding satisfaction.

Miss Bertie earned local appreciation and renown for her excellence and creativity in teaching third-graders, equipping them with solid achievement as they entered the upper grades. The Board of Education agreed she was an asset they couldn't afford to lose.

Bertie continued teaching for another thirty years, but the community never let her forget that she was—respectfully, of course—Boxcar Bertie.

Epilogue

Bertie and Ted were married for thirty-eight years, and if these two lovebirds could have made it longer, they would have. When she retired, he decided that Ted's Menswear should pack it in and he sold it. Now they had the freedom to travel abroad on several exciting trips. They lived in the same three-story house that Ted inherited, renovating it so many times that the final redo made it unrecognizable from the original. Together they weathered the Great Depression, World War II, and the Korean and Vietnam wars. Ted tried to enlist during WWII, but his age and a heart murmur kept him out. The Freemont marriage yielded two children. William became a civil engineer, married Mary Anne, and raised two grandchildren for Bertie and Ted. June became a lawyer, married Lt. Mike Borrows, and spawned three army-brat grandchildren.

Bertie managed to keep in touch with Velma Mason and daughter Liz. The Freemonts often spent weekends and some vacations on the Masons' farm near Acton, Mass. Velma never remarried, but Liz married and raised a family of two boys on the farm. There was always the weekly phone call that sustained the friendship.

After thirty-eight years of the Freemonts' blissful marriage, Ted suffered his fourth and fatal heart attack.

Even though Bertie lived and worked in the same town as her mother, she intentionally avoided contact. At various times, browsing through the *New Haven Register*, Bertie learned of the hit-and-run death of her stepfather; the sheriff's claim on the house for tax forfeiture; and, finally, the nursing-home death of Zelda Patchet.

For those of you who would like to know what happened to Bertie's boxcar buddies, here goes.

Arnie Folsome finally went back to college on a scholarship. He enjoyed college life so much that he became a professor and received tenure after twelve years of teaching. He remarried after his first wife died. He wasn't able to have children.

With the skills Stan Milhouse learned at the CCC camp, he became a successful home-building contractor, whose business took off during the post-WWII years. He and his wife had four children.

Bertie never got to meet up with the two men again. A few postcards and a couple of holiday cards were exchanged, but life got busy. Old friends have a way of fading away, but a memory pops up now and then.

We touch and are touched by all the people we have ever met, the good and the not-so-good alike. Consciously or unconsciously, we eventually become a product of them all.

The caboose always comes at the end of the train.

The Paco and Molly Mystery Series (#1)

Locks and Cream Cheese—In scandal-ridden Black Rain Corners, a Chesapeake Bay mansion harbors locked rooms and deadly secrets. A wily detective and a gourmet cook tackle the case.

The Paco and Molly Mystery Series (#2)

Hot Grudge Sunday—Bank robbers and conspirators derail the sleuths' blissful honeymoon at the Grand Canyon. Can they nail the suspects after they themselves become targets?

The Paco and Molly Mystery Series (#3)

Boston Scream Pie—A teenage girl's nightmare triggers a sinister tale of twins, two feuding families, and a blonde bombshell who hates being called "Mom."

Available on Amazon and all e-readers.

The Dan and Rivka Sherman Mystery Series (#1)

Death Goes Postal—Rare 15th-century typesetting artifacts journey through time, leaving a horrifying imprint in their wake. Dan and Rivka risk life and limb to locate the treasures and unmask the murderer. Not quite what they expected when they bought The Olde Victorian Bookstore. (**Also available as an Amazon Audible Audiobook**.)

The Dan and Rivka Sherman Mystery Series (#2)

Death Takes A Mistress—A young Englishwoman is murdered by her lover. Years later, her daughter, seeking revenge, journeys from London to Annapolis, MD to find the killer and her father. But to which family does he belong? Dan and Rivka set out to expose the true villain.

The Dan and Rivka Sherman Mystery Series (#3)

Death Steals A Holy Book—Dan and Rivka inherit a rare Yiddish translation of a 14th-century holy book, but it is stolen and their book restorer is murdered. Can they recover the book and nail the culprit?

Available on Amazon and all e-readers.

ALSO BY ROSEMARY AND LARRY

The Dan and Rivka Sherman Mystery Series (#4)

Death Rules the Night—Dan wants to know why all copies of an important book are missing, not only from the bookstore, but also from all the local libraries and the author's bookshelves. Who is trying to hide the book's secrets and what are they? Can stalking, threats, and even murder sway Dan from solving this mystery? Rivka fears for their lives.

Cry Ohana, Adventure and Suspense in Hawaii—A car accident, blackmail, and murder tear apart a Hawaiian *'ohana* (family). Kekoa, the teenage son, witnesses the murder and is forced into life on the run. Danger erupts at a Filipino wedding, a Maui resort, and the Big Island's volcanic steam vents. Can the family re-unite and bring down the killer?

Honolulu Heat—Leilani and Alex Wong anguish over son Noah, an idealistic teenager who teeters on both sides of the law. He meets Nina, his dream girl, but they unwittingly share horrific secrets. Noah finds himself immersed in a bloody feud between a Chinatown protection racketeer and a crimeland don who, ironically, is Nina's father.

Available on Amazon and all e-readers.

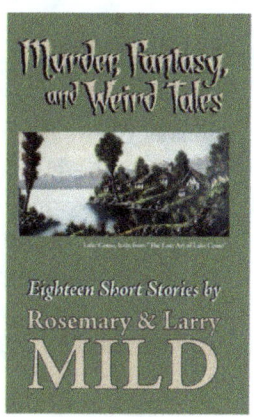

Murder, Fantasy, and Weird Tales

—Delve into tales of the brave, the foolhardy, and the wicked on their journeys to the unknown in Hawai'i, Japan, Cambodia, Italy, and elsewhere. Art lovers, hit women, a vampire, a lively hologram, and others reveal their secret compulsions.

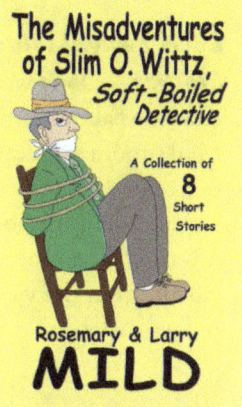

The Misadventures of Slim O. Wittz, Soft-Boiled Detective

—"If you're looking for a truly bumbling gumshoe, you want me, Slim. I'm frequently behind the eight ball and seldom paid. In eight complete mystery stories I always bump into criminals. And you're right: my case record is remarkably shaky."

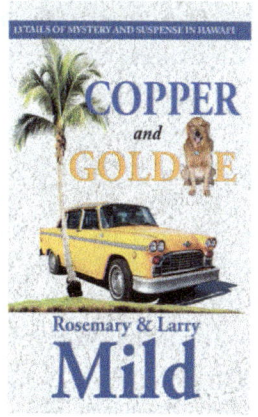

Copper and Goldie • 13 Tails of Adventure and Suspense in Hawaii

—Sam, a disabled ex-cop-turned PI, and his canine sidekick, Goldie, ply the streets of Honolulu in a Checker Cab, looking for fares and solving crimes.

Available on Amazon and all e-readers.

Miriam's World—and Mine

—Miriam Luby Wolfe, a junior at Syracuse U., spent her fall semester in London exploring her talents: singing, dancing, acting, and writing. But she never made it home. A terrorist bomb destroyed her plane over Lockerbie, Scotland. Learn about Miriam, the Pan Am families, the bombers, and the political fallout.

Love! Laugh! Panic! Life with My Mother

—Don't we all have mixed emotions about our mothers? Rosemary Mild's mom was super-achieving, but tough to live with. Luby Pollack was a journalist, popular book author, and psychiatrist's wife. Always the heroine, and sometimes the villain, from the viewpoint of her loving but ornery daughter.

In My Next Life I'll Get It Right—

is a collection of personal essays ranging from the hilarious to the serious—keen, sometimes wicked, observations on everyday life. And… wishful thinking mixed with tough reality. See how Rosemary views her two marriages, the good and the not so good. Join her as she takes on sailing, skating, Jazzercise, football, and more—and feel for a mother's heart-wrenching loss.

Available on Amazon and all e-readers.

Unto the Third Generation—Two young people, each unaware of the other, volunteer to become cryonauts—physically frozen in a life-suspension experiment. Leonard, a steel worker, and Francine, a waitress, postpone their destinies for untold generations. But their lives are in jeopardy —depending upon two world-shaking events.

Charley and the Magic Jug and Other Stories—Climb the mountain to the secret cave with Charley. Watch three brothers face a sweet but certain death. Learn how a tiny pill can changes lives. Get away through time with thieves. See what the winds reveal in "Tsunami!" Follow Casey as he chases the ladies. And witness much more, including quirky fairy tales.

Also by Larry

No Place To Be But Here—It is not only Larry's own story, but that of his family. Join him as he tells how his two wives, three children, and five grandchildren have shaped his life as much as he has molded theirs. Tragedy is certainly no stranger as he deals with death, cancer, murder, and global terrorism, not only on the written page, but in his own life.

Available on Amazon and all e-readers.

Larry grew up in New Haven, Connecticut and served in the U.S. Navy during the Korean War. After earning a BS in Information Systems Management from American U. he became a field engineer riding Navy ships for RCA. He spent most of his career at Honeywell/Alliant Techsystems, designing electronic equipment for the U.S. Government. Larry feels fortunate to have wed two terrific ladies. Losing Hannah to leukemia in 1986, he married Rosemary some time later. Together they launched their career coauthoring mystery, suspense, and fantasy fiction in their Honolulu condo overlooking the Pacific Ocean.

Rosemary, a Smith College graduate and former *Harper's* assistant editor, also writes personal essays, many published in the *Washington Post, Baltimore Sun, Chess Life*, and elsewhere. She was divorced when she met Larry on a blind date. He told her, "When I retire, I'm going to write a novel and I want you to help me." She knew he was Mr. Right, so she chirped, "Okay!" Twenty books later, Larry still conjures up their mysterious plots while Rosemary adds the pizzazz. And they haven't killed each other yet!

Email the Milds at: roselarry@magicile.com
Visit them at www.magicile.com

www.ingramcontent.com/pod-product-compliance
Lightning Source LLC
Chambersburg PA
CBHW070447120726
47910CB00003B/962